ASHES BENEATH HER

A NORTHERN MICHIGAN ASYLUM NOVEL

J.R. ERICKSON

COPYRIGHT

❀ Created with Vellum

Visit

JREricksonauthor.com

AUTHOR'S NOTE

Thanks so much for picking up a Northern Michigan Asylum Novel. I want to offer a disclaimer before you dive into the story. This is an entirely fictional novel. Although there was once a real place known as The Northern Michigan Asylum - which inspired me to write these books - it is in no way depicted within them. Although my story takes place there, the characters in this story are not based on any real people who worked at this asylum or were patients; any resemblance to individuals, living or dead, is entirely coincidental. Likewise, the events which take place in the novel are not based on real events, and any resemblance to real events is also coincidental.

In truth, nearly every book I have read about the asylum, later known as the Traverse City State Hospital, was positive. This holds true for the stories of many of the staff who worked there as well. I live in the Traverse City area and regularly visit the grounds of the former asylum. It's now known as The Village at Grand Traverse Commons. It was purchased in 2000 by Ray Minervini and the Minervini Group who have been restoring it since that time. Today, it's a mixed-use space of boutiques, restaurants and condominiums. If you ever visit the area, I encourage you to visit The Village at Grand Traverse Commons. You can experience first-hand the asylums - both old and new - and walk the sprawling grounds.

DEDICATION

For my husband and son who I often neglect in the final days of getting a book ready to release. Thank you for your patience.

1

SUNDAY, AUGUST 27TH, 1972

Liz

Liz felt her unease growing by degrees.

It was not as if Susie hadn't been late before. She was nineteen, a college girl, young and beautiful with a seemingly endless list of social engagements. It was normal for one of Susie's friends to see her roller skating or sun tanning in the yard, pull up and say 'hey, so-and-so's having a party.' Susan would throw on sandals, grab her red purse, and skip out the door.

Except even that scenario niggled at Liz's mind. Susan always left a note. She was a conscientious girl, a daughter any parent would have loved to call their own.

From Michigan State University that year, she'd sent both her mother and father handmade birthday cards. She even mailed a card on October 5th, their dog Howie's birthday.

When 7:30 rolled around, and it was time for The Dick Van Dyke Show, Liz found she couldn't pull herself from the picture window in the dining room. She gazed at their front yard, at the purple dahlias in large ceramic pots that flanked the driveway. Susie had helped her plant them several weeks before.

It was still daylight, would be for hours. In the street, a little girl pulled a wagon filled with a range of stuffed toys, and a beagle puppy, tongue lolling, eyes fixed on his owner's bobbing blonde head. The little girl's name was Becky. She lived three houses down in a blue Cape Cod with a bird fountain and a white porch swing. Liz knew her parents through neighborhood barbecues. They were a nice family. Their son, Jason was older than Becky by a few years and they had a new baby, though Liz couldn't recall her name - Barbara or Barbie.

"It's coming on," Jerry called from the sitting room.

Liz listened to the opening music, the upbeat instruments - horns and such - as Dick grinned from the desert backdrop.

She walked to the living room and put a hand on the back of Jerry's chair, willing the sound of tires in the driveway to drift in.

"Strange that Susie isn't back," she said.

Jerry, a bowl of popcorn balanced in his lap, glanced at his wife.

"Probably out with her girlfriends," he said, shoving a handful into his mouth.

Liz nodded but found her hands squeezing the chair back, her knuckles turning white.

"I think I'll give Hannah a call," Liz murmured.

Jerry nodded, watching the show.

"Course, if she's out with Hannah..." he said, implying that Liz would find no one at the other end.

Oddly, Liz knew an answering machine would be reassuring. Though more than likely Hannah's parents, Michelle and Frank, would be home. Michelle would know if Susie and Hannah had gone out together.

Hannah picked up on the second ring, and the sound of her voice caused Liz to start.

"Hello?" Hannah said a second time.

"Hi, Hannah. It's Mrs. Miner. Is Susie with you?"

"Susie?" Hannah asked, and she didn't have to say anymore for Liz to know the answer. "No, she's not. I talked with her this morning. She said she'd call me this afternoon to plan our camping trip next weekend, but she hasn't called. Is everything all right?"

Liz clutched the phone and stared toward the front door.

Walk in, Susie. Please just walk in. But the white door remained closed, and outside the world continued its business as usual.

"I'm not sure," Liz admitted. "I hate to sound like an old nag, but Susie wasn't home when Jerry and I got back from visiting his sister. She didn't leave a note, so…"

"Huh, yeah, that's not like Susie. She leaves a note if she walks to the mailbox." Hannah laughed.

"Can you make some calls? Find out if anyone knows where she is?"

"Oh sure, Mrs. Miner. Absolutely. A few people were talking about a beach bonfire. Maybe she tagged along. I'll track her down."

Hannah hung up the phone, and Liz listened to Jerry's laughter ring out.

"Liz, you're missing a great one tonight," he called.

She dropped the phone back on its base and walked slowly to the living room, glancing at the TV, and then at the window that offered an alternative view of the front yard and the street beyond.

"I think I'll walk next door," Liz said.

Jerry looked up and frowned.

He gestured at the TV.

"And miss this? Plus, you realize the Millers are watching this too?"

"Yes, but Joyce only half watches. She's got to keep her eye on the boys, after all."

Joyce was Liz's best friend. They'd gone to high school together, married their sweethearts who also happened to be best friends. It was no accident they lived next door. The girls had plotted everything, including having children, together. Unfortunately, God put a stop to their scheming right there. Liz got pregnant with Susie when she was twenty-one years old and was never blessed with another child. Joyce, on the other hand, tried to have a baby for years. It wasn't until she was thirty and had given up that she finally got pregnant with twins.

The ten-year-old boys were identical - matching sandy hair and green eyes, matching freckled noses, and matching wild streaks. On several occasions, Liz's husband Jerry had shooed the boys off their roof or scolded them for playing with firecrackers.

As Liz approached the back sliding door, she saw Ron in the living room, feet up on a stool, and Joyce hovering between the living room and hallway as if trying to keep an eye on Dick Van Dyke and the boys simultaneously.

Liz tapped on the glass. Joyce turned toward her, eyes lighting up.

"Oh, thank God," she gushed, opening the door. "I've spent all day with boys. Come in, come in."

"I'm not interrupting?" Liz gestured to the TV.

Joyce grimaced and sputtered.

"Most definitely not! I'll always take a good gossip over Dick Van Dyke. And to be frank, since they changed the show, I'm not impressed." Joyce waved dismissively toward the blaring television set. "Iced tea?" Joyce asked. "Or something a little stiffer?"

Liz glanced at the street through Joyce's living room window. The design of their houses was nearly identical. They'd chosen paint colors and furniture together. Sometimes it unnerved her how similar their homes were. It had a twilight-zone effect on days like today when Liz was especially ungrounded, drifty.

"Liz? What's wrong?" Joyce asked, frowning. "You looked… terribly sad just now."

Liz brushed a hand through her short, curly hair. It trembled.

"Did you see Susie today?"

Joyce shook her head, and then nodded.

"This morning. She was out roller skating. I can't tell you what time that was. The boys were complaining they were hungry, which you'd think would mean lunch time, but the boys say they're hungry twenty times a day, at least. I think it was around one."

Liz nodded, took the vodka tonic Joyce had made and sipped it.

"Her skates were by the door, so she made it home after skating, but…" Liz shrugged and offered an exasperated smile. "I'm being paranoid, right? She'll laugh at me when she realizes…" But Liz trailed off. The sinking feeling had returned, like a heavy dark fog descending over her, tugging her smile down.

"I've never known you to be paranoid," Joyce answered. She walked to the living room.

"Ron, did you see Susan today?"

Ron ignored his wife until she barked the question a second time.

He muted the TV.

"I'm sorry, what'd you say, hon?"

Joyce rolled her eyes at Liz.

"I said, did you see Susan? Your best friend's daughter. Remember her?"

He craned around in his chair and grinned.

"Hi, Liz." He offered her a little wave. "No. I was in the basement this morning trying to fix that God-awful water heater. This afternoon I built the ramp for the boys in the driveway, took a nap. No, I never saw her, Liz. Everything all right?"

Liz realized she'd slumped forward on the counter, knotting her fingers together. She stood up, blew out a shaky breath.

"Probably. But Susan leaves notes. We got home around four and haven't seen her. No note, no anything."

"Did you call Hannah?" Joyce asked.

Liz nodded. "She's making some calls. I should go back. Maybe she's called. I'm likely fretting for nothing."

"I'm coming with you," Joyce told her, grabbing both their drinks. "Ron, make sure the boys don't burn the house down."

They walked across the yard, the sky darkening as the horizon took on the fiery orange of the impending sunset. As Liz's feet met the steps leading to her back porch, she quickened her pace, and then burst through the sliding glass door into the kitchen, sure she'd heard the phone ringing, but only the sounds of Dick Van Dyke met her.

"Jerry did anyone call?" she asked, not bothering to kick off her sandals as she hurried into the sitting room.

His popcorn bowl sat empty on the table beside him.

He looked up, noticed Joyce, and started to speak, but then his eyes returned to his wife's face. She knew her fear warped her features. Her husband didn't miss it.

"Liz, why? Did you hear something about Susie?" He sat up straighter, lifted the remote and clicked it off. The ensuing silence rolled out like a tidal wave.

The phone rang, and Liz jumped.

"Do you want me to get it?" Joyce asked, pausing by the receiver.

"No, let me." Liz snatched up the receiver.

"Hello? Susie?" She couldn't help but say her name. She wanted desperately for her daughter's voice to come on the line.

"No, it's Hannah. Sorry, Mrs. Miner."

"Did you find her?"

"No, I didn't. I called everyone I could think of. No one has seen her. Greg said he chatted with her during her run. He was driving to the lake with a few friends and asked if she wanted to join. She said no."

"Did she tell him if she had other plans?"

"No, she didn't. I don't think he asked, but she didn't mention anything."

Liz closed her eyes, leaned hard against the counter, and felt the first tears prick the backs of her eyes.

Joyce watched her, eyes wide.

Jerry stepped into the kitchen. He too studied his wife, deep grooves in his forehead - his signature worried look.

"Hannah, if you hear anything at all, please let me know."

"I will. I promise. And Mrs. Miner, please ask Susie to call me as soon as she gets home, or if you talk to her. I'm sure she's fine. Any minute now, she'll walk through the door."

"I'm sure you're right, Hannah. Thank you."

Trembling, Liz hung up the phone.

2

Liz

"She's not that kind of girl," Liz told the deputy, hysteria rising into her voice. Jerry put a hand on her shoulder. There was strength in his grip, as if he feared Liz might lunge at the officer, pound on his chest like an animal.

"I understand, ma'am. But twenty-four hours is standard procedure, and-"

"Twenty-four hours?" Liz shrieked the words. "Do you have any idea how far she could be? What if someone took her? Susan wouldn't run off." She spun to face her husband. "Tell him, Jerry!"

Jerry pulled Liz against him, patted her head.

"Officer, my wife is speaking the Lord's truth. Whether you call that in isn't up to us, but in five minutes I'll have every friend of ours in town searching the streets, the woods, carrying pictures into shops. This isn't a runaway situation. Understand? Susie never ran away in her life. She's a good girl."

Officer Morrison was a young guy. Less than a year veteran of the Emmet County Police Department. He swallowed the lump gathering in his throat. He didn't know Susie. He grew up a few counties south, but he had a sister her age. A sister who loved to ride horses and who baked him a cake for his birthday every year. She too wouldn't run away. He imagined what he'd do if Jesse went missing.

"Okay," he said. "I'll call it in."

"Thank you," Liz mumbled into Jerry's chest. She pulled away and squared her shoulders. "Jerry, I'm going to call Susan's friend that works at the copy store and see if I can't get a picture down to her to make fliers."

"Good idea," Jerry agreed. "I'll finish up with Officer Kip."

It was after midnight. Liz had shifted from worry to panic hours earlier. Her body buzzed with adrenaline. Every noise sent her racing to the door. In her mind, she told herself she'd yell at Susie, stamp her foot and tell her she didn't care if she was a young woman, she had better never pull a stunt like that again. Another voice said no - give her a hug and never let go. The relief would be overwhelming, crippling. They would laugh about it over toast with peach jam - Susie's favorite - the following morning.

Joyce sat at Liz's kitchen table making lists. Lists of people they hadn't called, popular hangouts to visit with photos of Susan, how to coordinate a search party, and where. That was the scariest question of all. Where should people search?

~

The search party spread out in a single long line. Liz could not see the end. Heads of different sizes, different colors, some wearing hats, others in sunglasses, ponytails. Many young women, Susie's friends and peers from high school, long hair flowing down their backs, shoulders tanned, with odd looks on their faces as if they didn't quite know how to greet the day.

It was sunny and beautiful, a beach day, and yet they were picking through knee-high grass, brushing the earth with sticks looking for their friend, for one of their own, suddenly lost in the world.

Liz's arms were linked with searchers on either side of her. Jerry to her right, Gayle on her left. They were like her fortress, but Jerry's arm trembled like her own. She wondered if he was as terrified to peer into the grass as she. She imagined a shock of blond hair against the bright green grass, and then shook her head, cast the image away, and gritted her teeth.

The searches went on for days. They combed the woods that butted Tranquil Meadows - their little subdivision. They fanned out to surrounding state forest lands, hiking parks. Liz searched with the parties every day. She couldn't sit at home while Susan was out there.

~

Detective Hansen sat across from Liz and Jerry. He didn't look away and avoid eye contact. She wondered how he'd mastered that, looking people in the eye in such devastating circumstances. She didn't think she could do it.

"We've talked to everyone in your neighborhood, Liz. Everyone on Susan's list of friends, everyone she worked with."

"And?"

"And," he held up his empty hands. "Hannah was the last confirmed conversation."

"But-" Liz started.

The detective stopped her.

"We're not done. I have deputies talking to every business in town. There are pictures on the news and in the paper. People go out of town. If someone saw her, they might not realize it's important yet. Sometimes good leads take time."

"We don't have time," Liz choked out.

Jerry took her hand. His was hot, slick. His face was hard. Liz saw his clenched jaw beneath his lips.

"What can we do?" he asked, pushing the words out slowly, as if it took all his effort not to shout them, pound his fists on the desk.

"Keep spreading the word. Hand out fliers. Hand out a hundred fliers to everyone you know, and ask them to hand them out too. And keep thinking about any place Susan might have gone that day. Keep searching your memory for a comment, something you forgot."

Liz snorted.

"Hand out fliers? Try to remember? That's your big plan to bring our daughter home?"

The detective's eyes softened.

"Not *my* plan. The work we're doing is extensive. Every bit of manpower we can spare is on this, Mrs. Miner. I'm telling you what you and your husband should be doing."

3

Liz

Missing. Vanished. Gone.

Liz wrote the words on a little notebook next to the telephone, grinding the pen deeper into the page until it struck the wood of the coffee table beneath. Still, she could not stop. She shoved the pen down, holding it in her fist, willing the emptiness that the words summoned to become some sensation other than nothingness.

"Liz?" Joyce stood in the patio doorway, a pitcher in her hand. She wasn't smiling, but had the crestfallen, somewhat confused look Liz noticed on so many faces lately.

In the first week, Susie's disappearance mobilized them. Phone calls, search parties, fliers. There was a purpose, direction. Check the high school, the local hangouts, the beach. Each time, Liz swelled with hope. This time they would find Susie. But they didn't find her, not so much as a hair.

Liz didn't talk, just waved her in, glanced at the table where she'd gouged it with the pen. It stirred nothing, not even a shred of emotion. She could smash the table to bits and burn it in the backyard and doubted she'd even blink an eye.

Joyce poured them each a drink - sweet tea laced with rum.

Liz sipped it.

She considered pushing it away. She might say, 'I need to be clear if Susie comes home,' but too much time had passed. She understood the likelihood of Susie's fate, even if no one said it, even if her own mind refused to put the words together.

"Jerry's losing it," she said. "He screamed at a concession lady at Clinch Park yesterday when she couldn't remember if she'd ever waited on Susie. He's got all this rage, this emotion with nowhere to put it. He wants to blame someone. I can feel it hovering between us, like a balloon getting ready to explode."

Joyce put her hand over Liz's and squeezed.

"There will be answers," she said, though she did not sound convinced.

"You mean there will be someone for him to be angry with? Someone who-" Liz's sob strangled her words. It surprised both women with its suddenness. Liz buried her face in her hands. She couldn't imagine a bad guy any more than she could say the words. It all led to a single conclusion, an impossible truth. It was the sort of thing people didn't recover from. The death of a child. No, worse, the murder of a child.

Liz took her hands away, wiped the tears from her cheeks. She wanted that initial energy back. It had turned. Now she felt constant exhaustion coupled with jitters, an inability to sleep as she struggled to keep her eyes open.

"I don't know what to do, Joyce. Tell me what to do."

Her friend looked at her, her own eyes heavy with tears.

She pushed her drink closer.

"Just to take the edge off, Liz."

Liz took another drink. If she drank the whole pitcher, would she finally sleep? She doubted it. Instead, she'd lay in her bed, the room rolling, her stomach a mass of oozing nausea.

"Where is Jerry?" Joyce looked toward the front door, as if he might burst in at any moment and take out his directionless rage on her.

"At work," Liz said, puzzled. She had been angry when he went to work that morning. She'd screamed and cried. He left her on their bedroom floor, one of Susie's shirts clutched to her chest.

"Just a for a few hours," Liz added. "He needed to catch up on paperwork, insurance claims or something."

"That's good," Joyce said.

Liz nodded. It probably was good. They couldn't sit in the house together, Liz chewing her fingernails to bloody stumps, Jerry bouncing his foot until he wore a hole in the rug.

"Maybe I'm jealous," Liz whispered. "He has somewhere to go. I have nothing."

"That's not true," Joyce insisted. "There's still work to do, Liz. We will find her. You just need a rest. Your eyes look, well, like you haven't slept in days."

Liz knew it was true - the way she looked and why. She'd gazed at herself that morning in the bathroom mirror. She hadn't brushed her teeth or combed her hair, and she still wore yesterday's wrinkled pedal pushers and a saggy, sleeveless blouse.

She'd fallen asleep on the couch sometime around midnight and sat up wide awake just after three a.m. For an hour, she'd walked up and down the neighborhood streets, lightly calling out Susie's name as if she were a missing cat and not a grown woman. Did she expect Susie to burst from a shed, to wave wildly from a tree?

'I'm up here, Mom! I climbed up and got stuck.'

The thought caused Liz to stare into every dark tree, searching for movement, for the pale glimmer of a face.

4

120 DAYS SINCE SUSAN DISAPPEARED

Liz

Liz sat on Susan's bed, clutching Milo - the stuffed giraffe Susie had owned since she was little. Milo occupied a space amongst Susie's pillows until she was well into her teens. Around fifteen, Susie began to slip the plush toy into her bedside drawer, as if she didn't want her girlfriends to see him.

Milo's horns had long ago been rubbed off; its spots faded. Liz liked to think it smelled of her daughter, but she was no longer sure.

It was Christmas eve. The first Christmas without Susie.

Along the street, houses were lit with Christmas lights. Liz saw Christmas trees glowing through people's picture windows. In the house across the street, she could see the bright red and green of presents wrapped and stacked near the tree. The image made her feel hollow, terribly empty.

She closed her eyes and smelled the giraffe, conjuring a memory of Susan holding the stuffed animal on Christmas morning, wearing footie pajamas and hopping up and down when she opened the doll house Jerry had bought her. She'd fallen in love with the house months before, when she spotted it in Milliken's Department Store in Traverse City. Jerry had driven down the weekend before and bought it. Susan was seven. Her blue eyes sparkled in her soft, round face. Her hair was already long, nearly to her butt. Liz had braided it the night before. The doll house overshadowed her other presents. Each time she unwrapped another gift, her eyes wandered back to the gingerbread trim and the heart-shaped windows.

Susan barely left the dollhouse that Christmas day. The promise of chocolate pudding brought her to the dinner table. Otherwise, she would have happily played into the night without so much as a drink of water.

Tears poured over Liz's cheeks and soaked the giraffe. She'd been careful in the beginning about tainting the stuffed animal, avoiding anything that might remove its scent. Now she didn't care. She hugged it constantly, slept with it, cried into it. She'd spilled a cup of coffee on it the other morning.

Downstairs, Jerry was putting lights on the Christmas tree he'd arrived with that afternoon. He'd burst through the door, grinning, dragging the tree behind him. He had expected Liz to be happy. She saw the hope in his expression, which drained when he saw despair rather than joy on his wife's face.

In stony silence, Liz had walked upstairs and closed herself in Susie's room.

She heard Jerry downstairs, pulling Christmas boxes from the closet. He would string the lights and hang a few bulbs.

Why? Liz wanted to scream. She wanted to drag the tree into the snowy yard and stomp the bulbs into red dust. She wanted to run down the street and rip lights from people's porches.

Instead, she sat perfectly still, lest the grief catch hold and send her spinning into the black.

She had never imagined a Christmas without Susan. In the days, weeks, and months since that fateful August day, Liz found that she could live nowhere but in the moment. Thoughts of the past wrecked her with spasms of grief, the good times with her beautiful daughter like knives slicing and poking her psyche. Thoughts of the future, the futureless nothing, left her breathless, raw and exposed, hopeless.

But now, one such future had rushed up to meet her. The first Christmas without her child. It loomed, a blanket of heavy despair, a cold sweeping shadow that turned Christmas lights into the shining red eyes of a monster lurking in the darkness.

A knock sounded on the door downstairs, and Liz froze.

What if…? That was the thought every time the door opened or the phone rang. What if it's Susie? What if the person who took her decided to let her go? It was Christmas, after all. For a split second, the possibility, the all-encompassing joy of that possibility, sent her shooting from the bed. She pounded down the stairs as Jerry opened the door.

Detective Hansen stood on their stoop, his face grim.

Liz shook her head and walked backwards.

"It's not that," he said quickly at the look of terror on Liz's face. Jerry looked similarly horror-struck.

"I'm sorry, I shouldn't have," the detective stammered, pulling off his knit cap and scrunching it in his hands.

"No, come in." Jerry stepped back. He moved to Liz's side but didn't touch her. Touching had become hard between them, more and more rare, until even brushing against one another in the hallway felt like an electric shock.

"I was going to wait until after Christmas, but I thought you'd want to know right away."

"What is it?" Liz asked, squeezing the giraffe so tight her fingers hurt.

The detective held up a single tennis shoe. It was unremarkable, though clearly weathered. What had once been white now looked gray.

"Some kids found it. They were building a snow fort in the woods off Turner Street."

The woods off Turner Street were just blocks away. They were filled with bike trails and foot paths.

Sometimes Susie jogged in the woods on especially hot, sunny days - like the day she disappeared.

They had searched those woods.

Liz didn't speak, only continued to stare at the shoe.

The detective sighed, turned it so the heel faced them, and peeled back the tongue. The initials S.M., in blurred purple marker, appeared.

S.M. for Susan Miner.

5

THREE YEARS LATER

July 1975
Orla

Much like good deeds, Orla believed that no gift goes unpunished.

Though "gift" was a subjective term coined by her Aunt Effie who believed that, yes, Orla had a gift. Her father, on the other hand, called it a curse, and her mother pretended it did not exist at all. Any time Orla divulged a secret related to her "gift," her mother fluttered her hands, laughed shrilly and hurried from the room.

Orla learned quickly to be careful in disclosing the gift - which was not always easy.

Take, for instance, her second year in elementary school. She was skipping rope in the play yard with her best friend, Carrie, when a rock came whizzing from a tree and struck Carrie square in the forehead. Her skin split open and blood sprayed down her dress. She fell sobbing to the grass, clutching at her torn face. Without a thought, Orla bent over and picked up the rock. In an instant, she saw Marcus Riley, his buck teeth biting hard on his lower lip as he cocked his arm back and threw the rock. It wasn't Carrie he intended to hit, but Jessica, who stood a few feet away picking dandelions. Jessica had bested Marcus in the spelling bee three days before. As Carrie sobbed, and teachers rushed to her aid, Orla got the first sickening sense of knowing the truth and not revealing it. She wanted to. She desperately wanted to, for the sake of her distressed friend who still, more than ten years later, bore the scar.

Despite her silence, Orla did not sit idly by. A week after the rock-throwing incident, Orla spotted Marcus swimming naked in a forest pond. She stole his clothes and flung them into a high tree. At school on Monday, the cafeteria was abuzz with sightings of a naked Marcus as he darted down the street, holding a bushel of leaves in front of his privates.

In middle school, her mother sewed her a pair of beautiful white gloves to block the sensations. They weren't Orla's style. She liked bright, flowery things. Within two days, she'd soiled them black. Her mother fretted and tried black gloves, but Orla's mother hated black. The Irish Catholic in her viewed black as funerals and death, and she grimaced every time she saw Orla in the gloves.

Eventually, nude gloves appeared, and Orla attempted to keep them clean. After all, they blended in almost perfectly with her skin, so she could wear them discreetly. She didn't wear them all the time. Many things she touched barely left an impression. Some things created a spark Orla could ignore, like the sound of traffic on a busy street.

Now and then, she'd get jolted.

At fifteen, while visiting her cousin Liam, she touched his father's coat and realized her Uncle Clancy was having an affair with a woman he'd met at a pub. He'd been with her that morning.

The gift had peaked in her adolescence. Between the ages of twelve and fifteen, the sensations were so overpowering, she wore her gloves almost constantly, but then they faded, and she learned to control them. If she didn't attune to the touch, she could almost avoid the images altogether. But still, she wore the gloves often. It wasn't that she didn't want to know; she was curious. But she had a keen understanding of the old adage *ignorance is bliss*. Once you knew something, you couldn't unknow it.

Orla lifted the nude gloves from her bedside table, and slipped them on. It was a habit by now. At twenty-years-old, she no longer even thought about the gloves. Putting them on was as natural as wearing lip gloss.

She grabbed her canvas bag of books, and trotted down the stairs two at a time.

Most of her roommates had already left for the day.

She spotted Hazel in the garden, offered a quick wave, and pulled her bike from the shed.

It was the perfect day for a bike ride.

~

"Can I give ya a hand?" Orla asked the man.

He stood near his car, studying a flat tire as if he hadn't a clue what to do about it.

He glanced up, expressionless.

Orla gazed back, lifting her eyebrows and wondering at the blankness in his dazzling blue eyes.

He blinked, looked back at the tire, and then grinned. The smile lit his face, erasing the strange absence.

"Looked like you were buggin' out for a minute there," Orla told him, returning the smile.

He laughed and gestured at the tire.

"I was trying to remember if I had a spare. I had flat a few months back."

"Got it. Well, I happen to know how to change a tire, so if you need some help...."

"You know how to change a tire?" The man surveyed her, not in the usual revolting way that men looked at Orla, their eyes hungrily bouncing along her curves, over her long legs.

"Yes, believe it or not, there are girls in the world who don't look at cars like bug vomit."

"Bug vomit?"

"Yeah, you know, bugs are often gross to girls, so is vomit, put the two together." She waved her hand to imply the rest.

"Ah, good to know. So, you aren't afraid of bugs or vomit either, then?"

Orla shrugged.

"Natural things in the world, aren't they? I'm more afraid of politicians and atomic bombs."

He smiled.

"I'm afraid of those too. Though I know a handful of politicians, and they're not all bad."

"Do you, now? Rubbing elbows with the man? I do get the strait-laced vibe from you. Don't tell me, you're a lawyer? Or a banker?"

He cocked his head to the side.

"Somehow you just made both those professions sound less appealing than bug vomit. I'm a graduate student in psychotherapy."

"Yikes, a head-shrinker. The most scary option of all."

He stared into her eyes.

"Tell me, Miss, how's your relationship with your father?"

Orla rolled her eyes.

"Grand. It's my mother where the problems lie. But if we're going to change this tire, we'd better hustle. See that orange sky?" She pointed at the tree line. "It means the sun is heading for a long sleep."

He glanced at the horizon over the trees, and then stuck out his hand.

"I'm Spencer Crow."

She shook it.

"Orla Sullivan."

"Orla? Now that's an interesting name."

"It's a very Irish name, of which I am. In fact, Orla Delaney Sullivan - it doesn't get more Irish than that."

"Irish," he scanned her. "Shouldn't you be covered in red hair and freckles?"

"Very few of us fit that terrible stereotype. Though I have a cousin who looks the part. Open your trunk."

"Yes, ma'am." Spencer gave her a single firm nod of the head and walked back to the trunk.

Orla grabbed the spare.

"Here, let me," he said.

She laughed and pulled the tire away, carrying it to the side of the car. "You grab the jack," she told him.

As Spencer cranked up the car, Orla pulled her long black hair into a ponytail.

"Do you come here often to hike?" Orla asked him, setting the spare on its side as he pulled the flat off.

"No, this is my first time," he admitted. "How about you?"

"At least once a week. I ride my bike out here. It's such a peaceful place. There's a bald eagle's nest about a quarter mile down the creek."

"Really?" He looked toward the trees.

The small dirt parking lot that bordered the trailhead was completely deserted. Orla rarely saw cars in the lot. She'd been surprised to see the shiny gold Corvette sitting there when she'd emerged from her hike earlier. Equally surprised to see the clean-cut man beside it, wearing white tennis shorts and a yellow t-shirt. His sandy blonde hair brushed the tops of his ears. Oddly, she thought she'd seen a mustache on the man when she emerged from the forest, but upon closer inspection, his face was clean-shaven.

"This is a pretty isolated place. You must ride your bike a long way."

"It's about ten miles. I live near the college. Long rides are my drug of choice. I once rode to the Mackinac Bridge."

He grimaced.

"I'm more of a wine man, myself. That sounds like an exhausting trip."

She smiled and shrugged.

"I stopped along the way and met up with some friends in Gaylord. There's an amazing mind space when you ride for hours. It's like your thoughts switch off, and you can just be."

"Do you have a car?" he asked.

"Yep. Nothing like this." She patted the side of his car, and she noticed his eyes linger on the spot where her gloved hand had rested. He didn't ask about the gloves, and she was grateful, though she'd created a story years earlier about skin sensitivity. "It was my mom's car, but she rarely drove it. She walks to her store every day - even in the winter. If the weather is terrible, my dad drives her. She gave me her car when I turned eighteen. I wanted to move out, and she feared me hitchhiking."

"It can be dangerous," he said. "I love my car, my freedom. I live in an apartment at U of M during the school year, in a carriage house at my mom's on the Leelanau Peninsula in the summer."

"A carriage house," Orla murmured. "Sounds fancy."

"It has its perks."

Orla rolled the flat toward the trunk, but he grabbed it before she could pick it up.

"I've got this," he told her.

She glanced in his trunk, noticing a sheathed machete poking from a duffel bag.

"Doing some bushwhacking?" she asked.

He grinned and zipped the bag closed.

"I like to explore new places. Sometimes it comes in handy. Listen," he glanced toward the empty road. "Would you like to come back here tomorrow? Have a picnic. I'd love to see the eagle's nest."

Orla studied him. He wasn't her type. She preferred shaggy men with liberal political views who didn't mind smoking the occasional joint and opted for live music over white linen dinners. But then again, she hadn't been on a date in weeks, and Spencer intrigued her. Something seemed amiss beneath his clean facade. Maybe there was more to him than his preppy image.

"Sure. I'd love to. Noon?"

"Noon is great. I'll put my bike rack on my car tomorrow, so I can give you a ride home. We can probably cram it in the backseat now..." He trailed off, and Orla had the sense that cramming anything onto the leather seats of his car would put Spencer on edge.

She shook her head.

"I like the evening ride. There's another hour of daylight, anyhow. Once the sun sets, I'll get a few more hours of purple twilight. I wouldn't want to miss it."

"Purple twilight," he murmured, smiling. "Sounds like a song. It was nice to meet you, Orla. I look forward to tomorrow."

Orla offered a little wave and grabbed her bike from where she leaned it by a tree. She pedaled off, not turning to see if he watched her as she rode away.

6

Orla

Orla leaned back on her bike, pulling her hands away from the handlebars and opening her arms wide. The blacktop rushed beneath her, the trees ticking by one after another, and up ahead the expansive blue of a cloudless summer day almost convinced her she could fly. She lifted her gaze from the road, the wind whipping her hair back, and laughed.

The opening night of Phantom of the Opera at the Old Town Playhouse had been a hit. The costumes she'd made were beautiful. Ginger, the lead actress, had gushed over the design and insisted she would appeal to the playhouse owner to bring Orla on full time as the costume designer. The mere thought of the possibility made her giddy.

Orla gripped the handlebars and opened her feet to the sides as she slowed and coasted into the dirt parking lot at Birch Park. As she rounded the welcome sign, she glimpsed a young woman at the edge of the forest. Around Orla's age, with long blonde hair parted in the middle, and wearing a yellow t-shirt and shorts, she had looked lost for a moment, even fearful.

Orla pushed her bike into high weeds behind a tree and walked back across the lot to offer the woman help. Perhaps she'd gotten lost hiking.

The stretch of forest appeared empty.

Orla frowned, walked to the trailhead, and gazed down the grassy footpath. No sign of her.

"Hello?" she called out, but her voice was muffled by the sound of a car pulling in behind her. Orla turned to see the gold Corvette.

Spencer parked and waved out the window.

"Hey there, Orla Delaney Sullivan," he called, before stepping out.

"A bona fide picnic basket," Orla announced when Spencer plucked the basket from his backseat.

"My mother owns every food-related item ever created," he told her. "Is it fondue you're after? She's got a set. Or how about a teasmade? No one wants to bother with a teapot anymore. That's so 1950s."

Orla laughed.

"A teasmade! I happen to love my teapot. Your mother sounds like an interesting woman."

His eyes darkened, and then he smiled.

"Yes, she is interesting."

"Does she work?" Orla asked, picking up the plaid blanket he'd brought folded in the trunk. The items made her want to laugh - they seemed pulled from an advertisement. *Accessories for the Perfect Picnic,* it would say in red, bold letters against a backdrop of blue sky, and a grassy field with a smiling, blonde, blue-eyed family.

"She doesn't work. She inherited money after my dad died..."

"Oh, I'm sorry," Orla apologized. "That's terrible."

"I wasn't even two. I have no memory of him."

Orla followed Spencer onto the forest trail, thinking of her own father. He was big and loud and kind. She couldn't imagine life without him. Her mother was his polar opposite, and yet somehow, they functioned together.

Spencer had traded in his tennis shorts for jean cut-offs and a plain white t-shirt. A red ball cap covered his blond hair. His white tennis shoes looked squeaky clean, as if he'd never worn them outdoors.

White rarely made an appearance in Orla's closet. She'd thrown on flowery shorts, yellow Converse tennis shoes and a billowy black tank top. In truth, she'd gazed for a few seconds at the long red and orange dress she'd just finished making the week before. It was backless with slits up the sides and a plunging neckline. It was completely unrealistic for a bike ride or a picnic, but she'd considered it for half a second, mostly because it looked so lonesome hanging in her closet.

Orla walked ahead of Spencer, keeping her eyes peeled for the young woman in the yellow shirt, but not a trace of her remained. Orla pointed out a leafy tree fat with black elderberries.

"That's an elder tree," she told him. "You know, there were cultures who called the elder tree the Witch's Tree. They believed every elder tree had a resident witch, and that a witch could turn into an elder tree."

He plucked one of the black berries.

"Would this be her eye, do you think?" He popped it in his mouth, letting some red-black juice squirt between his lips.

Orla made a face and laughed.

"Does it taste like an eyeball?"

He shook his head.

"Not very sweet though."

"Look." Orla pointed to a tall beech tree. The eagle's nest perched huge and gnarled in the high branches.

Spencer gazed at it for a long time. Orla studied the line of his jaw, his tan neck. He had the body of an anatomy model. Like Leonardo da Vinci's Vitruvian Man stretched out in a star, everything perfectly proportioned. Orla had an eye for proportions. A quality she'd inherited from her mother, useful in making and mending clothes.

He caught her looking.

"Do I have a stain on my shirt?" He examined the fabric.

She laughed.

"No. You're very symmetrical. I was just noticing."

He lifted an eyebrow.

"I've received a few compliments in my life, but symmetrical is not one of them."

She grinned and shrugged.

"Life of a seamstress."

He watched her for a moment.

"Orla the Seamstress. Has a nice ring."

"And Spencer the what?"

"Spencer the hungry," he said, grabbing the blanket and fanning it out. He shook it high, and for an instant the fabric covered her, darkened the forest, and then it slid down and she could see once more.

~

Rain poured over the windshield, and the wipers swished dizzyingly but couldn't keep the glass clear. Spencer appeared relaxed, unaffected by the storm.

"Well, that was sudden," Orla murmured, putting her hand on the armrest in the car and trying not to squeeze. She didn't like thunderstorms, never had. Her father claimed she got lost once during a rainstorm when she was only a toddler. They'd been at the beach with friends, and she'd wandered down a sand dune, just out of sight. The rain came from nowhere, a deluge of sharp water that blurred the already dreamy quality of the sand dunes. Orla's father had found her within minutes, clutching a tree and shrieking.

Orla had no memory of the day, but she couldn't deny the unease that coursed through her during heavy storms.

"Wow. Did you see that one?" Spencer asked as lightning shattered the sky. For an instant the wet, leafy trees glowed white.

Spencer pulled down a long driveway shrouded by trees. Orla squinted at the mailbox, but could not read the name or number.

Through the rain, she saw little - the muted lights of a front porch, the vague outline of a large house.

She wondered about her choice to accompany Spencer home. The conversation had been so easy, the wine dulling her inhibitions.

Spencer jumped from the car, pulled a light coat from the backseat, and ran to Orla's door. He opened the door and held the coat over their heads as they dashed into the garage beneath the carriage house. Orla made out the shapes of two cars in the darkness. Spencer took her hand and led her, laughing, up a set of narrow stairs.

He pushed through a door, Orla behind him. The door swung

closed, and Orla stood in complete darkness. She blinked into the room, her breath catching as she waited for the light to turn on. Seconds passed.

"Spencer?" she asked, the first seedling of doubt rooting in her mind. She had followed this man, a complete stranger, to an isolated house in the woods.

The lights flipped on washing the room in a yellow glow.

"Sorry." He grinned. "Took me a minute to find the switch."

Orla gazed around the apartment. The ceilings were high. Bookshelves lined the large window that looked over the driveway. A modern black sofa sat on a white shag rug. Above the sofa, a canvas hung, the paint a splattering of blacks and reds.

It was a studio apartment, but spacious. The bed stood in the main room, tucked behind a Chinese screen. The apartment was clean; spotless, really. Orla glanced down where three rows of men's shoes stood in a row. She imagined her own room, the bed unmade, books strewn haphazardly on the bedside table.

"Don't take this the wrong way, but does your mom clean your apartment?"

He walked to the little kitchen complete with a narrow, pea-colored stove and refrigerator. From a cupboard, Spencer produced two wine glasses. He grabbed a bottle of red wine from a rack on his counter.

"Do you like Merlot?" he asked.

"Sounds great."

"And no, my mother doesn't clean my apartment. I'm tidy. I realize it's unusual, but I prefer it this way." He gestured at the apartment.

Orla walked to the bookshelf and scanned the titles. He read mostly nonfiction. She peered at dozens of titles about psychology and sociology. A stack of magazines sat on one end of a shelf, and she looked at the cover.

"True Detective," she murmured, gazing at the image beneath the headline of a terrified woman with a knife pressed against her throat. A masked man stood behind her. Orla grimaced and pushed the magazine away.

"Have you ever read it?" Spencer asked, startling her from behind.

She jumped and shook her head.

"Not my style. It looks creepy." She took the glass he held out.

"True enough, but it's real life. Better to be prepared than-"

"Surprised?" she interrupted.

"Dead," he finished, clinking his glass against hers. "But let's not talk about death. I want to know more about you, Orla Delaney Sullivan."

She followed him to the couch and sat down, sipping her wine and continuing to gaze at his impeccably clean apartment.

"I'm marveling at this place. Where's the pile of dirty laundry?"

He laughed.

"I'm guessing you're not a neat freak. If you were, this would make complete sense to you." He pointed at a little door near his bed. "That's called a closet. It contains a hamper. Inside, you'll find my dirty clothes."

"Wait. Those plastic things with the handles? Those aren't for books and unmatched socks?"

He widened his eyes and groaned.

"I guess that's another use for them."

She smiled.

"I'm not as bad as I sound. I do, however, like to drop my dirty laundry in the corner, and then kick it down the hall to the laundry room."

"I had no idea we'd be having such a scintillating conversation."

Orla cocked an eyebrow.

"With all those psych books, you're clearly interested in people's idiosyncrasies. What's more revealing than laundry habits?"

He leaned toward her, eyes twinkling.

"Sexual habits are pretty revealing."

7

Orla

Orla laughed, color rising into her face.

"I'm gonna need more than one glass of wine to reveal those secrets."

He pointed at the counter.

"I've got bottles."

She glanced at the rack.

"Tell me about you, Spencer. You go to the University of Michigan, you're studying to be a psychiatrist. Do you have a girlfriend?"

He balanced his chin on his hand and studied her.

"Do you think I'd bring a woman home if I had a girlfriend?"

"You wouldn't be the first man who did."

He shook his head.

"No girlfriend. I've dated at school, but I'm busy. Most women aren't keen on spending Saturday night in the library."

"I love the library," Orla admitted. "Though our reading preferences differ considerably."

"Which is the perfect moment to pivot to you, Orla. Tell me about your life."

"That's a long tale."

"We've got all night."

"Do we, now?" She took a sip of wine and leaned back on the couch. "Well, I was born in Detroit in 1955. My parents are Patrick and Fiona. We lived for a few years in a little apartment. Dad worked for the Chrysler factory. My mom stayed home with me and worked part-time as a seamstress. They were Irish immigrants, and both had family in Detroit, but my dad's cousin, Uncle Martin, moved to Traverse City. He'd gotten construction work. He wrote to my parents, said it was beautiful, simple. So, they packed us up, and we drove north."

"Are you an only child?"

"Yes and no." Orla thought of the wooden crib in her parents' attic engraved with the name Cillian. "I had a brother. My mom had him when I was five, but he only lived for a few days."

"I'm sorry."

Orla sipped her wine.

"It's sad, in a mysterious way. Like when you're walking through a graveyard and see a child's tombstone. But I was young when he lived and died. I have no memory of it. Do you have any siblings?"

He shook his head.

"I don't think my parents planned for any children. I was an accident."

"A happy one, I'm sure."

He shrugged.

"Maybe."

His comment surprised Orla. She wasn't exactly bosom buddies with her parents, but she'd never doubted their love for her. Even her mother, who often drove her nuts with her constant fretting, loved Orla to near suffocation.

"How did your father die?"

Spencer shook his head.

"I don't know. A heart attack, maybe. One morning my mom found him dead."

"Had he been ill?"

"Not that I'm aware of, but she doesn't like to talk about it. I've accepted that I'll never know much about him or his death."

"She doesn't talk about him as a man? As a person?"

"He was a dentist. She met him when she got a root canal in Chicago. He liked to golf, and he liked to read. That about sums up what I know."

Orla started to ask another question, probe the mysterious dead father, but she noticed the grim look in Spencer's eyes and closed her mouth.

He swirled the wine in his glass, and then looked at her conspiratorially.

"Tell me the worst thing you've ever done, Orla."

She paused at the abrupt change in topic and tried to conjure a list of the bad things she'd done her life.

"I once ran over a chipmunk with my bike. It was horrible. I crushed him, and I kept riding. I couldn't stand to look back and see what I'd done." She chuckled and looked at her wine. "I've never told anyone that. This wine must be going to my head."

"A chipmunk. I think if that's the worst you've done, you're in good shape."

"And you?"

He leaned back on the couch and draped an arm behind her shoulder.

"I wrecked my mom's prized possession - a 1964 Aston Martin. I wrapped it around a tree."

Orla watched the little smile on Spencer's lips. He held an expression of guilt coupled with exhilaration. It was a strange sight, and Orla set her glass on the table.

"Did you get hurt?"

"No. Miraculously according to the doctors, but... well, I knew I wouldn't get hurt."

"Did you plan it?" Orla asked, goosebumps rising on her arms.

He looked at her, his eyes glassy, and then blinked. His normal gaze returned, and he laughed.

"Of course not. I'd have to be crazy to do something like that on purpose."

He reached out and touched her long black hair.

"You're stunning," he said.

Orla smiled, tucked her hair behind her ear.

"Thanks."

He leaned in and kissed her. His lips were soft and warm, and she felt him holding back. When he pulled away, he slipped his hand into hers, pausing and looking down at her hand.

"Why the gloves?" he asked.

She blushed. It wasn't the first time someone had asked. Intimacy always ended up there.

She started to offer her rehearsed response - dry skin, etcetera. Instead, she told him the truth.

"Sometimes, if I touch things with my hands, I receive impressions."

He looked at her curiously.

"Impressions?"

Something in his face stopped her. She had been ready to reveal all, but quickly pivoted, choosing the safer, more sane response.

"Just tactile sensations, you know? Like every ridge and bump. I can't describe it, but it's unnerving. I keep them on to reduce that."

He nodded and studied her gloved hand.

"Can I refill you?"

She shook her head.

"I think I've already passed my limit."

"A lightweight." He stood and took her glass.

Something had changed between them. Orla couldn't place it, but the near-revelation with the gloves had closed off some part of Spencer.

"Listen, I'm not trying to be fresh, but do you want to spend the night?" he asked, turning on the faucet and putting the glasses in the sink. "I can drive you home. I don't mind at all. I was just thinking about driving up to Leelanau State Park for a hike tomorrow. I thought you might like to join."

Orla glanced toward the clock over his refrigerator. It was going on midnight, and the drive back to town would take forty-five minutes. She wasn't tired. She imagined they could stay up all night talking, and she'd wake refreshed when the sun peeked over the horizon. But then she remembered his look when she talked about her hands…

"Sure," she said. "On the couch, though. This will suit me fine." She patted the leather sofa.

"Not a chance." He shook his head. "You get the bed. I'll take the couch."

~

Orla stepped from the door of the carriage house. Flowering trees and high, dense bushes shrouded the building. It was a beautiful spot. The sun slanting through the branches made her want to step out, press her face into the soft petals of the pink flowers on a nearby bush.

Spencer had left to pick up pastries and coffee, insisting she take her time waking up, have a shower if she'd like.

Dark pink flowers, heavy and sagging from the lattice, wound up the garage's side wall. Orla heard the frenzy of bees as they hovered over the fragrant flowers.

The rain left a sparkling sheen on every surface.

She looked at the huge oak tree, whose roots rose and fell within the green grass, and imagined an enormous bark-colored octopus reaching out from a secret sea hidden beneath the earth.

Slipping off her gloves, she tucked them in her jeans pocket. At the flowers, she cupped the fleshy petals, savoring the sensations. Warmth spread through her hands.

The driveway was a menagerie of glittering stones. As she walked, she stared down at their shapes and colors. Pausing, she reached down and picked one up, turning the stone in the sun, watching the dazzle of light off its sharp surfaces. She reached for a second and a third. It was the fourth that rocked her. She hadn't been paying attention, simply plucked one from the ground, and the moment her fingers grazed the object - not a stone at all - a terrible vision tore across her mind.

A young woman stood on hands and knees, bleeding from a head wound and staring at her own bloody teeth knocked from her mouth by a terrible blow.

As the image vanished, Orla lurched backwards, almost toppled over, but managed to shuffle her feet and stay upright. She looked at the tiny, hard item in her hand. It was not a rock, but a tooth, perfectly intact. A molar.

The sound of feet crunching over gravel brought her back to the moment. A woman stepped into the glare of the sun.

Orla stuffed the tooth in her pocket, her stomach a soup of

nausea. Fear had not yet arisen. The shock of the vision still lingered, overwhelming her other senses. In her mind's eye, she saw the girl who'd been struck - blonde hair falling over her battered face, destroyed by… a rock, yes, Orla thought someone had hit her in the head with a large rock.

The woman who'd walked from the main house had not seen Orla. She was middle-aged, her dark hair neatly pinned up, and she wore dark slacks and a navy blouse. Dark lipstick lined her small, thin mouth.

"Excuse me?" The woman's voice stopped her cold.

Orla looked up, struggled to meet the woman's cold stare.

"Are you Spencer's friend?"

Allowing her hair to fall over her face, Orla nodded and pretended to look at the flowers. She took a few steps backwards into the driveway and bolted. She'd get to the road and hitch a ride back into town. The tooth hung heavy in her pocket, though she knew it weighed nothing at all.

"Wait," the woman commanded.

Orla's legs wanted to keep running, and for a minute they did. It took all her willpower to slow and turn.

The woman walked toward her. Orla realized she should say something, apologize for taking off, but her mind could not find a suitable excuse.

"Spencer is always in such a rush. Won't you join me for breakfast?"

Orla swallowed and shook her head.

"I better not. I forgot about some sewing I'm supposed to have done. Let Spencer know I'll call him. I've really got to run."

The woman took a step closer, still smiling, and then another.

"Where's your car, dear?"

Orla's mouth hung open.

"I don't live far," she lied.

"You have such beautiful hair. May I?" The woman was right in front of her now, reaching out a pale, slender hand.

Orla's eyes bulged as she watched the hand as if were a tentacle. She wanted to slap the woman's hand away, turn and run, but the woman had sunk her hand into Orla's hair. Orla saw the woman's other arm slip from behind her. She held something that glinted in the sun. Orla stared, perplexed, as the woman's hand lifted, hovered, and plunged a syringe into Orla's neck.

Orla shrieked and wrenched away, but the woman depressed the syringe. Whatever it contained rushed into her body.

Orla fled, not down the driveway, but into the dense forest that butted it. She fought the branches away as they snagged her hair and face. She'd barely gone a few steps when her legs gave out and she fell into a tree, wrapped her arms around the trunk, but could not hold herself up.

Darkness descended like a wave. It fled down the sky, erasing the trickle of sunlit blue. It washed over the trees and swept Orla away.

8

Hazel

Hazel shuffled her tarot deck. She spread the cards fan-like on the dark blanket beneath her and gazed at the sparse early morning traffic from her front porch. It was her morning ritual. Draw four cards, one for each girl in the house, and slip them under everyone's respective coffee mugs.

For herself, she drew the six of cups. The card was not a surprise. Her mother's birthday was less than a week away. She would have been forty-six that year, but she'd never seen forty-three. Ovarian cancer had stolen her from the world, not quietly, but with a roar after months of near-constant pain. In her final days, a drugged haze was the only existence her mother could tolerate. The cups were cards of emotions; the six of cups spoke of nostalgia, romanticizing the past. Since her mother's death, Hazel had found herself weepy-eyed in July, wanting to do things she and her mother used to do, hoping to keep her memory alive.

She pulled the second card for Bethany - the ten of wands. Bethany occupied the room across the hall from Hazel. She was two years her junior at eighteen, newly graduated from high school, and intent on living independently from her parents. She worked two jobs, one as a waitress, the other babysitting a family down the street. The card made sense. Bethany was pushing to stay ahead of things, falling into bed exhausted most nights.

The third card went to Jayne, the wanderer. At twenty-one, she'd already lived in Thailand, California, and a series of cities along the East Coast. She'd left home at fifteen years old with nothing but a backpack and hitched her way around the world. She was a restless spirit and had a lot in common with Orla, their fourth roommate, who occupied the attic room at the top of the house. Jayne received the Hermit card - part of the high arcana. Hazel laughed and shook her head.

"Not likely," she murmured. The card implied that Jayne needed to fold in, spend time at home, deepen into silence and stillness. Hazel drew the Hermit card for Jayne at least twice a week, but Jayne never heeded its call. She said she intended to embody the hermit when she reached ninety and settled into a farmhouse filled with cats and marijuana plants.

Hazel shuffled and drew the fourth and final card, studying the image of the half-man, half-goat with black wings. It was the Devil card, a strange harbinger for Orla, who genuinely lived in the light. The Devil represented the shadow - a darker side of the self, or of another. Hazel sensed the card did not represent Orla at all. An omen, perhaps.

Hazel tried to remember if Orla mentioned any conflicts at work, anyone who might be deceiving her. She didn't think so.

The morning before, Orla had given Hazel a quick wave goodbye as she pulled her bike from the shed. She'd pedaled off, her canvas bag of library books slung over her shoulder. Hazel hadn't asked where she was headed.

Usually, the four roommates reconnected over dinner. They took turns cooking each night, but Hazel went out to dinner with her boyfriend, Calvin, the night before and missed their communal meal.

Hazel carried the cards into the kitchen, made a pot of coffee, and pulled each girl's mug from the cupboard. Orla drank from a brown mug decorated in orange and green flowers. Hazel's eye lingered on the card as she slid it halfway beneath the mug. She took her own coffee and returned to the porch.

~

"No Orla?" Hazel called, watching Bethany and Jayne on the porch swing, drinking their coffee and talking.

Hazel stood in her garden, pulling handfuls of weeds up by the roots and tossing them to the side.

Orla typically woke up before the other two girls, shortly after Hazel. It was nearly ten a.m., and no sign of her.

"Nope," Jayne said. "She wasn't here for dinner last night, either."

"I haven't seen her since breakfast yesterday morning," Bethany added.

"Did she say where she was going?" Hazel asked, brushing her dirty hands on the skirt she wore in the garden. It was a light, cottony fabric, dark-colored with big pockets to drop vegetables into. Orla had made it for her.

"Nope, I slept late yesterday," Jayne said.

Bethany nodded her head.

"We talked in the morning about the book she was returning. God's eyes or something," Bethany said. "But I didn't ask about the rest of her day."

"Their Eyes Were Watching God," Hazel corrected. She had recommended the book to Orla. "I think I'll run up and check on her," Hazel told them, walking to the house and taking the stairs two at a time.

The doorway to the attic lay at the bottom of a second, narrow stairwell. The door was ajar - strange, since Orla closed it when she went to bed.

Hazel knocked on the door before calling her friend's name.

"Orla?"

No answer.

She crept up the stairs, not wanting to wake her on the chance she'd been out late and decided to sleep in.

Orla's bed stood beneath a window overlooking the garden. Her bed was rumpled; typical. She only made her bed once a week, after she'd stripped and washed the sheets and replaced them with clean.

It was obvious Orla had not come home the night before. Hazel gazed around the room. A book lay spine-up on Orla's bedside table next to a half-glass of water. On one side of the room, her sewing table stood beneath the slanted ceiling, a swath of olive fabric next to the machine. The room was neither messy nor clean, a certain organized chaos that Orla thrived in.

Orla had moved into the house a year and a half earlier. She attended Northwest Michigan College, taking general studies courses but had little interest in school.

Hazel picked up a yellow bandana on Orla's nightstand.

In white stitching, she read *Memory Keeper*.

She had her own bandana with those words sewn along the edge. Orla had made them a year earlier, in July, as they approached the dual anniversaries of Hazel's mother's birthday and death-day.

It was a pact they'd made just months after Orla moved into Hazels house. They'd been awake long into the night often those first few months. It was like dating someone knew; they wanted to discover everything about one another. For the first time since her mother's death, Hazel had found someone she could genuinely confide in. She and Orla clicked.

Hazel remembered that balmy summer night, sitting on the porch, crying into a glass of raspberry wine, as she revealed the story of her mother's death to Orla. Orla, in turn, revealed her strange gift.

Hazel had slipped her mother's wedding ring into Orla's hand and she had cried when she held it.

"Your father bought this in Scotland when he was stationed there..." Orla had murmured. A little smile played on her lips and then her mouth turned down. She touched her belly and winced. "The pain, your mother was in such terrible pain, but," she looked up at Hazel, her eyes shining, "you brought her the most indescribable joy, Hazel. She was not afraid in the end, but she despaired to leave you behind."

Hazel had taken the ring back and marveled at the gold band before slipping it into her pocket.

"Sometimes, I miss the memories most of all," she had said to Orla. "My mother told me the stories of our life together. We talked about what we'd done and seen. She kept the memories alive. Now that's gone. I have no one to remember her with."

Orla had been reclining on the porch against the little wooden rail, but she scooted to Hazel and wrapped an arm around her back.

"I will be your memory keeper, Hazel. And you can be mine. Tell me your stories. In time, they will become my stories, too."

And the following summer when July approached, Orla had come down to breakfast one morning with the bandanas - ordinary colorful bandanas with that reminder stitched into the fabric: Memory Keeper.

Hazel held the bandana to her heart, for a moment, and then returned it to the table, before slipping out of Orla's room.

As the day progressed, Hazel tried not to worry about Orla, but looked up eagerly each time the front door opened. It was always Jayne or Bethany. In the afternoon, her boyfriend Calvin walked in. He looked a little hurt when her excited face turned to a frown as he breezed into the kitchen holding a potted plant.

"Rosemary," he announced. "My mom took it from her garden. What is it, honey?" he asked at the worried look on Hazel's face.

"Orla never came home last night."

He pulled open the refrigerator door, rummaging for a snack.

"It's Orla. She probably crashed with someone."

Everyone took the same nonchalant tone, but Hazel didn't think so. Orla was free-spirited, but she always told the other girls where she was going. And they had a perfectly good telephone. Why wouldn't she call and let them know?

Orla had recently started part-time work at Zander's Cafe, an organic restaurant in town. All the girls posted their work schedules on a big calendar next to the kitchen table. Orla was supposed to work the following morning, Monday, at nine a.m.

"Did you call her parents?" Calvin asked, selecting a block of cheese.

"That's the last place she'd crash," Hazel mumbled.

"Not if her mom was sick, or it was her dad's birthday. I think you're worrying over nothing."

Hazel didn't nod her head. Instead, she walked to the counter and frowned at Orla's empty coffee mug and the devil card beneath it. She couldn't bring herself to put the mug away and remove the card.

~

Hazel's concern intensified the following morning.

The phone rang at 9:15 a.m.

"Hi, this is Stan at Zander's. Is Orla there?"

Hazel's chest tightened, and she put a hand to her heart.

"No. She didn't show up for work?"

"Not yet. We expected her fifteen minutes ago. I was hoping you would say she was on her way. We'll be swamped today."

"I'll tell her to call as soon as I hear from her."

When Orla hadn't come home again the night before, Hazel almost called her parents. However, Orla had confided in Hazel about her mother's fragile and worrisome personality. Hazel didn't want to scare them, and she didn't want to anger Orla if she'd merely stayed with a guy, or at a friend's.

Orla had moved into the house to escape from the judgmental gaze of her parents. Hazel feared it would be a betrayal of trust to tell Orla's parents she'd missed work, not come home, and was acting irresponsibly.

"But it's not Orla," Hazel whispered. She sat at the table, tapped her fingers, and watched the clock.

~

Orla's father worked for Clark Construction, and her mother owned a little seamstress shop on Union Street.

Hazel recognized Mr. Sullivan immediately. He was tall and dark like his daughter, with piercing blue eyes and a no-nonsense expression. He sat on the back of his pickup truck, eating lunch from a metal box.

"Hi, Mr. Sullivan?" Hazel was aware of the construction men's eyes on her. Not because she was beautiful, per se. She wasn't. Pretty, according to some, but Hazel considered herself average. Her clothes, on the other hand, were not. They were bright and flowery and almost always eye-catching.

He gave her a mystified stare, and then nodded.

"You're Orla's roommate," he said, wagging his finger. "I remember. You lived in China or something."

Hazel shook her head. "Our roommate, Jayne, used to live in Thailand. I'm Hazel. I'm sorry to bother you on your lunch. I'm wondering if you've seen Orla."

He put his sandwich back in the box and shook his head.

"About two weeks ago, I guess. She stopped at the store to get thread."

Hazel bit her lip, tempted to turn and leave. She didn't have to say anything more but knew if something had happened to Orla, she'd regret her silence for the rest of her life.

"Orla hasn't come home for two nights. She missed work today, and I'm worried."

Mr. Sullivan unscrewed the cap on his thermos and took a drink, swishing it in his mouth, and then spitting the water off to the side of the truck.

"Sorry. Fiona uses this mustard that leaves a funny taste in my mouth." He replaced the cap. "Orla hasn't been home." It wasn't a question, but a statement. "And you find that unusual?"

Hazel nodded, despite the skeptical look on his face.

"I know Orla is spontaneous. But I've lived with her for almost two years," Hazel explained. "She's never done anything like this before."

"Stayed with someone else for a couple of days?"

"Left without telling anyone. We're like a family. We keep tabs on each other. I wasn't very worried the first night, but then when she didn't show again last night and also missed work… It's not like her. And she's supposed to make dinner tonight. We rotate. It's just… it's not right."

He lifted an eyebrow.

"You call any of her other friends?"

"Of course," Hazel said. Before she'd driven to the construction site, Hazel called everyone she could think of. No one had spoken with Orla. "She left Sunday morning to return a library book. That's the last time anyone has seen her."

Mr. Sullivan put his lunch things away and picked up his hard hat, but Hazel saw the troubled look in his eyes.

"I'm off in three hours. If Orla doesn't show up to make dinner, call me. I'll call the police."

At the mention of the police, Hazel drew in a sharp breath. She didn't quite know why. Maybe because the police felt like strange heroes considering they were living in a time of near-constant strife between the free-spirited folks like Hazel and the men who claimed to uphold the law. Twice, she'd been arrested for protesting the war in Vietnam. She hadn't even thought about calling the police.

Their mere mention cast Orla's disappearance into a darker and more frightening light.

9

THE NORTHERN MICHIGAN ASYLUM FOR THE INSANE

Orla

Orla swam in darkness. Beneath her eyelids, a black navy reigned supreme. When she opened her eyes, more darkness greeted her. It was not altogether unpleasant, rather like the one time she tried magic mushrooms.

She'd been at a party when a boy thrust the gnarled-looking fungus into her hand.

"Most amazing ride of your life," he'd said, popping one of the dried gray mushrooms into his mouth.

The fungus had tasted earthy, dank. She choked it down and followed it with a gulp of Coke. Afterwards, she drifted on a river of color and sounds, which collided, merged, and wove a beautiful tapestry of light tendrils connecting everything. It had been tranquil until she drifted back toward reality. She grew exhausted, but when she tried to sleep, the river continued to sweep her down and down.

This moment felt similar. Except it didn't seem like a moment at all, but a million moments, an ocean of time lapping, rolling, returning to a giant darkness, ever moving with no end.

A coldness enveloped her - the only sensation of discomfort. The chill penetrated her flesh, moved through her blood into her organs. Strange thoughts slipped by. She wondered if her spleen was cold, or was that her pancreas? She had paid little attention in anatomy class. If faced with identifying the location of an organ, she'd likely pick the wrong side of the body.

Now and then, she attempted to move. Wiggle a finger, lift her head, but her sense of her body was as boundless as time. She couldn't seem to isolate a limb to move it, and the effort so exhausted her that she'd slip back into the abyss, only to emerge a short time later, flutter her eyelids, part her lips, and then recede again.

When Orla finally woke, the drug's effects had faded. Her conscious mind no longer held any trace of the peaceful tranquility of her drugged sleep.

Her eyes flew open - not to darkness, but the drab gray of medical walls, a brick ceiling, a bit of light snaking beneath a doorway.

Heavy fabric bound her arms against her sides. Straps wrapped across her shins and over her thighs, pinning her to the bed. An additional bind cut into her forehead, pressing her skull against the hard surface beneath her.

She wanted a sip of water and to cry out, but something had been stuffed in her mouth and strapped in place. It cut into the tender flesh of her cheeks and the creases of her lips.

Her final memory appeared vague and dream-like. The woman in Spencer's driveway sinking a needle into her neck. Where had the woman taken her, and why?

She wondered at the tooth in the driveway, the vision of the blonde girl gazing in horror at her own blood.

Adrenaline pumped through Orla's blood, creating an infuriating sensation of wanting to rip from her binds and sprint from the room, but she could do nothing.

She lay gagged and bound and terrified at what lay ahead.

10

Liz

"Fiona Sullivan?"

Fiona looked up from the sweater laid out on her table. She'd been fussing the seam for over ten minutes, unable to concentrate on the tiny thread.

A woman stood inside the shop's entrance. She looked about Fiona's age, with short blonde curls and a grim, sad smile. Wearing a wrinkled gray blouse and too-tight jeans, she appeared mildly disheveled. She had the air of a woman on the edge, a feeling Fiona was all too familiar with.

Fiona smiled, set the sweater aside and stood, frowning at the ache in her lower back.

"Yes. I'm Fiona Sullivan. How can I help you?"

The woman stepped forward, glanced around the shop at the piles of neatly stacked clothing pinned with the names of their owners waiting for pickup.

"My name is Liz Miner. I heard about your daughter."

"Orla?" Fiona asked, though of course it could be no one except Orla. She had only one child.

The woman nodded. She clutched her handbag as if it held her together. If she dropped it, the woman herself might collapse as well.

"My daughter was Susan Miner, Susie. Have you heard of her?"

Fiona frowned, trying to recall the name.

"Is she a friend of Orla's? I can't remember all her friends. She rarely brought them home, such a secretive girl."

Liz shook her head. She drew a folded piece of paper from her purse and strode across the room, handing it to Fiona.

Fiona studied the page. She took a moment to realize it was a missing person's poster.

Missing: Susan (Susie) Lynn Miner

D.O.B.: April 7th, 1953

Last Seen: Sunday, August 27th, 1972

In Petoskey, Michigan

Wearing: A yellow Rolling Stones t-shirt with red lips and tongue. Blue or black shorts. White tennis shoes.

Fiona stared at the pretty blonde girl in the photo. Her wide-set eyes looked light, probably blue. Her nose was little, dotted with freckles over a wide smile with two rows of straight teeth. Hoop earrings poked through her long blonde hair.

"She's still missing?"

"It will have been three years on August 27th."

It was July 13th. Little more than a month from the anniversary.

"I'm so sorry," Fiona said, her guts twisting as she considered her own daughter, missing now for five days. But Orla was different, bohemian, reckless in some ways. Surely, she had just hitched a ride with friends. She'd be back any day.

"I'm not sure how I can help, Mrs. Miner."

"Please, call me Liz."

Fiona offered her a polite smile and handed the poster back.

"There have been other missing girls, Fiona. Five I'm aware of. Six, if I include Orla."

Fiona frowned and shook her head.

"Orla's not missing. She just..." Fiona twiddled her fingers. "Left town for a week. She's a wanderer. My husband's mother was an Irish traveler - a Minkier. That's where she gets it."

Liz frowned and tucked the paper back into her purse, but stood firm.

"I don't think so," Liz disagreed.

"How do you know about Orla?"

"A friend who's investigating the cases told me."

Fiona held her up her hand, her voice rising.

"Orla is fine. She-"

"Three years," Liz interrupted. She swallowed and shook her head, as if tasting something horrible. "Three years without my Susie. I'd give anything to get her back. I'd die if she could come back. But she's dead. I know it. In my heart, I sensed it that very night when she didn't come home. Fiona-"

"Orla is fine!" Fiona snapped, her voice shrill.

The bells on the door tinkled as they swung in. It was Patrick.

"Pat," she sobbed, running across the room and clutching him. She buried her face in his chest and cried.

He patted his wife's back.

"What is it, Fiona? Hmm?" He spoke in a gentle voice, low and husky, as if his wife were a child rather than a grown woman.

Liz stepped forward.

"I'm sorry," she stammered. "I didn't mean to upset her."

"Who are you?" Patrick asked, taking his wife's shoulders in his hands and gently steering her back to the sewing table.

She sat in her chair heavily, staring at her hands clasped in her lap.

"My name is Liz Miner. My daughter disappeared three years ago. I came here because-"

"Orla? Do you know where she's at?" His face shifted, concern softening his otherwise hard features.

Liz shook her head.

"No, but there have been others."

"She just took a little trip," Fiona interrupted, again the shrill edge, her eyes taking on a wild sheen.

Patrick rested a hand on his wife's shoulder and shook his head.

"No, Fiona. I don't think so. I reported her missing two days ago."

"You what?" Fiona stood up, her lips pulling away from her teeth, her hands reaching toward him with claw-like hands.

"Honey." He took her hands, folded them against his chest. "I didn't want to scare you. Okay? But I made a few calls. No one has seen Orla since early last Sunday morning. It's going on a week."

"Women have been going missing for four years," Liz said, taking a second bunch of papers from her purse. She stepped to the table. "May I?"

Patrick looked at Liz, and then at his wife.

"Head home, Fiona. I'll lock up the shop. Have a bath. I'll be home in an hour."

To Liz's surprise, Fiona didn't argue. She hung her head, her eyes red-rimmed. She took her purse from the floor near her chair, slung it over her shoulder, and shuffled from the store, the bells tinkling behind her.

"I'm sorry," Patrick said, sighing. "Fiona is a very sensitive woman. She's afraid for Orla. So afraid that she's pretending everything is fine."

Liz bit her lip, tempted to tell him that was the worst thing Orla's mother could do, but she withheld her judgement. After all, she too had desperately tried to dismiss Susan's disappearance as a spontaneous adventure. In her gut, she knew better, but oh, how she wanted the alternative to be true.

Liz spread the papers on the desk. Five sheets, each featuring a different young woman beneath the word *Missing*.

He frowned and bent over, studying their faces.

"All these girls have disappeared?"

"Yes." Liz tapped the first face. "Sherry went missing in the summer of 1971 in Gaylord. My daughter was next, Susie in August 1972. There were two in 1973 - Darlene in Traverse City and Rita in Beulah. This spring another girl went missing, Laura in Cadillac. And now your daughter, Orla."

"What makes you think they're connected?"

"A few things. One, all of them are between the ages of eighteen and twenty-one. They're all young, pretty, disappearing in the summer and without a trace. No purse left behind, no note. As if they were plucked from thin air and didn't leave even a stick of gum behind. No bodies have ever been found. All within a two-hundred-mile radius. That's an awfully small space."

"Have the police connected them?"

"They won't confirm it. But I've been working with a journalist who's convinced they're connected. Detective Hansen in Petoskey is also investigating a connection, though not publicly. They're all in different jurisdictions, and-"

"Orla doesn't look like these other girls," Patrick said, frowning. "These girls are all blonde. And reading about their appearances, they all seem rather small. Orla stood almost five-feet-nine inches tall, long black hair. It would take a strong man to abduct her."

"Or a man with a weapon. I agree, she's an anomaly. But I still think she's connected. In my heart, I feel it. I've developed something from studying these cases, Mr. Sullivan. A sixth sense, if you will."

Patrick gave her an odd little smile.

"What?" she asked.

"Just the sixth sense thing. Orla had something like that. I sometimes called it her bullshit detector, but it was more than that."

"More how?"

He laughed, his face growing pink, and scratched at his short dark hair.

"Sometimes when she touched things, she got ideas about 'em. Like one time she picked up a pipe in my desk and said, 'This belonged to Pap and he liked potatoes.' Crazy thing was that the pipe had belonged to my grandfather - a man who died long before Orla was born. He was a potato farmer in Ireland."

"Was his name Pap?"

Patrick grinned and shook his head.

"Seamus. But our family called him Pap."

Liz glanced toward the window, sun streaming through, and considered his story.

"Your daughter never came home?" Patrick asked, looking suddenly older than his forty-three years.

"No. But I intend to change that. I've let go of finding her alive. I'm not naïve. But I want a proper burial for my child. I want to lay her to rest next to my mother. I want to plant flowers and clean her headstone and have a space to be near her again."

Patrick rubbed his slightly bristly jaw.

"Fiona would..." he trailed off. "It would kill her if Orla never came home."

Liz nodded, gathered the papers into a pile.

"I once believed that too, but it's almost cruel what we can survive."

11

Hazel

Hazel's head hit the pillow, and she fell into an instant sleep.

She woke surprised at the darkness. When she'd crawled into bed, the half-light of evening had left her room awash in a warm summer's glow. Now the black of deep night surrounded her.

She had been exhausted, still was, but an insatiable thirst turned her mouth dusty.

She swung her legs down and felt along the floor for her slippers.

"Hazel." Her head snapped up at Orla's voice.

"Finally," Hazel huffed, her relief instantly turning to irritation.

Orla had come home.

She pushed through her door into the hallway and found her friend hovering at the top of the stairs, but she looked all wrong. A blindfold covered her eyes, a dark strap stretched over her mouth, and her wrists and ankles showed angry red welts.

"Orla," she shrieked, running to her friend. But as she reached out to grab Orla, who appeared to be falling down the darkened stairs, her friend vanished.

Hazel teetered on the edge of the top stair, her torso jutting forward, hands flailing at the emptiness, and she started to fall.

She let out a little squeal, seized the bannister and caught it with one hand. The momentum of her body rocked forward, but her grip pulled her hard sideways and she crashed into the wall, twisting one ankle painfully as she missed the second step and landed awkwardly on the third.

The hallway light flicked on. Bethany hurried to the top of the stairs, her long t-shirt stopping above her.

Hazel still clutched the bannister, balancing her weight on her good ankle, breathing heavily and unable to shake the image of Orla, bound, calling out for help.

"Are you okay?" Bethany asked, squinting at Hazel while holding up a hand to block the glare from the lightbulb.

Hazel pushed away from the wall and winced at the pain in her ankle.

She sagged onto the top step.

"I heard Orla," she murmured.

"Here? Is she home?" Bethany peered into the dark stairwell, but Hazel shook her head.

"No. It was like a dream, but it wasn't a dream. I don't know." She pressed a finger against her already swelling ankle.

"Did you hurt it?" Bethany squatted next to her.

"Yeah. Could you get me a towel with ice and a glass of water? Sorry to be a pest, but I think walking down the stairs might do me in."

"Yeah, no problem."

Bethany hurried down the stairs.

Hazel stood shakily and limped back to her room. She turned on her bedside lamp and picked up her tarot cards, shuffling several times, envisioning Orla. She pulled a card from the top.

The Devil stared back at her. She pulled a second card - the ten of swords - an equally, if not more, ominous card that depicted a man lying face-down with ten swords jutting from his back.

Bethany hurried in, handed Hazel the water.

"Here, let's prop your leg up." Bethany stacked two pillows and helped Hazel lift her leg on top. She laid the towel with ice over her leg. "Are you worried about her?"

Hazel nodded.

"I know there's something wrong. I know it."

More than a week had passed since Orla disappeared. The searchers gathered at Birch Park, a natural area Orla often rode her bike to. Hazel knew if they found Orla in the woods, she'd likely be dead. That was the terrifying aspect of disappearances. If people could come home, they would.

Cars crowded the parking lot and bikes lay in heaps along the tree line. The police weren't involved. Hazel wondered if they'd do it all differently.

"Here." Calvin handed her a walkie-talkie. He'd tucked his long, dark hair behind his ears and opted for jeans over his usual shorts.

Hazel had planned the search, but Calvin organized it. Though he worked in a bookstore, detested law enforcement, and fit snugly into the 1970s counterculture many young people preferred, he came from a military family. He understood how search parties worked. Despite their political differences, his father and two brothers had volunteered their help. They'd also brought maps of the natural area marked into grids to organize searches, walking sticks, two-way radios, and jugs of water.

Hazel smiled gratefully at Calvin's father and gave him a quick hug. Tall and broad with buzzed hair, he looked the part of a soldier, as did Calvin's two brothers, who fanned out giving people directions.

"How ya doing, honey?" Calvin asked, trotting over.

"I don't know," she admitted.

Thoughts jumbled her mind. Fear of discovering Orla's decomposing body had soured her sleep for two nights. She searched the sky for crows and vultures, some signal that death lay near.

"You don't have to give any directions. I'll lead this group. My dad's taking searchers west. My brothers are covering the group along the road. If you spot anything," he pushed the red button on the side of the radio, "give your location."

Hazel nodded and started forward with the searchers. She saw neighbors, a woman who Orla mended clothes for, and many people she'd never met. Orla's father, Mr. Sullivan, arrived with a pickup truck filled with the same men she'd seen at the job site. He offered her a nod but didn't say hello.

As she walked through the knee-high grass, she concentrated on the ground. Twice, other searchers paused, exclaiming they'd found something, only to hold up empty pop cans or discarded food bags.

"Is that a shoe?" a woman several paces to Hazel's right, asked.

Hazel rushed over.

The woman pointed at a dark blob that appeared to be leather. Hazel stared at shoelaces tangled in the object. Moss covered most of the boot.

"It's not Orla's," she sighed.

~

After the search, Hazel gulped water from a jug Calvin handed her.

The searches had come up empty. Hazel felt hollow. Perhaps Orla had not gone to Birch Park at all, and Hazel had wasted everyone's time searching the wrong woods.

Across the parking lot, a man held his camera up, snapped a shot of the group, twiddled with the lens and took another, and then another. He didn't speak with other searchers and appeared to be on his own. A notepad hung by a string around his neck.

"Are you a reporter?" she asked, stopping just short of him, blocking his shot.

He lowered the camera.

"Yes, with Up North News." He held out a hand. "Abraham Levett. I prefer Abe."

Hazel looked at his hand and felt torn. Was she supposed to befriend this man, beg him to print a story about her friend? Or did he intend to act as so many others had, as if she were making a spectacle out of a girl who'd hitchhiked out of town and would be back any minute.

Finally, she offered him a limp shake.

"I'm Hazel. Why are you here, Abe?"

He glanced toward the woods where more searchers trickled in, their faces sunburnt, their shoulders slumped.

"To cover the story of a missing woman."

"So, you don't think she just took off?" Hazel asked, an edge in her voice.

"Have you heard of Rita Schneider?"

Hazel frowned. The name sounded vaguely familiar.

"She vanished from Beulah the summer of 1973. That's where my father lives, where I grew up. She used to feed his cat if he went out of town. On July 17th, 1973, she rode her bike to Platte Bay and vanished without a trace."

Hazel blinked at him, a cold, sinking feeling in her stomach.

"And you suspect her disappearance is connected to Orla?"

"Orla doesn't fit the type, but maybe."

"The type?" Hazel asked, irritated.

"It's not an insult. If you truly want to know, I'll explain it."

"I do, but I need to help Calvin wrap this up. Can we meet in a few hours?"

Abe looked at his watch, a raggedy thing with a cracked face and a worn leather band.

"Sure. I'll come by your house."

"How do you know where I live?"

"I'm a journalist. That's my job."

12

Hazel

Abe knocked on Hazel's door moments after she poured herself a glass of water and slumped onto the couch. Calvin had gone home with his dad to drop off the search supplies and would return in the evening. Hazel wanted to curl up and sleep. Her feet and lower back ached. She was in good shape, but trooping through the woods, hunched over and squinting at the ground until her eyes crossed had worn her down.

In the end, they'd found nothing.

She pulled open the door.

Abe still wore the same blue jeans, rolled at the bottom, and brown t-shirt. His hair was black, curly and just above his ears. His beard and mustache were not unruly like many men Hazel's age, but neatly trimmed. Though Abe looked young, she suspected he wasn't her age - closer to thirty than twenty.

A black camera bag hung over one arm, a folder tucked into his armpit, and he held his notebook in his hand.

She smiled and almost threw the door open wide to invite him in. Instead, her mind drifted back to the Devil card she'd pulled for Orla days earlier. She quickly stepped onto the porch and closed the door behind her.

"We can talk out here," she said, leading him to the patio furniture at one end of their long front porch. It was white aluminum cushioned in green floral fabric. It had belonged to Hazel's mother. Every night, Hazel carried the cushions inside and stored them in the closet.

Abe sat in a chair and opened his folder.

Hazel looked at a map of northern Michigan spotted with little red dots.

"What are the dots?" she asked.

"Where each girl went missing."

"Wait." She looked up, startled. "Each? You mean there are more than two?"

"Six, if we include Orla. Six women have disappeared since 1971."

Hazel gaped at the page.

"How come I haven't heard about this."

Abe looked at her squarely.

"Because there are no bodies. Without bodies, there's no conclusive evidence of foul play. Worse, there's no evidence at all. Maybe they took off, started a new life, hopped on a plane."

"Maybe they did," Hazel said.

"They didn't," Abe told her. He pushed the map aside and pulled out paper-sized photos of each girl. "I've spoken with their parents, their friends. These weren't runaways. They didn't hitchhike. Most of them didn't smoke pot. Not one of them had ever taken off, not even once. Rita left three hundred dollars in cash in the bureau next to her bed. Susie had plans to go camping for Labor Day Weekend."

He pointed at pictures as he spoke.

"Orla was making costumes for Harvey at the Old Town Playhouse," Hazel murmured. She imagined Orla's room with the book laying open, the tepid glass of water, the beautiful dress she'd made days earlier hanging unworn in the closet. It was not the room of a woman leaving town.

"Why haven't they been in the newspapers?" Hazel asked, growing angry.

"Why isn't Orla in the paper? We're coming out of a time when a lot of women took off, when they hopped in a van and moved to

California to drop LSD and sleep on the beach. Unfortunately, most of our law enforcement view the '70s girls the same way they did the '60s girls. They assume the parents are being paranoid, over-reacting."

"But six girls in four years!"

"Exactly. But they're all in different jurisdictions. Or they were, until Orla."

"Who's the other girl from Traverse City?"

"Darlene Rice." He slid out a Polaroid of a smiling girl with long blonde hair pulled over one shoulder. She was leaning her head on a large man, her father perhaps. In her arms she held a struggling puppy.

"Her name sounds familiar, but..." Hazel shook her head. Had she read about the girl? Seen a missing poster? She wasn't sure.

"Her case is especially difficult. She was vacationing here with her parents, renting a house in town. Her mom and dad and two brothers went to get ice cream and watch a movie. They'd been here for a week and were beached out at that point. Darlene wasn't. She took her beach bag and walked out the door, and they never saw her again."

Hazel lifted the photo to look closer and wanted to cringe away from the smiling face. How could someone vanish without a trace?

"No one saw her? How is that possible?"

"People saw her up to a point. But she disappeared on a Tuesday in the middle of the day. A wooded trail offered a shortcut to the beach. The last sighting of Darlene was by a woman driving, who glimpsed her walking into that park. No sightings after that. No one saw her at the beach."

"She disappeared in the woods? Which means you think someone is taking them - going into the woods and abducting them?"

"That's my theory."

"You said *Orla doesn't fit the type*. What did you mean?"

Abe pulled out more photos of the girls. He spread them on the table.

Hazel studied the pictures.

The first thing she noticed was their hair. They were all blonde.

Their hair appeared mostly long and straight. Their eyes were light colored, blue or green.

"You can't tell in all the pictures, but the girls were also petite. Most of them were no taller than five-foot-four inches and weighed less than one-hundred and twenty pounds."

"Orla's tall."

"I know. But she's the right age, and the circumstances are similar. Her hair is dark, but it's straight. And I think she's connected."

"Why?"

Abe gazed at the images before him, as if the answer lay within the faces of the missing girls.

"Call it a hunch, a somewhat confirmed hunch."

"Confirmed?"

"I've been talking with Susan Miner's mother for a year. The morning I saw the news brief about Orla, I knew he had taken another one. Susan's mother called me fifteen minutes later. She had the same instinct."

"He?"

"In cases such as these, it's usually a man."

Hazel swallowed. She remembered her vision of Orla. It had not been a dream; of that she was sure.

"I want her to be in a car somewhere, driving to Vermont to a music festival or visiting her cousin in Detroit. I want so much to believe she's going to pop through the door, apologize for taking off, and act shocked that we raised the alarm."

"But you don't believe she will."

"No, I don't."

"You mentioned her cousin in Detroit. Who's she?" Abe flipped open his notebook.

"It's a he, Liam. Why are you taking notes?"

He glanced up at her.

"Because I'm investigating her disappearance. I've been investigating all of them. I'm writing a story about these women. It's going on the front page next week. I'm going to be under the wire, but I want Orla in that article. I need to gather as much information as possible."

"For your story?" she demanded.

He laid his pencil down and regarded her.

"To find out who's behind this. To stop him before he strikes again."

Hazel studied his face.

"Why haven't you written it yet? If these girls have been disappearing for years..."

"I only learned of the disappearances last year. Liz Miner contacted me. I knew of Rita's disappearance, but local gossip claimed she took off with a boyfriend. After Liz reached out, insisting she'd spoken with the other parents, I started looking into it. I realized she was on to something. I've spent the last year talking to families, pouring over police reports, trying to find the link."

"And you haven't found it?"

"Not exactly, no."

"How do I help?" she asked. "I need to help."

13

NORTHERN MICHIGAN ASYLUM FOR THE INSANE

Orla

Orla woke to discover someone had moved her. The white hospital walls and dim lighting no longer surrounded her. She lay in a dark space, cave-like, except the walls were brick rather than stone. Lights flickered from torches lining the walls. Gleaming silver instruments and a glass bottle sat on a metal table beside her. The label on the bottle read 'sodium thiopental.'

She turned her head to the side. A man in a white coat hunched over another metal table.

When he turned, she noticed a startling resemblance to Spencer, the man she'd spent that final night with. He'd told her his father was dead.

Did he know what happened to her? Or worse, was he in on it?

"Who are you?" Orla croaked, mouth gritty.

"At last she wakes," the man said, unsmiling.

He pushed the needle into the bottle and pulled the syringe back.

"Please," she murmured.

He didn't respond but stepped to the bed and slid the needle into her neck. She tried to cringe away, but the straps held her in place.

He returned to the metal table.

"We'll give that a little time to do its work, shall we?" he asked.

He walked away from her, disappearing into a dark tunnel.

When he returned, Orla studied him.

His thick, dark hair was combed away from his forehead. Piercing blue eyes gazed out from his tanned face. Like Spencer, he had a sharp nose and a square jaw. Handsome, but cold. In his fifties, she thought, or older.

"Truth serum," he told her, picking up the bottle and tilting it in the firelight. "Have you heard of it, Orla?"

"Yes." She closed her mouth, surprised at her answer. The moment he'd uttered truth serum, she'd intended to clamp her mouth shut and not speak a word.

"Good, that's very good. And can you tell me your name?"

Orla tried to shake her head, but again spoke. It seemed impossible not to. As if the part of her that wanted to lie still and silent wasn't in complete control, some automatic part of her brain took over.

"Orla Delaney Sullivan."

"And I am Doctor Crow. Nice to officially meet you. How old are you, Orla?"

"Twenty. Please, I'd like to go home now. I feel dizzy."

"Soon," the man told her. "Just a few more questions. You visited a young man, Spencer, at his home in Leelanau. What did you find?"

The tooth rose in Orla's mind, and she knew she couldn't speak of it. If she revealed her vision, she'd be dead.

"A tooth," her mouth said anyway.

"A tooth?" he asked, lifting his eyebrows.

"Susan's tooth," she added. She clenched her eyes shut and ground her teeth together.

"How do you know it was Susan's tooth?"

Orla wiggled her gloved fingers.

"I see things with my hands. It's a gift." She laughed, and tears slipped over her cheeks.

"You see things? Explain that."

"It's like the residue of an experience, energy, I guess. Sometimes when I touch things, I catch images, experience feelings, receive information."

"And you found a tooth at Spencer's house. The tooth of a woman named Susan?"

"Someone murdered her." Orla gasped as the words slipped out. She had revealed everything, and she couldn't take it back.

"How did she die?" he asked, calm, voice unmoved.

Orla squinted. She glimpsed the image again, the brief flash of something striking Susan in the face.

"A rock, I don't know. Someone hit her with a rock."

"And did you see who killed her?"

Orla shook her head no.

"What happened after the rock hit her?"

"I don't know," Orla whispered, and she didn't.

Her face ached from the effort of not speaking, but she had spoken.

The man watched her with a troubled, and intrigued, expression.

"We have work to do, Orla. You and I."

14

Abe

Abe pulled into the small parking lot at Birch Park's trailhead. Another car, invisible from the road, was parked half in the overgrowth. Abe studied the gold sports car, surprised the owner would leave it where pine sap might fall onto the hood. It appeared as if the driver wanted to conceal the car from the road.

Abe peered at the photo of Orla he'd taped to his dashboard. She sat cross-legged in the grass with a pile of kittens crawling in her lap. She gazed down, and grinned at the kittens, her black hair falling over one shoulder. Hazel had loaned him the photo. It made Orla real. A breathtaking young woman with a smile and a heart and a life.

Abe stepped from his car, jotted down the license plate of the gold sports car, and walked closer. He peered in windows at the clean leather interior. Shiny clean, as if the owner had detailed the car that morning. Abe searched for personal items and spotted none. Not a pair of sunglasses or a discarded candy wrapper lay in sight.

"Can I help you?"

The voice startled him, but Abe didn't react.

He lifted his gaze, offered a smile, and nodded at the car.

"She yours?"

The man was around his height, six foot, with sandy hair, tanned skin, and bright blue eyes. He was handsome, clean-cut, a college boy. Abe had been a college boy too, but he had never owned tennis shorts in his life.

The man hooked one thumb in his pocket and nodded.

"Yeah." He smiled, losing the hardness of his jawline for a more relaxed expression. "Got her last year. My baby." He stepped to the car, patted the hood, and pulled keys from his pocket.

"Hiking?" Abe asked, gesturing at the trees.

"Actually," the man gave him a sly smile. "I was taking a piss."

He got into his car, offered a salute, and started the engine.

Abe walked backwards.

His own car, a Rambler bought cheap the year after he graduated from college, made a sad comparison to the Corvette. He watched the car drive from the lot. The driver's eyes flicked to the rearview mirror for half a second before he pulled onto the road and was gone.

Abe glanced at his notebook where he'd written the license plate number.

"It doesn't take that long to piss," he murmured, looking toward the trailhead where the man had emerged. And why walk into the trail at all? He'd parked right next to a grove of dense trees. He could have stood next to his car and remained unnoticed.

Walking the trail, Abe searched for the man's footprints but quickly lost them in the trampled grass left by the search party. It was unlikely there was anything left to find.

A half-mile in, a shadow passed over Abe and he gazed toward the sky to see an eagle, its white head at the tip of huge, dark wings, soaring into a tree.

Abe cut through the trees, leaving the path to get closer to where he thought the eagle had landed. He found it. A huge nest sat high in a tree. He heard the eagle, but the leafy branches blocked the bird from view.

Scanning the ground beneath the tree, Abe saw nothing, but continued his search squatting low, brushing the ground with fingertips, and then moving on.

After fifteen minutes, he stood and walked back to the base of the tree. He inspected the bark, the low branches.

He almost missed it. As he ducked beneath a branch, something wispy caught in his beard. A spiderweb, he assumed, and started to bat it away and then paused, his eye catching on the color. It was black. He reached up, pinching it between his thumb and forefinger.

He stared at a long strand of black hair.

~

Hazel

Hazel saw Abe's car pull into her driveway, and she scrawled a quick note to her roommates before hurrying out.

She climbed into his passenger seat, stepping on several Styrofoam coffee cups.

"Sorry," he told her, leaning over to gather them up and toss them into the backseat. "I like to call her my mobile think-tank." He patted the dashboard.

"I can imagine the inside of a brain looks something like this," she admitted, glancing into the disarray of his backseat.

"Do you know anyone who drives a gold sports car?" Abe asked, backing down the driveway and turning onto the road.

Hazel shook her head.

"Why?"

"I went to Birch Park this morning and met a man who drove a distinctive gold car. I thought he might be one of Orla's friends."

Hazel tried to remember the few men Orla had gone on dates with, but didn't land on anyone with a sports car, especially a gold one.

"No, nothing. Did you find anything else?"

Abe gestured to his glove box.

Hazel popped it open, but the door stuck. Papers stuffed into the small space blocked the hinge. She reached in and pulled out a paperback.

"It's in the book," he said.

She flipped open the cover and stared at a clear plastic bag. Inside, she saw a long, black hair.

"Is there any way to know if it's hers?"

"Microscopic hair analysis could get pretty close to a verification, but right now, there's no detective willing to consider it."

Hazel looked out the window. Sun-baked beaches speckled with bright towels and umbrellas stretched along the bay. Beyond them, Lake Michigan seemed to doze beneath the hot midday sun.

The summer temperatures peaked in July and August. Hazel looked forward to the evenings when the sun's intensity subsided. Still, she woke many nights sweaty, summoning a breeze that rarely arrived.

"Do you mind?" she asked, touching the dial on the air conditioner.

"Not at all. Crank it. The heat today is already unbearable, and it's not even noon."

Hazel turned the air to high and sighed back in her seat as the cold rushed out.

"I didn't sleep well last night," she admitted.

"Me neither," he said, turning a vent so it blew into his face. "If this heat holds up, I may need to shave."

She looked at his beard and grimaced.

"I'd have shaved weeks ago."

He smiled.

"I woke up at 3:11 on the mark. Dead asleep, and then just wide awake."

Hazel frowned and stared out the window.

"I did, too. 3:11 exactly. Two nights in a row."

He glanced at her.

"Really?"

"Yes, but I… I heard Orla. She said my name - Hazel - just like that. I opened my eyes, and sat up, but no one was there."

Abe looked troubled. More than troubled.

"Did you hear her too?" Hazel asked.

He shook his head.

"How could I know? I've never met her, but no, I didn't hear her."

Hazel studied his jaw, where he was chewing his cheek. She felt sure he was holding back.

"But you heard something? Right?"

"I don't know, Hazel. It seemed odd how I woke up out of the blue. I wondered if I heard something."

"Turn on Hammond," she directed him.

They were tracing one of Orla's usual routes. Abe wanted to see all the places she might have ridden to.

"The police asked me a few questions, but they haven't been back," Hazel murmured. "Are they doing anything?"

Abe shook his head.

"I work with a lot of cops. Some of them are great. When someone commits a crime, they're on it. Unfortunately, they don't work well with ambiguity. Detective Moore has been assigned to this case. He and I have butted heads a lot. He thinks Orla took off. When Darlene disappeared, he said the same thing."

"A girl running away while on vacation with her family? That's ridiculous."

"That's what I said."

Hazel shook her head, glared out the windshield.

"Even though everyone who knows Orla says differently? How is that okay?"

"Because people don't know it's happening. It's that simple. Until you're a victim of a crime or know someone who is, you don't understand the criminal justice system. And I'm not saying it's all bad. It's not. But there's a lot of missed opportunity in investigations because they waste time. One issue is that most parents will claim their kid wouldn't run away. Even if the kid runs away every other week, packed a bag, and stole a wad of cash. They'll still insist it's not a runaway. Cops get jaded, start seeing every missing person's case as a runaway."

"So, what do we do?"

"This." Abe beckoned toward the road. "We investigate, we figure it out. For my part, I'm writing an article that's going to blow this thing wide open. People will be aware for the first time that we're not talking about one missing girl, but six. Good luck finding a person who's not terrified by that. That puts pressure on the police. They form a task force, more manpower gets assigned to the cases, more money funnels into the investigation. It's bureaucracy, a slow-moving glacier, but once she picks up speed…"

"So, they'll help us if they're getting paid more?" Hazel grumbled.

"Not exactly, but in a way, sure. Otherwise, the administration has to allocate the funds more evenly. The job of the press is to inform the people. The people then have to mobilize, make their voices heard, put pressure on the politicians. It's coming, Hazel. But in the meantime, we're following the leads, because otherwise they'd get cold long before the police got to them."

Hazel nodded, and tried to find his words uplifting.

"There's a detective in Petoskey who's been working Susie Miner's case from the beginning. He also believes there's a connection, though he won't admit it on the record. He's committed a lot of hours to this case. The problem is, he's the only detective in the office. He's overloaded."

"And you think us driving around, searching for clues, is helpful?"

"I know it is. I've met people who solved the murders of family members, who found missing kids. The closer you are to the crime, the more access you have to the truth."

15

THE NORTHERN MICHIGAN ASYLUM FOR THE INSANE

Orla

Orla watched the young man move through the room. He was awkward, long arms past his waist. His greasy, dark hair hung over his face, shielding his eyes. He moved through the room mopping up her vomit.

The medicine Crow gave her in the morning upset her stomach, likely a result of her refusal to eat breakfast. It was a futile, and foolish, rebellion. Starving herself would only make her weak and incapable of escape, but when Crow presented her with a bowl of mush sprinkled with raisins, she'd still turned her head away.

He warned her the medicine would make her throw up.

"Good," she said. "A quick way to get it out of my system."

And it had been.

The doctor cursed when she'd thrown up. Unfortunately, he'd merely returned a short time later, the smell of her vomit sour in the room, and injected the medicine into her arm.

Now she lay dazed, not having eaten all day, the sedative effects wearing off.

She'd noticed the man before. He'd been standing in the hallway when the doctor had rushed in, his hands shoved in his pockets, staring at the floor.

"Help me," Orla croaked.

The man froze, the mop clutched in his hand. After several seconds, he returned to his mopping as if she hadn't spoken.

"He abducted me," she whispered. "My name is Orla Sullivan. Please…"

The man continued mopping in silence, lifting the mop into the bucket and then plopping it onto the tiles.

As he pushed the bucket toward the door, wheels squeaking, he glanced at Orla.

For an instant their eyes connected.

His widened and then darted away.

Orla lifted her fingers, reaching, but he'd already slipped from the room.

16

Liz

Liz waved at Patrick as he entered the diner.

"Abe, this is Patrick Sullivan. Patrick, Abe Levett. Abe's a reporter at Up North News."

Patrick narrowed his eyes.

"I thought that paper mostly wrote fluff about left-leaning political heroes."

Abe shrugged.

"What paper doesn't write those?"

Patrick nodded.

"I see your point."

Liz patted an empty chair, and Patrick sat down, eyeing the other patrons in the restaurant wearily.

He looked tired, skin sagging beneath his blue eyes, lips turned down. If he'd showered and changed his clothes that day, you wouldn't know it.

Liz remembered those days, the first weeks after Susie disappeared when showering was an afterthought. Sometimes she'd climb into the shower at two a.m. and let the water rush over her. A few times, she fell asleep beneath the hot spray and woke up shocked when the water had turned cold.

"How's Fiona?" Liz asked, signaling to the waitress to bring another coffee.

"Wound up like a ten-day clock. If I sneeze, she practically jumps into the ceiling."

"It's hard," Liz recalled. "Every sound could mean…"

"She's home," Patrick finished. "But she's not."

Patrick held an envelope in his hand. He opened it, and several photos spilled out.

Abe leaned over the table for a closer look.

"The many faces of Orla," Patrick said, touching one of the pictures.

She was a beauty - dark hair, bright blue eyes like Patrick's. Her long, sinewy frame looked strong, like an Amazon woman.

"She loved her bike. Rode it everywhere. For her sixteenth birthday, she didn't beg for a car. She wanted a new bike. The Schwinn Super Sport in lemon yellow."

"Nice-looking bike," Abe said.

Liz studied the young woman's face.

In one photo, she sat on a paisley couch next to a boy about her age, with a shock of red hair and a freckled nose.

"That's her cousin, Liam. My sister's son. He lives in Detroit."

Orla smiled in the photo, but not a big, toothy grin. Instead it was a small smile, as if she and Liam had just shared an inside joke the photographer was unaware of.

"This is the most recent." Patrick pointed at the last picture.

Orla stood next to a small woman with a pinched smile.

"That's my wife, Fiona," he told Abe.

A distance separated the two women, despite Orla's long arm draped over her mother's small shoulders.

"It was Fiona's birthday. Orla took us out to dinner at Paulie's. She'd just started a new job and was excited to have extra money to treat us."

"What was the new job?" Abe asked.

Liz watched him pick up his pen. His eyes drifted back to the photos for an instant, a sadness gathering, but then he shifted, looking at Patrick dispassionately.

"Waiting tables at a cafe called Zander's. They serve funny food, like raw sandwiches or something. You couldn't pay me to eat there, but these younger generations." Patrick waved a dismissive hand. "It's not a long-term option. Orla takes classes at the college. She teaches sewing, makes costumes for the playhouse shows. She's an unusual girl, gets bored easily. She makes handbags and sells them at the farmer's market, among other things."

"Did she mention anyone from the cafe? Anyone who made her feel uncomfortable? Or anywhere else in her life?"

"I wish I could tell you, but you're barking up the wrong tree. Orla doesn't talk to me or her mom much about personal stuff. She hasn't lived at home for a year and a half. Her girlfriends would know those things. And Liam." Patrick picked up the photo of Orla with her cousin. "My sister and I call 'em bacon and cabbage."

Liz saw the same confused expression on Abe's face.

Patrick shrugged.

"Guess you have to be Irish. Our mam cooked bacon and cabbage every day she could get her hands on some good meat. They go together - so to speak."

"Does Liam have any theories about Orla?" Abe asked.

Patrick shook his head.

"I've talked with Effie, my sister, a few times. She said Liam's as mystified as the rest of us. He's been itchin' to come north, but he's got a pregnant wife and a big job. Can't exactly take off."

"He'd be open to talking with me?" Abe asked.

"Sure, yeah."

"Can you give me his full name, phone number, and address?"

Patrick rattled off Liam's contact information.

"How do you feel about this one?" Abe asked, pushing Orla's senior picture to the center of the table.

"It was taken two years ago," Patrick said.

"I know, but it's a clear headshot, which is helpful. I'd like to use this one in the article."

"What article?"

Patrick and Abe both looked at Liz.

"Abe's writing an article about the disappearances - all of them," Liz told him. "He and his editor have been working on it for months. Orla's the… the last straw, I guess."

"If the police won't link them," Abe said, "we will. The public deserves to know about this and make their own conclusions."

"But you said she didn't fit," Patrick said to Liz almost accusingly.

"I also said it was the same man," she responded, eyes hard.

"This may be your only chance, Patrick. Don't turn away from this. Go home and prepare Fiona."

"There's likely to be a media response," Abe said. "And hopefully a police response. It's time to get their attention."

"When will the article appear?"

"Five days. It's coming out in Sunday's paper. I have a few more interviews to do. I'd like to talk with Liam, and chat with Orla's co-worker, but it's getting close."

~

Hazel

"Hazel!" Miranda rose from one of several card tables where people, mostly women, sat with spreads of tarot cards scattered before them. "I hoped you'd come today."

Miranda took Hazel in her large, soft arms and pressed her into a hug. The woman smelled of a heady blend of lemon and peppermint oils. Her thick, dark hair was piled and clipped on her head.

"I read about Orla in the paper. Any news?"

"No." Hazel shook her head. "That's why I'm here, actually. I thought maybe we could do a collective reading. See what everyone gets."

"Yes!" Miranda's head bobbed up and down, orange teardrop earrings bouncing. She maneuvered her round body through the tables and clapped her hands.

"Lovelies, can I have your attention, please?" There were eight people in the room, two per table. They were all readers, but they practiced on each other. Six women and two men gazed at their unlikely leader. "Our dear friend Hazel has come to us for help."

Several people shifted to Hazel, offering little waves and nods.

Hazel smiled at them. She had met with many of them for years.

She knew their stories, both from readings and the small talk that inevitably followed the group's sessions.

"We're doing a reading for Orla Sullivan. Orla has been missing for more than a week. Got a picture, sweets?" Miranda shifted to Hazel.

Hazel drew several photos from her purse, and Miranda quickly dispersed them amongst the tables.

~

Hazel sat alone with Miranda after the group had disbanded and the others had trickled out.

The tarot consensus had been clear - Orla had come into contact with someone devious. The Devil cards had shown up a startling number of times, accompanied by the Tower, and the ten of swords.

Miranda shuffled her own stack, closed her eyes, and flicked the cards onto the table.

She flipped over the top card.

The knight of swords stared back at them.

"A young man, quick-thinking and fast-acting. Driven by intellect, strategy. This is your helper." Miranda tapped the card. "Be watchful for this person."

"He's already arrived," Hazel said, thinking of Abe.

"Yes, good." Miranda flipped another card. "The Magician." She studied the card. "You have everything you need, but you must call upon all of your faculties - beyond the intellect, you must use your intuition, your compassion. I believe you will help to balance this individual." Miranda touched the knight card again. "This problem cannot be solved by mind alone. There are forces beyond us. Remain open to receive their messages."

17

Abe

Abe spotted Liam easily. He stood over six feet tall, with coppery red hair and a full beard to match. He looked older than twenty, big and lumberjack-like as he growled at a man sitting on some scaffolding, smoking a cigarette.

"That's your third smoke break in an hour, Pete. Get back to work," he snapped.

The man shook his head, but as Abe watched, he caught the eye of another construction worker and winked. The man grinned at the young foreman.

"Liam Byrne?" Abe called, stepping around a pile of bricks and hopping over a length of steel.

"Sure am," Liam said. "You lookin' for a job?" Liam eyed him up and down.

Abe was almost as tall as Liam, but the Irish man likely outweighed him by a hundred pounds. Abe had a writer's body - thin and pale with soft hands.

"No, I'd puke if I had to climb up there." He gestured at the high building. "I'm a reporter from northern Michigan."

Liam blinked at him.

"You're here about Orla? Have you found her?" Liam asked, a hopeful tinge in his voice.

The concern in his face transformed the strapping man he'd witnessed seconds earlier.

"No, I'm sorry. I'm here to ask you some questions about her. Sometimes little details, can open up new avenues for investigation."

Liam's mouth turned down.

"You came all the way down here to ask me questions. Why didn't you just call?"

"Because that's not how I operate. Do you have lunch soon? Maybe we could meet somewhere?"

Liam gave him a wry look.

"I don't take lunch. Gotta be on these guys like foam on a pint." He bent over and grabbed a plank from the ground, plunking it on top of two saw horses. "Our very own park bench," he announced, dropping onto the board. It groaned beneath him, but held.

"That works," Abe told him, sitting next to Liam and pulling out his notebook and pencil. "This seems like a big job for someone so young."

Liam laughed. "I've got a fourteen-month-old and another one on the way. Gotta feed 'em somehow."

Abe shook his head, incredulous.

"Sounds like a lot of pressure."

"Nah." Liam braced his hands on the board and stretched his legs out. "I always wanted a big family. Erin, my wife, did too. Our little girl, Aileen, wasn't an accident. People like to think she was because we were so young, but when you know what you want, why wait?"

"Well said. I'd like to have kids someday, but..." Abe shrugged.

"But what? No woman?"

Abe laughed. "For starters, yeah, no woman. I work a lot too. I'm not sure I'm ideal husband and father material."

Liam slapped him on the back.

"You're wrong. Don't ask me how I know, but I do."

Abe grinned and wrote Liam's name in his notebook.

"Do you have theories about Orla? About what might have happened?"

Liam's face fell. He leaned forward and braced his elbows on his knees.

"Whatever it was, she didn't run off. I can tell you that right now. Orla and I have been like this," he held up his hand, the index and middle fingers crossed, "since diapers. She's not the type to go bananas. If she wanted to leave, she'd leave, but first she'd say goodbye to her parents and her roommates. She'd call me and fill me in on the big plan."

"Has she ever done that before? Taken off, or talked about it?"

"Nope. She travelled around Michigan, came down here a few times a year. She's not a California girl. My ma said a rumor is floatin' around up there. Orla is proud of this place. She loves Michigan, up north especially. She's been haggling me to bring Erin and Aileen to visit since Aileen was born. We would've gone too, but then Erin got pregnant again and..." He held up his hands.

"When's the last time you spoke with her?"

"The Friday before she disappeared."

"Can you tell me what you talked about?"

"Sure, nothing major. She told me she's been reading a lot. Talked about costumes she made for a play. I told her Erin was finally over the morning sickness and now eating everything in the house. Aileen got on the phone and baby-talked with her. Aileen only has a handful of words - Orla is one of them."

"So, you're still close? Despite the distance?"

Liam gave him a sidelong glance.

"Distance doesn't matter. Not when you're connected. Orla and I are connected. I've got four siblings, and not a one of them share what Orla and I have."

"How often do you talk?"

"At least once a week, sometimes more. She talks with Erin a lot too."

"Does she know Erin?"

"Course she does. I introduced Erin to Orla before she met my parents. They were fast friends."

"Erin was never jealous of your relationship with Orla?"

Liam laughed.

"No. Erin calls Orla a bonus. She can pick her brain about me, and she can vent to her. Orla knows me better than anyone. Erin loves that. She got a husband and a great friend, too."

"And Orla mentioned nothing to you or Erin about going anywhere that Sunday? Even just around town? Or having met someone?"

"Nope, and if she'd have met someone, we'd have heard about it. She's dated a few chumps. Erin and Orla loved to laugh about these nightmare dates she had. She went out once with a guy who brought his cat in a duffel bag. The damn thing jumped out while they were eating dinner and almost scratched Orla's eyes out."

Abe laughed.

"That sounds like the date from hell."

"Yeah, and he was one of the better ones."

"So, she's had trouble with men? With finding someone?"

Liam scratched his chin.

"Orla's never been into finding someone, not like a lot of girls. When we were younger, she complained how all her friends talked nothing but boys. She had other things on her mind, big dreams. She never found anyone who trumped those."

"Has she ever dated bad guys?"

Liam grinned.

"Depends on your definition of bad. They weren't Pat and Fiona approved. In our family, your ideal mate is an Irish Catholic with eight siblings, and parents who fly back to the motherland every year to celebrate the St. Patrick's Festival - not Orla's type."

"What was her type?"

Liam scrunched his brow.

"Guys with an axe to grind. That's the one trait I remember from the few I met. They hated the man, or the pigs, or their parents. They walked with a kind of righteous indignation. Problem was, they seemed to get stoned more than do anything about it."

"Does Orla use marijuana?"

"God, you sound like a cop."

Abe smiled.

"Sorry, when I get rolling, I'm all professional."

Liam shook his head.

"Once in a while. We smoked grass a handful of times."

"Has she ever used other drugs?"

Liam shrugged.

"Here and there. She wouldn't say no if the mood was right."

Abe watched the men on the scaffolding. They walked with ease, as if there wasn't a forty-foot drop beside them.

"I wish I could help more, man. I do. It's been killin' me not being there, looking for her. My ma's been on the phone with Fiona every night. Pat's fit to be tied. I'm stuck here. Never felt that way before, but with Orla missin', that's just how I feel. Trapped."

"Is there anything else? Anything that might have gotten Orla into trouble."

Liam set his jaw and his eyes darted away. There was something. Abe recognized the look, the holding back. He waited, not wanting to push him the other way.

"Maybe," he said finally. "Orla wouldn't like me tellin' ya."

"I won't write about it," Abe told him. "This is off the record. I'm a reporter, but I'm on this story for different reasons. I have no interest in making things hard for Orla. I want to find her while there's still a chance-"

"That she's alive?"

Abe nodded.

"Blimey," Liam muttered, kicking at a rock with his huge boot. "Orla sensed things if she touched them."

Abe frowned, made a note.

"How so?"

"She, ummm…," Liam reached out and cupped his fingers, "got feelings when she touched objects. If she touched my car keys, she could tell me the last place I drove, or maybe the song I was singing in the car. It was weird, but cool. We experimented with it a lot as kids, and she was dead-on every time. It scared the stuffing out of her ma. But my mom, Effie, said God had blessed Orla. Tomayto-tomahto, you know?"

Abe scratched words onto his notebook, puzzling at the ink letters.

"So, if she touched this pen, what? She could say I wrote the word 'blessed'?"

Liam nodded.

"And she could probably say you were talking to me, and add something quirky like how you felt when you wrote it."

"A psychic ability?"

"Sure, yeah. It's not like we ever had a name for it. She started wearing gloves as we got older, because it bothered her. She knew things she shouldn't. Sometimes she learned things that upset her. She was dating a guy in high school, and she touched his locker one morning and saw him standing there making out with somebody else."

"Ouch."

"Yeah, and I'm sure that was the least of it. She probably sensed some pretty terrible stuff. After we were about fifteen, she rarely took the gloves off."

~

Abe drove home and mulled over his conversation with Liam. His eyes flicked between Orla's picture and the road.

He wondered if she'd kept one of the kittens, named it something quirky like Gatsby. According to Hazel, Orla loved both the novel and the movie that had come out the year before. Abe too had loved The Great Gatsby, required reading in twelfth grade English, but found Daisy to be a frustrating object of affection for the much more complex Gatsby. He had read the book several times over, and often imagined Daisy had a secret internal world of depth and mystery that Gatsby instinctively sensed, even if the author never managed to portray it.

Abe considered Orla's strange ability to sense things. It troubled him.

The sun cast a harsh glare in Abe's eyes and he reached up, pulling his visor down. A piece of paper fluttered out, and he caught it before it drifted into the backseat.

He read the series of letters and numbers, trying to place it. Then he remembered the gold car sitting in the parking lot at Birch Park. He had meant to call his friend at the police station and ask him to run the plate. He made a mental note to call it in the following day.

18

THE NORTHERN MICHIGAN ASYLUM FOR THE INSANE

Orla

Dr. Crow watched Ben wrap gauze around Orla's head, covering her hair and face, even her eyes. He left only her mouth and nose exposed.

"Orla," Crow said, his voice close, as if he'd stepped right to the bed. "We're taking you down the hall for a shower. You are to remain silent. If you ignore my orders, I will punish you. Do you understand?"

"Yes," Orla mumbled, though she had no intention of remaining silent.

Crow didn't want anyone to recognize her.

He'd sedated her hours earlier and the drug still held her, made her head heavy, eyelids droop, but she fought to hold onto a shred of consciousness.

She listened as the wheels on the gurney slid over the floor, the rhythmic pat, pat, pat as they spun. Bright lights, brighter than she'd seen in days, pierced the flimsy gauze. They had strapped her arms down, but her legs were free. She waited until she heard voices, and then she screamed.

"Help me!" she shrieked, thrusting her head up on the bed, turning her head from side to side, where she could see the silhouettes of other people. "Please, they have taken me against my will. My name's O-"

But someone had thrust a wet towel over her head, covering her face from her nose down to her chest. It didn't merely lay there, but pressed hard, flattening her nose into her face. Orla couldn't breathe. She choked against the towel and tried to cry out, kicking her legs and thrashing. She threw her lower body sideways. It slipped off the gurney, and the towel pulled free.

"Orla," she howled, but the towel was already back. The gauze had slid down, and for a split second she'd glimpsed a man wearing blue jeans and a green sweater, his eyes wide.

Her head jerked back as Crow snapped the towel down hard. Rough hands shoved her legs back on the gurney and secured them with straps.

She could hear Crow's breath, unsteady. The young man too, Ben, huffed and let out a little moan, as if he'd strained a muscle. But she couldn't concentrate, because again the towel - heavy, thick, immovable - suffocated her. She bit at it with her teeth, tried to turn her head from side to side, panic building. The lights dimmed, and she felt a soft prick in her arm. Orla slipped into unconsciousness.

She woke with a searing headache and burning eyes.

Lying still, she listened.

"Never again. Never again," Crow's insistent and angry voice repeated.

She cracked open her eyes and saw a shadow moving to her right. Tilting her head, she watched him.

He slammed his fist down on a metal table, and glass bottles flew to the floor, shattering.

"Clean those up," he barked.

Orla shifted her head to the other side and saw Ben hovering near the door. He dropped to the floor, and with bare hands brushed the glass and pills and liquid together.

"Are you a goddamn fool?" Crow shrieked, walking over and kicking Ben's hand aside. "If you cut your hand and get insulin in your wound, you're liable to go into insulin shock right here on the floor. Fucking idiots, the lot of you. Get up." He yanked Ben up by the scruff of his shirt. "Get the broom."

Orla trembled.

She wanted to touch her nose, which felt raw and sore where the towel had crushed it. She'd passed out. The man had suffocated her with the towel until she passed out.

"Give her a goddamn shower. Never again," he hissed. "She can rot in her own filth, for all I care. The stink will kill her as quickly as anything else."

He ripped his coat off, dropped it on the floor, and stormed from the room.

19

Abe

"Can you run a background check on this guy?" Abe handed Deputy Waller the sheet of paper containing the license plate number from the gold car.

"Already got a suspect?"

"Hardly. I saw him at the park where Orla might have gone hiking the day she disappeared. Just chasing a hunch, I guess."

"Sure you don't want to be a cop? You've got more fire under your ass than half the guys I work with."

Abe slapped his friend on the back.

"I'm afraid I'd shoot myself in the ass. I like to track 'em down and leave the hard part to you."

Waller grinned.

"I'll call you tonight."

~

Abe hung up the phone. The man's name was Spencer Crow with an address at 311 Sapphire in Leelanau County. No prior record, nothing so much as a speeding ticket on his license plate.

He drew little arrows pointing at the name, wondering why he couldn't let the guy go. It was wrong to be thinking of him. This was exactly the sort of tunnel vision that screwed up investigations. Too often hunches were proved wrong, and yet cops and journalist could spend months, years, trying to pin the guy they had a bad feeling about for a crime he never committed.

azel

Hazel carried a crate of cucumbers from the back of a pickup truck.

"Here, let me," Abe called, hurrying over.

She shouldered him out of the way and cocked her head back toward the truck.

"Grab the beets if you want to help."

He snatched the wooden crate of beets and hurried to catch up with her.

At first, they were both silent, pondering the same question - Have you heard anything?

Hazel spoke. "I talked with her dad last night. He said he met you."

"He's a nice guy. I spoke with Liam, too. Orla's cousin."

"But you haven't found anything more about Orla?"

"I don't know. That's why I'm here."

Hazel dropped the crate of cucumbers on a long wooden table. She put a little cardboard placard on the front that read 'Cucumbers 5 for $1.'

She faced Abe, waiting.

"Do you know a guy named Spencer Crow?"

Hazel frowned, glanced at the vegetables as if searching for the name, and then shook her head.

"Doesn't ring any bells. Did he have something to do with Orla's disappearance?"

"I'm not sure. He's the guy I mentioned who drove the gold sports car. Something about him…"

"The Devil."

"What?"

"Sorry. I was just thinking back. The day we realized Orla was missing, I pulled the Devil from the tarot. I draw a card for the girls every day."

"And the Devil means what?"

"Someone who's up to no good. Not always. It's symbolic, it can mean a lot of things, but that was my first impression. As soon as I saw the card, I sensed it portrayed a man with ill intentions."

"And you think Spencer's the guy?"

"No." Hazel shook her head, arranged the beets sideways, and then turned them back straight. "I don't know who it applies to, but it's possible. Why was he in the park?"

"He told me he stopped to pee."

"But you didn't believe him?"

"No. And I usually have a good sense of people. There was something about him."

"I'll ask our roommates," Hazel sighed. "Unfortunately, if I didn't know about him, they probably won't either."

Abe nodded.

"I'd like you to meet Liz Miner. Susan Miner's mom. She's been working with me on this case for a long time. She's kind of my right hand, or maybe I'm hers."

"Sure," Hazel agreed. "Anything to help find Orla."

~

be

Abe pulled his car off on the side of the road. A high iron gate, doors open, stood at the end of the tree-lined driveway for 311 Sapphire Lane in Lake Leelanau. The driveway curved, blocking the house that lay at the end.

The mailbox did not contain a name, only the numbers 311. He stared at them, a flicker of something trying to surface in his mind. Had he visited the house before? No. He would have remembered.

"Can I help you?" A woman's voice startled him.

He put a hand to his brow, blocking the sun.

She looked at him from the rolled-down window of a black Cadillac Eldorado. Her dark hair was pulled away from her lined, but pretty face. He saw the sparkle of a diamond earring in one earlobe. In a word, he would have called her elegant.

"Hi. Is this your home?" he asked.

She watched him behind dark sunglasses.

"Yes, and you are?"

He held up his press badge, always dangling from his neck for moments such as these.

"Abraham Sevett. I work for Up North News."

Her expression did not change.

"And you're here because…?"

He glanced at the mailbox, and then at the woman. The man was surely her son, based on the resemblance around the nose and cheekbones.

"I'm researching historic homes on the peninsula, and I stumbled across yours. I wasn't going to trespass. I thought I might see it from the road."

She took off her glasses. He saw the same startling blue eyes he'd stared at in her son's face. And like his, they had a coldness, maybe even an emptiness.

Abe glanced down the deserted road, unease settling in.

"It's not a good day for me," she said finally. "Give me your card. Perhaps I can give you a tour when it suits."

"Umm sure, yeah." He searched his pockets, came up empty, then jogged back to his Rambler, again looking sad and grimy next to the shiny Cadillac she drove. He pulled a coffee-stained card from his cup holder and returned.

She took it in her manicured hand, nails painted with a clear polish and sharp, as if she filed them to points. She slid the card in the visor, pushed her sunglasses back onto her face, and turned into the driveway without another word.

~

Abe

After Abe picked up a printed copy of Spencer Crow's driver's license, he drove to Hazel's house.

"Hi," she said when she opened the door to find him on the porch.

"I've got a picture of Spencer Crow. Have a minute?"

"Yeah, sure." She stepped onto the porch and took the paper.

"Never seen him," she sighed. "311 Sapphire Drive," she read aloud. She cocked her head to the side and frowned. "3-1-1," she said again. And then her eyes widened as she looked at him. "Three-eleven."

"I'm sorry, what?" But then he stopped. It was the odd time of night they'd both awoken at. Except now, he'd awoken at 3:11 a.m. for the last six nights.

"It's happened since that first night," she said. "And the night I dreamed of Orla, I think I woke up at three-eleven that night too. I didn't look at the clock until I was back in my room. It said 3:14 then, but I bet you anything."

Abe sighed, took the photo back, and folded it in half.

"Abe," Hazel said, touching hand. "What can it hurt to open your mind a bit? Hmmm…? Maybe we're getting clues, and…"

"From who, Hazel? From what? God? The Devil? You think there's a God sending us little clues but allowing young women to get snatched from the street, brutalized, murdered? He has the time to wake us up in the middle of the night, but not to stop a homicidal maniac from killing in the first place?"

He threw up his hands and stomped down the porch steps, half tempted to kick over the pot of pink flowers near the sidewalk. He resisted.

"Abe," Hazel called out. "Wait, okay?"

She followed him down, her long red skirt swaying. "Come in and have dinner with us. Jayne made chicken salad. Calvin brought over a cherry pie. You need a break. You look exhausted."

He bit back his angry words. The words that would imply she

should be doing more herself. He had obsessive tendencies, and yeah, he also had his reasons, but people had to go on. That was the truth of life, no matter the trauma, injustice, devastation - people had to go on.

He brushed his hands back through his messy hair and nodded.

"Yeah, okay. I could use dinner that's not from a can."

20

Hazel

Hazel stepped from Abe's car. He'd parked in the driveway of a little fifties-style bungalow. The houses on either side burst with summer flowers, neat rows of bushes stood beneath windows. This house held no such color. The drawn shades and closed garage door gave the house an air of abandonment.

"She lived here? Susan Miner?"

Abe had explained his relationship with Liz on the drive. Not only had she motivated him to begin the investigation, she'd fielded tips, had a thousand theories, and worked night and day to solve Susan's disappearance. She was also his way into the families - after all, she was one of them.

Abe knocked on the door.

After a moment, a man pulled it open.

He looked prematurely gray, wore a sweater despite the summer heat, and offered them a strained smile.

"She's in the study," he murmured and wandered back into the living room, returning to his chair where a muted television played.

Cold churned from a window air conditioner, turning the dark rooms and hallways frigid.

The study occupied a small room lined with long tables. The

tables held stacks of fliers, and a network of corkboards with maps, missing girls' posters and tips plastered the walls. A telephone sat on one desk.

A woman stood staring at the map, her hand poised as if she'd been reaching up to adjust something and gotten lost in thought. She'd clearly not heard the knock on the door.

"Liz?"

The woman gave a start, dropping her hand.

"Abe. I didn't hear you come in."

She blinked at him, and then at Hazel. Her short curly hair lay flat in the back, as if she'd recently slept on it. She wore pleated jeans and a loose button-up men's shirt.

"I was trying to make sense of the abduction sites. I mean, the probable abduction sites. We can't know for sure, but…."

"Liz, I'd like you to meet Hazel. She's Orla's roommate and close friend."

Liz stared at him for a long moment, as if processing his words took time She smiled and crossed the room.

"Yes, of course. Abe said you were coming. Delighted to meet you, Hazel."

She turned back to the map, frowned, and then shook her head.

"I can't make heads or tails of it."

"Maybe it's time for a break?" Abe asked. "From the room, anyway?"

Hazel had the sense the woman spent a lot of time in the room, too much time.

She continued to stare at the map until Abe cleared his throat.

"Yes, a break. You're right."

They followed Liz to the kitchen.. She opened the refrigerator door, and it surprised Hazel to see bare shelves. A half-empty gallon of milk sat on the top shelf.

"I should have made tea," she murmured.

"No. You didn't need to go to the trouble. Let's drive into town. Jerry, can we bring you back lunch?"

Abe stepped into the living room, where Jerry sat watching the still-muted TV.

He looked up, then craned toward his wife.

"I'll have what you're having, dear."

Liz nodded, brushed at the flat curls on the back of her head.

She picked up a red purse from the counter.

"This belonged to Susie," she told Hazel as they left the house.

The sun shone blindingly bright after the dim interior.

"It's nice," Hazel told her.

Hazel watched Liz's eyes drift to the neighbors' yard, a self-conscious expression flitting across her face. She reached up to her hair, and then touched her shirt, pausing. She looked down.

"Good grief, I'm still in Jerry's shirt. Give me five minutes to change?"

"Take your time," Abe told her.

Liz disappeared back into the dark interior.

Hazel watched her. "It's like her life was-"

"Frozen," Abe finished. "Pretty much. Everyone handles it differently. Liz abandoned the person she used to be. She told me that once, she felt like she'd stepped out of that woman's skin and left it in a pile on the floor."

Hazel grimaced at the analogy.

"Do you think she'll ever…?" Hazel trailed off. She didn't know how to finish the question: get over it - move on - be normal again?

He gazed down the roadway, where freshly washed cars gleamed in driveways.

"I don't know. When she gets answers, when she is freed from the purgatory of not knowing, that's when she might be able to rebuild again. Figure out who she is on the other side of all this."

Hazel imagined years down the road, walking through town and glimpsing a streak of long black hair, wondering if it was Orla - never knowing what had become of her friend.

She took an uneasy breath, chased the image away. She wouldn't forsake her friend by giving up.

"Do you guys get tips? Is that what her phone is for?"

"We advise people to send tips to the police, but every flier also contains her phone number or mine. We both take calls."

Liz bustled out several minutes later in a clean blouse and less wrinkled jeans. She'd pulled her short curls into a tiny ponytail at the base of her neck.

"Much better," she announced.

The restaurant had a fifties theme, and Hazel followed Abe and Liz's lead by ordering a chocolate milkshake. It arrived in a tall, old-fashioned glass smothered in whipped cream and dotted with a red cherry.

"This has become our little ritual," Liz said, plucking her cherry from the white froth and gazing at it. "Susie loved this place, the milkshakes in particular. Jerry and I always gave her our cherries." Liz put it in her mouth, rolled it around. "I eat it now. For her. I used to order it without one, but now..." She stopped, and her eyes welled with tears.

Abe took her hand and squeezed.

"Here's to Susie," he said, clinking his milkshake against each of theirs.

"And to finding the son of a bitch who took her," Liz added, renewed strength in her voice.

"The story will hit the stands Sunday," Abe said. "We have to be ready to field calls, they'll be pouring in. And Liz, expect the cranks again. If people call your home line, let the machine pick up."

"Let 'em call," she said. "A few words from me and they'll never do it again."

Abe chuckled.

"Has anything of the women's ever been found?" Hazel asked. "A purse? Or a wallet? Anything?"

"Susie's shoe is the only physical evidence the police have ever found in connection with any of the girls," Liz offered. "The other missing girls left nothing behind. But what it tells us is that someone abducted her in the woods."

Abe spread out a map that labeled the state forest area where someone had discovered Susie's shoe. "There's a series of marked trails maintained by volunteers. Then there's a dozen other trails formed by deer and mountain bikers. They found her shoe on one of those. There are three marked parking lots for this forest. Based on where her shoe was, our guy was parked here." Abe pointed to a darker square. "This location is also important because it's shielded from the road. You can easily park there and conceal your car."

"On a Sunday afternoon? Why wasn't he worried about hikers?"

"A few reasons. One, by Sunday afternoon most of the tourists are heading out of town, families are getting ready for the work week. And for those not doing that, it was hot out. People went to the beach, not hiking. But this guy is careful. He can abandon his plan at any time. He nabbed her close to the trailhead near his car. I'd say he could see his car and the lot. The coast was clear, so he grabbed her. We assume there was a struggle, and that's how she lost her shoe. He carried her to the car."

"Orla would not have been easy to carry," Hazel interrupted.

"I agree, but if we assume she vanished from Birch Park, he didn't have to worry about other hikers. That place is empty most of the time. So he didn't have to move as fast. If she was hard to carry, he could take breaks. And she might have gotten in his car willingly."

Hazel frowned.

She wanted to disagree, but Orla was not a suspicious person by nature.

21

THE NORTHERN MICHIGAN ASYLUM FOR THE INSANE

Orla

The familiar bottle of sodium thiopental, or truth serum as Crow called it, stood on the metal table near the bed.

Crow sat in a wooden chair, watching Orla.

"What time is it?" Orla asked.

"The time is not relevant."

Orla screwed her eyes shut and tried not to scream. They'd been sitting in the room for a long time. Crow rarely spoke to her until the medicine had plenty of time to enter her system.

"Are you going to kill me?" she asked.

He glanced at his watch.

"I'm a doctor."

Orla scoffed and turned her head away, preferring to stare at the wall rather than Crow's cold eyes.

"When did you first experience impressions with your hands?"

Orla pressed her lips together, tried not to hear him. For several seconds it worked, and she didn't speak.

He snapped his fingers and without intention, the words poured out.

"I was four."

"Tell me about it."

"No."

Again, she pressed her lips together.

He stood and marched to the table, took her chin in his hand and jerked it toward him.

"You have no idea what I could do to you in here, Orla. Do you understand? As far as the world knows, you're gone. You belong to me."

Rage bubbled in her stomach. It rose hot and acrid into her diaphragm. She clenched her hands into fists and imagined wrenching them up, grabbing his head in her hands and tearing the eyes from his head.

He seemed to recognize the anger in her face, and a small smile spread across his mouth.

He slipped an object into her bare hand.

Before she could drop it, an image of her father emerged in her mind. He held flyers in his hand, his heart heavy, his hands shaking as he lifted the pages, gazed at his daughter's face, and stapled the paper to a telephone pole.

Orla lifted from the bed, straining into her elbows, crushing the paper in her hand. She sagged back, head flopped down, heart thudding.

Crow opened her fingers and removed the page.

"Anger amplifies the impressions, doesn't it?"

She turned her head away. The tears she'd held back earlier poured over her cheeks. She wanted her father, to lean into his broad torso and his big arms. She wanted to smell his Teak aftershave with the sweat and dirt combination of a day on the job. He would kill this doctor. If she ever escaped and told him what happened, he would crush the man's head beneath his boot.

Orla snorted laughter, and the doctor stepped away.

He eyed her wearily.

The door opened, and Ben shuffled in holding a tray in his hands. Orla gaped at a piece of toast and a glass of water.

Her stomach cramped at the sight. She hadn't eaten since the morning before.

"Are you hungry?" Crow asked. "Of course you are. And after you answer my questions, you shall have breakfast."

"Fruit," Orla said, staring hungrily at the toast. "I want an apple."

Crow sat back in his chair, leaving Ben to fidget by the door.

"A request?" He laughed, but the sound was humorless and cruel. "An apple must be earned."

He turned to Ben.

"Leave. Come back in an hour with an apple. We'll see if she earns it."

Ben backed from the room.

Dismayed, Orla watched the toast disappear from view.

"Tell me about your first impression through your hands."

Orla closed her eyes and sighed. The answer came easily, she'd recalled it many times over the years. The challenge was offering up such a vulnerable part of herself to this man.

"I had pneumonia, and they hospitalized me for three days. I don't remember the sickness. My dad said I nearly died. When I woke up, my mother was beside me, crying and praying. She put a wooden cross in my hand. I saw…" Orla pressed her eyes tighter, the memory making her miss her mother. "I saw a robed man waving incense over the cross. My mom was kneeling beside him. I felt how her knees hurt against the prie-dieu, the prayer bench. I tried to tell her about the vision, but she just cried and shook her head and lay across me."

"Did you tell anyone else?"

Orla bit her lip. She remembered stepping into the confessional in her family's church. Father Flannery had listened to her story, reminded her of the common fever dreams of illness, and assured her not to give it another thought.

"I told our priest. He said I was dreaming. But then it happened again."

"How soon after the first occurrence?"

"I don't know, a week or two. My parents took me to the park. Some kids were playing ball, and it rolled over to us. I picked it up and saw Andy, the kid who owned the ball, getting hit in the back with it. When he did something bad, his dad threw the ball at his back over and over to punish him."

Crow took notes as she spoke, somehow filling the page with her scant words.

"And you told your parents?"

"Yes."

"What did they say?"

"My mom pretended she didn't hear me. My dad didn't know what to do. He put us in the car, and we went home."

"Did you ever undergo medical testing?"

Orla gazed at him, confused.

"In a laboratory, where they questioned you about the abilities while checking heart rate and other vitals?"

Orla shook her head.

"It became a secret. My mom made me gloves. I learned to control it."

"Someone taught you to control it?"

"No. Every time I told someone about the experience, they either didn't believe me, or it turned out poorly. I learned to keep my mouth shut and wear my gloves. If I didn't wear the gloves, I learned to ignore the impressions."

"How?"

"I don't know how," she snapped. Her stomach growled.

"And you've never used the gift for your own benefit?" Crow's voice rose as he spoke.

"How so?"

"I can think of many ways, but let's start with blackmail. I'm sure you learned dark, secret things about people. Did you ever use that information to attain money or favors?"

Orla frowned.

"I'm not a thief."

"That's not what I said."

"I'm also not a morally shallow bitch."

Crow gazed at her steadily.

"But you wanted to, didn't you, Orla? All that power, literally at your fingertips…"

Orla glared at him. No, she hadn't wanted to. It had never crossed her mind to use the knowledge to control people, but this man wanted to.

22

Hazel

Hazel didn't bother to muffle her cries as she watched Abe pull into the driveway and climb from his car.

"Today is my mother's birthday," she sniffed. She wiped her eyes with the hankie she'd brought into the garden. She sat next to a pile of weeds, gazing at their tangled roots.

Dead, gone, ripped from the earth. Did they know? Did the surrounding flowers realize she'd uprooted their earth-mates to ensure the weeds didn't steal the nutrients from her valuable flowers and vegetables?

"I'm sorry?" Abe faltered.

She offered him a sympathetic smile.

"She's dead. That's why I'm crying."

"Damn. Well now, I'm doubly sorry."

She waved a weed.

"You don't need to be sorry. She was suffering. I try to remember that. It makes the missing her a little easier. How can I want her here when she was in pain? I can't, simple as that, but I miss her just the same. And now the anniversary is coupled with Orla." Her voice hitched. "Do you think she's dead, Abe?"

He gazed at her for a long time, and then beyond her, through her.

"After forty-eight hours, the likelihood of finding an abducted person alive is much smaller. But it happens."

"We're not searching for Orla, are we? We're searching for a body or for a madman, but not for my friend."

Abe nodded.

"There's a good chance, yes."

"You'd make a terrible grief counselor," she told him.

"Yeah. I'm built for what I do and little else."

"Speaking of what you're built for, how's the story coming along?"

"Good," he said. "That's why I'm here. I'd like you to read the portion about Orla. Make sure I've got my facts straight."

Hazel stood and brushed off her skirt, gathering the weeds in her arms and dumping them in her compost pile.

"Go ahead and have a seat." She gestured to her patio furniture and slipped inside to grab a plate of cookies and pitcher of mint tea she'd made from her garden.

Abe picked up a cookie, took a bite, and made a face.

"They're sage shortbread. Orla's favorite," Hazel told him.

He took a second bite, cocked his head and nodded.

"Not what I expect in a cookie, but intriguing."

He set the cookie down and ruffled through his briefcase. A huge stack of typed pages emerged.

"Is that your story? It looks like it will take up the entire newspaper."

He shook his head.

"I write the story ten times, ten different ways. Then I ask everyone to check their pieces. I do my final fact check, and then I modify the story that most jumps out on my second read-through."

"Sounds like a lot of work."

"The twenty hours I spent writing these," he touched the pages, "don't compare with the work of the last year of my life. It made me sick to cut so much."

Hazel lifted a cookie for a bite, and then returned it to the plate. She'd lost her appetite. She pulled the page with Orla's story closer and read.

~

"Do you believe in fate, Hazel?"

Hazel looked up from the sheet of paper.

Abe sat across the patio table, his eyes distant.

"Yes, though I think there are many fates, and we determine the path. Why do you ask?"

"When you consider the missing girls," he started. "Every single one of them vanished without a trace. Not a single witness saw them get into a brown truck or walk into a certain store. What if they'd varied their choice by some tiny thing? Left their house fifteen minutes later? I bet we'd be staring at different girls' faces. This guy chose them because there was no possibility someone could trace the abductions."

"Which implies you don't think it was fate, but an opportunity that put each of them in danger."

He frowned.

"It's a notion I've struggled with my entire life. Is it all random? Is there no lesson in all of this? No greater truth?"

Hazel looked at her garden. Some flowers would live, others would die. Who made the call?

"I like to believe there's something more… but maybe it's not dictating our lives."

He shrugged.

"How could they disappear without a trace? Without a fucking trace?"

Hazel sighed.

"The woods. Right? Isn't your theory that they all vanished in the woods?"

Abe frowned, chewed his lip.

"Rita was afraid of the woods. Her dad told me she never hiked, hated camping. She got lost in them once when she was young. They found her within a few minutes, but it had a lasting impact."

"How do you know so much about all of them?"

His expression had grown distant as he gazed at the photos.

"Because how can we discover the choice, that tiny imperceptible moment that put them in the path of this man, if we don't know everything about them? She didn't go hiking in the woods. That's not where he found her."

"Where did she like to go that's remote?"

He smiled.

"Now you're thinking like an investigator. She liked to go to the beach, once beach in particular, where she searched for Petoskey stones."

"A beach is not exactly isolated."

"Some of them are. And she went on gray, windy days, because she often found more stones. She polished them. She covered her dresser in jars filled with Petoskey stones. He's local, he's an opportunist. He does not target these girls before he takes them. The who doesn't even matter. Here's what matters: their long blonde hair. I suspect that's the focus. Long blonde hair and a moment of opportunity."

"Orla has dark hair."

"Orla was an anomaly. I haven't made sense of it yet. Maybe the urge was too strong, or she had some other trait that made her desirable. Something..." he trailed off.

"It's great," Hazel finished, pushing the paper back across the table. "You captured the spirit of Orla in this. One little thing, though, she prepped food at Zander's. She didn't wait tables."

Abe grabbed a pencil and crossed out a line, put a note beside it.

"Pat said waitress."

Hazel smiled.

"Pat probably assumes the only work for women in a restaurant is waiting tables. Orla joked that she'd forget the water if she had to waitress."

~

be

Abe sat on the long wooden bench, staring into Detective Moore's office. The shades were drawn, but the door stood open. He'd tried to walk directly in, but an eager young deputy refused to let him pass. After fifteen minutes, he shifted his attention to the deputy. The moment something distracted him, Abe was making a move for the office.

Detective Moore stepped from the office, his suit coat clutched in his hand. His eyes found Abe, and he froze, and then started to turn as if he intended to slip back into the office. His gaze darted toward desks containing deputies, up to the wall clock, and then finally back to Abe.

"I can give you five minutes, tops," he barked, waving for Abe to join him.

Abe stood and followed the burly man into his office. Paperwork flooded the detective's desk. Family photos lay jumbled at the back, some fallen over, as if edged aside to make room for more paperwork.

"Any developments on the Orla Sullivan case?"

The detective sat on the edge of his chair, not settling in. Abe preferred to stand. After a moment, the detective stood as well, clearly not comfortable looking up at the young journalist.

"The suspected runaway? No."

Abe blew out a frustrated sigh.

"She's not a runaway. Are you incompetent? Does anyone in this office actually investigate crimes?"

Abe should have bit his tongue. It didn't pay in his profession to be on the bad side of the cops, but unfortunately Detective Moore rubbed him the wrong way. He seemed to view anyone under the age of thirty as a lazy, pot-smoking communist. Abe was no exception.

The detective rested his hands on the desk and leaned toward Abe.

"Be careful, young man, or I'll make sure you never squeeze a tip or so much as a fart out of this office again."

Abe tensed his jaw, glaring at the detective.

"I assume you're not connecting Orla to the other five missing girls?"

The detective cocked an eyebrow.

"I get it. You want your big story. But guess what? In my line of work, the crime has to fit the evidence. Where's the evidence, Abraham? Where's the eyewitness connecting a single perp to these women? They're from different cities, they didn't know one another, they disappeared years apart. Visit any state in the country, and you'll find scores of missing young women. Could you lump 'em all together and cry connection? Sure. Would you be a damn fool for doing so? Absolutely."

"I'm not the only one who sees this, Detective. You want to know what I think? You've lost your instincts, your gut. You can't see the connection because you're blinded by your own prejudice."

The detective flicked his finger at the door.

"Get out of my office. I don't have time to talk conspiracy theories today."

Abe didn't go home. He'd given Moore one last chance to prove his competency, and the detective had failed.

He drove to the newspaper and delivered his story. His editor was on the phone, but grinned and gave him a thumbs-up when Abe rested the pages on his desk.

23

Abe

Abe stepped into the office. He could see his editor on the phone, his face red, his eyes lit as if he were in a heated conversation. Throughout the office, phones rang. Several other reporters scurried to answer them, jotting down hurried messages.

When Brenda, who wrote obituaries and entertainment stories, spotted Abe, she grinned.

"Oh my God, Abe!" she squawked. "People are going nuts."

She held up a copy of Up North News, his headline plastered on the front: *The Missing Girls of Summer - Are the Police Paying Attention?*

He paused, his breath catching as he gazed at the six women staring out from their black-and-white photos. A sensation of exhilaration, floating on a tremor of fear, coursed through him.

His editor Barney walked from his office, his glasses askew, his eyes wide.

"That was Detective Moore. He's livid!" The editor grinned and clapped Abe on the back.

"Well done, Abe!"

It was not a typical reaction. Many editors would be furious if their head reporter ostracized the police, but Barney was old-school. He believed that journalists were the watch dogs, whether they were outing the criminals, the cops, or the politicians. More than once, he'd proclaimed their reaction to the missing girls as gross negligence bordering on criminal.

"What did he say?" Abe asked.

"Oh, the usual. Reckless journalism, jumping to conclusions. We've created a shit storm, and vigilante parents will soon fill the streets with their rifles and a hangman's noose."

Abe considered the accusations, listened to the phones ringing, and smiled.

"Maybe we're finally gonna nail this guy."

"You the one writ' them articles?"

Abe looked up from the table, where he had notes spread from the sugar canister to the table's edge. A fidgety man gazed down at him.

"Yeah." Abe stood, brushed the crumbs from his toast off his shirt and held out a hand. "Abe Sevett. You got a tip?"

Abe had set up a makeshift office in Grady's Diner. They served hot coffee and cheap breakfast and didn't mind if he took over an entire booth. Certain types of people wouldn't set foot in a police station, or a newspaper, to offer information. He'd let his editor know to send tipsters directly to the diner, and Grady seemed grateful, though he grumbled about the few who stopped in without buying a cup of coffee.

The man shifted his eyes around the diner. He looked one loud sound away from spooked.

"Here, have a seat, man." Abe shoved the papers to one side of the table, clearing a space, and gestured at the opposite seat. "Can I get you a cup of coffee?" He watched the man's eyes rove across the counter, pausing hungrily on the glass case of pie.

"Or a piece of pie? Peach or blackberry?"

The man blinked at him, eyes watering, and nodded.

"Peach," he mumbled

Abe walked to the counter.

"Mona, can you grab us a piece of peach pie and a coffee?"

"Sure thing," Grady's wife told him, offering a thumbs-up as she grabbed a plate of eggs from the hot window and slid them in front of two men eating at the counter.

"You got a name?" Abe asked, sitting down. He rarely bought food for strangers who may or may not have anything of significance to tell him, but the man looked like a runner, and on the skinny side. He'd count it as his good deed for the day.

"Stuart," the man said, glancing at the papers on the table.

Abe was careful not to leave anything exposed that wasn't already public knowledge.

"I seen her," Stuart whispered, leaning forward. His hand snaked up from the beneath the table, tapped quickly on Orla's picture, and then rushed back down.

"On the day she disappeared?" Abe grabbed a clean sheet of paper and wrote Stuart's name at the top.

Stuart shook his head.

"Three days ago - no, four." He shook his head, frowned as if days were hard to follow. Stuart dropped his voice to a whisper "At the big hospital."

"The big hospital?" Abe asked, confused. "You mean the asylum?"

Stuart's eyes darted around, and when Mona arrived with the pie, he jumped and nearly sent the pie flying. Mona pivoted away and kept the plate balanced on her hand, spilling only a sip of coffee on her white apron.

"Barely a drop," she announced, grinning. She slid the pie and coffee on the table and turned without another word.

Stuart blinked after her, and then turned his eyes to the pie. He licked his lips and leaned close, sniffing it. He glanced around again, studying Mona before lifting his fork, carving out a bite, and touching his tongue to the pie. Abe wondered about his strange behavior.

"Is there something wrong with it?" he asked, though he suspected the pie wasn't the issue.

"Can never be too careful," Stuart told him, taking a bite and chewing slowly.

"You saw Orla Sullivan at the Northern Michigan Asylum?"

Stuart's head bobbed up and down.

"Doing what, exactly?"

Abe didn't want to write the man off, but he'd been hoping for a more plausible lead.

"Screaming. Her head was all wrapped up." He gestured to his head as if wrapping it in a towel. "Her arms was strapped down. She looked me right here." Stuart pointed two fingers square at his own face.

"Stuart. It's public knowledge that Orla is missing. I find it hard to believe a doctor, a nurse, or an administrator at the asylum wouldn't have called the police immediately to let them know."

Stuart took another bite, watching Abe as he chewed.

He turned his head slightly, as if someone had whispered in his ear.

"I did it," he said. "I told him. Not up to me no more."

"I'm sorry, what?" Abe tried to make sense of his words, though he doubted the man had been speaking to him.

Stuart lifted the plate, licked off the pie residue, and stood. He hurried from the restaurant without another word.

Abe watched him through the window. He cut across the parking lot and disappeared into a thicket of trees at the road's edge.

Despite his doubts, he jotted down the man's tale.

"More coffee, hon?" Mona asked, pausing by his table with the pot.

"Yeah, thanks. Do you know him, Mona? The man who just came in?"

"I've seen him around. He's a patient at the asylum, but he gets town privilege a few times a week. He's never come in before - usually just walks up and down the roads. Harmless, but an odd ball."

"Thanks."

Abe tapped his pencil on Orla's picture. It was a ridiculous claim. Unless somehow, she'd been admitted without a name. Could she have fallen, ended up with no memory of who she was? Could they somehow have not recognized her?

Abe shook his head and shifted back to his other notes.

~

Hazel

Hazel pulled into the diner. She waved at Abe seated inside.

As she turned toward the door, she spotted Orla's dad at the telephone pole across the street, stapling a flier to the wood. She caught Abe's eye, pointed at Orla's dad, and held up a finger, signaling she'd be right back.

"Mr. Sullivan," Hazel called, hurrying across the street.

He looked up, more fliers tucked beneath his arm, a determined look in his eyes. When he noticed her, his face lightened.

"Hi..." He paused as if searching for her name.

"Hazel," she reminded him.

"Yes, Hazel, sorry."

"Are those fliers for Orla?"

He sighed and held them up.

"Yeah. Fiona had an episode yesterday over the other fliers. They didn't depict her eyes properly. So..."

"May I?"

He handed her the stack, and she looked at a picture of Orla in a high-neck dress, long black hair sweeping over each shoulder, wide blue eyes fixed on the camera.

"It's a beautiful picture."

Patrick nodded, taking the fliers back and dividing them in half.

"Do you mind?"

"Not at all," Hazel said. She took the stack. "I had more fliers made up two days ago and already passed them out."

He nodded, looking down the street.

"Have you heard anything more from the police?"

He shook his head.

"They still think she left on her own. This character who writes for Up North News might be our best hope."

"Did you read the article?"

He nodded and stopped, an odd gurgling sound rising from his throat. He rushed across the street. His fliers exploded into the air and floated in lazy circles to the hot pavement below.

Hazel watched, awestruck, as Patrick slammed into the side of a man on a bicycle - and not just any bicycle, but Orla's yellow bike, with the little purple basket painted with yellow flowers.

24

Hazel

The man on the bike flew sideways, his body hitting the pavement hard, but Patrick wasted no time. He lifted him by his shirt and held him dangling above the ground.

Hazel almost picked up the discarded fliers but, realizing the situation in front of her was more dire, ran across the street.

"Where's Orla?" Patrick shouted into the man's startled face, and Hazel realized he was barely a man at all, maybe sixteen, with terrified brown eyes and an ugly red scrape where he'd landed on his left forearm.

"Mr. Sullivan," Hazel whispered, touching his arm.

Patrick didn't seem to hear her or notice the gathering people who'd stopped to watch the assault unfolding.

The boy shook his head, gave Hazel a panic-stricken glance. His Adam's apple bobbed in his thin throat.

"I don't know. I'm sorry. I think you've got me confused."

The boy didn't break away when Patrick spoke. Instead, he pulled his head back into his face, as if expecting the man to punch his teeth in. Hazel wouldn't have been surprised if Patrick did just that.

"You've got my daughter's bike." Patrick jerked his head toward the fallen bike. "Now, I'm going to ask you one more time-"

"I found it," the boy squeaked. "I swear. I passed it a few times just laying beside a tree. I thought…" But he didn't finish as Abe ran up beside them.

"Mr. Sullivan. Somebody called the police. You better set the kid down." He put his hand on Patrick's arm and pushed it down, encouraging him to release the boy back onto his feet. "Don't even think about running," Abe told him.

Hazel knew he had no such intentions. His skinny legs quaked beneath his shorts. She wouldn't have been surprised if he wet himself.

"He has Orla's bike," Patrick told Abe, jabbing an accusatory finger at the yellow bicycle.

Abe nodded.

"The police will be here any second." Abe glanced down the road, where cars had slowed and more people stood in small groups on the sidewalk, sharing their stories. "When did you find the bike?" Abe asked.

"Umm, on like Thursday," the boy stammered. "Yeah, it was Thursday. In Elder Park. It was just lying there, honest to God. I walked by it a few times and figured somebody dumped it."

"Where's the park?" Abe asked.

The kid scratched his head, avoided eye contact with Patrick, and gestured toward the north. "A little north of the bay. On Cherry Bend Road."

"How long was the bike there before you took it?"

Hazel observed Abe's brain working behind his eyes. He wanted to question the boy before the cops arrived.

"Umm… like two days. I just thought somebody left it."

Patrick stood frozen in place, glaring at the kid as if he wanted to pummel him despite the story. Hazel had the sense Patrick's anger had been building ever since Orla went missing.

Hazel stepped toward the bike. She needed to set it upright. Orla loved her bicycle. She'd hate the image of it lying on the pavement, discarded.

"Don't touch it," Abe told her. "It's evidence - already contaminated by this kid, but at least he found it, and now we have it. They need to dust it for fingerprints."

"Am I in trouble?" the boy asked, as if the mention of fingerprint dusting had sealed his fate.

"Not if you're telling the truth," Abe told him. "So, give that a good think. If you're lying, now's the time to come clean."

"Did you see anyone with the bike or around it?" Hazel cut in, squatting next to the bike. She pulled out a sprig of pink flowers tangled in its spokes.

The kid glanced at her, looked scared all over again, and Hazel knew he had. Abe, too, seemed to notice the slip.

"No," he murmured.

Hazel held up the flowers.

"Water willow," she told them. "They grow in Birch Park along the stream. I've picked them there myself."

When the squad car arrived, two uniformed officers stepped out. The one in charge, clearly the senior of the two, was graying around the temples and wore dark sunglasses. He was handsome and reminded Hazel of a cop from a movie. His partner was young and fresh-faced, with an eagerness in his gait as he stepped onto the sidewalk.

"We received a call about a disturbance," the senior office started, and then he spotted Abe. A little smile flitted across his lips, but he quickly returned to an impassive expression.

"Deputy Waller." Abe nodded his head toward the officer.

"Mr. Sevett, everything all right here?"

"No," Patrick interrupted. "This punk has my daughter's bike."

The younger officer looked between Patrick and the teenager, and then to Deputy Waller for instructions.

"Deputy, this is Patrick Sullivan, the father of Orla Sullivan," Abe explained.

Waller's expression softened.

"I understand. What's your name, young man?" the deputy asked.

The younger officer pulled out a notepad and pencil.

"It's, uh, Luke Dixon." He fiddled with his hands, shoving them in his pockets.

"And how did you come into possession of Orla Sullivan's bike?"

"I found it on Cherry Bend Road, like I told these guys. It was left there, on its side, like somebody didn't want it no more."

"Where exactly on Cherry Bend Road?"

"Elder Park."

"I will need you to show me the exact location. Officer Petty, call the station and request a tech to come secure the bike. There's no room in the squad car. Luke, we'll drive you to your parents' house for permission, but I need you to take us to the place you found the bike."

"Sure, yeah." He shot a furtive look at Patrick, and then at his feet. "My ma's workin' at the grocery store, but we don't need permission. She'll get mad if we bother her."

"How about your dad?" Waller asked.

Luke shook his head.

"He split when I was little."

"Okay, go over to the squad car. Officer Petty will help you into the back."

Luke cast terrified eyes at the car but did as he was told.

"Anything I need to be aware of?" Waller asked, shifting his gaze from Abe, to Hazel before falling on Patrick.

Patrick no longer looked angry. It had been the boy's comment about his father splitting. Hazel had watched Pat's mouth fall a bit at those words.

"I picked him up by his shirt. Scared him pretty good. I shouldn't have done that."

"No, you shouldn't have," Waller said, "but under the circumstances, it's not a surprising reaction. Did he tell you anything else about the bike?"

"Yeah, he found the bike on Thursday, but it sat there for two days before he took it," Abe told the officer. "And he's holding something back. He saw someone around that park. I'd press him."

Several minutes later, a van pulled onto the scene and a man in dark slacks and a white coat got out. He collected the bike, pushing two long metals rods between the spokes to lift it.

Hazel watched Orla's bike suspended over the rods, the man in gloves putting it in the back of the white van, and shuddered. It all seemed so wrong. She witnessed a similarly haunted expression in Patrick's eyes.

Hazel heard Abe talking quietly with Detective Waller.

"The office is in an uproar. I'll give you the exact location, but only after we've swept it. Understand?"

"Of course." Abe held up his hands. "Thank you for taking this seriously."

Waller winked.

"More than a handful of us agree with you, Abe. We've been looking at these crimes as a series, but without proof…" He held his hands out, and then dropped them. "But that article lit a fire under some butts. A task force is being assembled. The wheels are turning."

"Good. I hoped for nothing less."

~

"I've got to get back inside." Abe gestured toward the diner. "I've turned this into my home base for the rest of the week, and I promised my editor I'd be here at the diner for people to stop in with tips. Plus, Mona will have my hide if I take up a booth all day without an hourly order of coffee."

"Your article was…" Patrick paused, blinking a few times and giving his head a little shake. "Good. It was real helpful to get an idea of all that's gone on. Scared me, too."

Abe nodded.

"Sometimes, I struggle knowing the parents will read it. I tried to be honest and objective, but I also wanted people to get to know the girls, daughters, sisters, women with dreams. It changes people's perspectives when they get close."

Patrick nodded, rubbed his jaw.

"I shouldn't have picked that kid up. He hurt his arm. I…"

Hazel put a hand on Patrick's shoulder.

"Mr. Sullivan, you acted on instinct. Had you not run across the street, he might have pedaled away. We might never have found him."

Patrick tried to smile, but it came out as a frown.

He sighed and looked at the street where fliers lay plastered along the cement. A few blew up when caught in a rush of wind by passing cars.

"I've got those," Hazel said. "Abe, I'll meet you in the diner in a few minutes. Mr. Sullivan, I'm happy to put those up. Why don't you go home?"

Patrick started to argue, but Abe cut him off.

"It's best if you're close to home, Mr. Sullivan. That article is already producing leads. One might come direct to your house. I'm sure it'd be best if you took the call."

Patrick's eyes widened, as if imagining Fiona answering the phone.

"Sure, okay. Thanks again."

He walked back across the street. A flier blew up, and he reached out, snatching it in his hand and holding it to his chest as he returned to his truck.

"Any leads?" Hazel asked. She ordered a cup of tea and gazed at the frenzy of notes on the table.

Abe nodded.

"A dozen, at least. A few worth following up on."

"Any good ones?"

Abe shook his head.

"I don't think so, but I'll track them anyway. After people see the girls' pictures, either on fliers or in the article, some create false memories. It's strange, but I've seen it in other cases. They see Orla in so many pictures, they superimpose her on strangers."

"A lot of extra work for nothing, then."

"Yeah, exactly. Fortunately, most people don't call in tips unless they're sure, but there's always a handful of eager helpers who are not helpful at all."

"You know the cop outside?" Hazel asked.

Abe nodded.

"Deputy Waller. He worked with my dad for a lot of years. I consider him a friend, and he's offered me guidance on several stories."

"Was your dad a cop?"

"No, a prosecutor."

"Deputy Waller believes the girls are connected?"

Abe nodded.

"He hasn't put it in those words, but he's encouraged the direction of my investigations."

"Well, I'm done at the market for the day. How can I help?"

Abe shuffled some papers aside.

"Liz is visiting the gas stations along 210, the road to Birch Park. Want to cover the territory along M-22 leading up to Cherry Bend? Take a flier, ask if anyone's seen her, find out who was working the day she disappeared. Ask about any suspicious people or vehicles. Ask if anyone saw Orla's bike."

"Sure. I'm on it."

"One more thing," Abe said. "I advertised a five-hundred-dollar reward in the article. Patrick offered that, but the higher the better. The family of Laura, the girl from Cadillac, got creative to fund her reward. They did a garage sale, held a pancake breakfast. See if you can't think up some options to raise money for Orla's reward."

Hazel nodded, relieved. Organizing a fundraiser was something she could do.

25

THE NORTHERN MICHIGAN ASYLUM FOR THE INSANE

Dr. Crow

"This way," Crow told Dr. Knight, leading him into the restricted wing of the hospital. They ducked beneath heavy canvas sheets meant to stop the spread of any leftover disease after a flu outbreak the previous spring killed ten patients.

"Very wise choice," Knight told Crow. "Though how can you be sure the cleaners won't come through here?"

"They're scheduled for August 20th. Believe me, they're as terrified of the flu as a black plague. They won't step foot into this hallway until the last possible second."

Crow opened the door into Orla's room. It was a large, square room, used for operations, with a drain in the center of the floor, no windows, and a long metal table and sink along one wall.

Orla lay on the bed, staring at the ceiling.

"Benjamin, fetch my bag," Crow told the man who hovered in the corner.

Benjamin nodded and scurried from the room.

"How do I get one of those?" Knight asked. "If I ask Nurse Polly to hand me a tissue, she near melts me with an angry stare."

Crow ignored the question, stepping beside Orla and placing a hand on her pulse. Her heart was racing - good.

"I've brought someone who's interested in your gift, Orla. This is Dr. Knight."

Orla's gaze remained transfixed.

"Maybe she belongs here, after all," Knight joked, moving closer to the bed and staring into Orla's face. He touched a strand of her long black hair.

Ben returned to the room carrying a black leather medical bag.

Crow took it and shooed him away, before pulling out a white doctor's coat.

"Is that Kai-"

"Shh…" Crow snapped. "Watch."

Orla curled her fingers, but Crow forced them open.

"Remember what we discussed, Orla. You don't want to upset me."

She allowed him to shove the coat into her hand.

~

Orla

She wanted to resist, but Crow's words rang in her mind.

"The grave is already dug," he'd told her an hour earlier. A grave meant for her. If she disobeyed, if she refused to reveal her secrets, he had no use for her. She would die, be buried. Her parents would never know her fate.

The stiff white cotton touched her palm, and the images poured forth.

"Doctor," she muttered. "Stephen Kaiser. Murderer, matricide, but now I'm a doctor, Mother. Don't you see? The girl who speaks with ghosts. The ghosts are everywhere, eating me, they're eating me," she screamed and clenched her eyes shut.

The second doctor, Knight, had backed away as she spit the words out. He watched her with curious dread.

Crow pulled the coat away and folded it over his arm.

"You see?"

Knight looked at the coat, and then at Orla.

"But how?" he stuttered.

"Good God, Knight. How many patients have you observed in the chamber? You still approach the supernatural with such reverence and naivety. It's alarming."

Knight touched the white coat tentatively, as if he feared the same images would arise in his mind.

"It's just a coat," he murmured, and then he shot a skeptical eye at Crow. "Did you prepare her?"

Crow nodded.

"I told her if she didn't share the vision, I would kill her."

"That's it? You told her nothing of Stephen Kaiser?"

"Not so much as a name. But don't take my word for it," Crow added. He pointed at Knight's watch.

Knight looked at it and shook his head.

"My wife-"

"Shut up," Crow snapped.

Orla closed her eyes. She wanted them to leave. Alone, in the silence, she could continue to plot her escape.

Reluctantly, Knight removed his watch.

"Put it in her hand."

Knight placed the watch in Orla's hand.

"Sears, Roebuck and Company, a gift from your wife for Christmas, she bought a matching one for her father. You dropped it in the bath last week, feared you broke it. Your dog's name is Critter."

Orla gazed into Knight's astonished eyes.

In truth, she was astonished too. She'd never spent so much time tuning into her ability. Each vision seemed to grow stronger and more pronounced. They flooded her brain, tricked her emotions so that for those minutes of seeing, she lost Orla and took on the life of the object in her hand.

"Interesting, she would pick up the name of your dog. Was she correct?" Crow asked.

"Yes," Knight breathed. He lifted the watch and returned it to his wrist. "Critter licks my watch when I sit with her on the floor."

"There you have it," Crow said, clapping his hands.

Orla watched, dismayed, as Crow took a needle from his coat and slid it into her arm. He drugged her every day before he left the hospital. If she awoke at all during the night, she was disoriented and barely able to open her eyes.

"The others must see this," Knight added.

"In time," Crow said.

~

Dr. Crow

Crow invited only five other doctors of the brotherhood to the chamber. They did not record their findings in the Enchiridion. It was unorthodox. No, it was forbidden, but he couldn't risk putting Orla on display for the entire Umbra Brotherhood. What if one of them considered the experimentation too risky?

The publicity surrounding her disappearance put all the men on edge. They were used to working with the forgotten, the abandoned, the lost.

Crow glanced at Orla, bound to a heavy wooden chair. She glared at the other doctors. During his observations, he noticed that the clarity of her impressions improved when she was upright. He wondered if increased blood pressure amplified her perceptions.

She watched the men with hooded, angry eyes. Her temper never waned, and she was surprisingly strong. The first time he took her to the chamber, she nearly broke free. Had he not sedated her, she might have escaped.

Crow bribed her to ease their transition to the chamber. In the beginning, threats of death were enough, but then she started to challenge him.

"Go, then," she'd growl. "Get it over with."

The bribes were more to his liking. That day he'd given her a set of clean clothes and a cup of coffee. If she obeyed him during the session, a pear would be her reward.

"I'd like to consider an injection of-" Dr. Knight started.

"No drugs," Orla snapped. "I'm sick of your fucking drugs. I swear, I'll never speak another word if you stick that in my arm."

Her eyes paused on the syringe resting on the little metal table.

"Fair enough. For today," Crow told her.

He picked up a cup and placed it in her palm. Her arms were bound with her palms face-up so they could put objects in her hands.

"Margaret, waitress, she's fifty - no, sixty, chipped a nail this morning. Black coffee, bitter. Customer's always right. None of her business if the man wants to burn a hole in his stomach."

Crow beamed, his head bobbing up and down.

"Very good."

The other men surveyed their notes. They'd each brought an item, prepped each other beforehand on what they knew. Crow laughed at Margaret's displeasure in his choice in black coffee. He didn't care, but it was intriguing. Private thoughts on display through the touch of a coffee cup.

Crow took the mug away.

Dr. Hues stood, a blue winter scarf clutched in his hand. He'd been at the previous two sessions, brought menial things. In the first, a pen from his banker, the second was his dog's leash. Today his hand trembled as he rested the scarf on Orla's palm.

"Kenneth. His mother bought this for him at Bergdorf's. He hates it but loves his mother. A woman brushed her face against the fabric. It tickled, and she laughed, put the scarf over their heads, and kissed him."

"The woman's name?" the doctor demanded, color flushing his neck.

Orla blinked at him, narrowed her eyes.

"Are you sure?" She glanced at the other men. Crow understood the unsaid things.

Dr. Hues did not need to hear the name spoken out loud, his wife's name, and yet he nodded.

"Beverly," Orla told him.

Dr. Hues face fell. He stood and ripped the scarf from her hand, shoving it into his suit coat.

Crow did not know Dr. Hues' wife. The man worked as a psychiatrist in Pontiac. The men of the brotherhood did not socialize, but over the years, they learned things about one another. Dr. Hues' wife worked as a secretary for a dentist. Crow wondered if the dentist's name was Kenneth.

Orla offered Hues an expression of sympathy, which hardened when the next man, Dr. Frederic, stood. He smiled cruelly at Orla and pressed a small, sharp knife into her hand.

She bucked in her chair and gasped before emitting a loud, piercing scream.

~

Orla

Orla closed her eyes. When she opened them, the men waited with matching expressions of curiosity. The doctor who killed the rabbit wore perverse pleasure on his sharp features.

The same pleasure aroused him when he sliced the rabbit open, killing it not swiftly, humanely, but slowly. He had watched the light drain from its small, terrified eyes as blood seeped from its open belly.

"What did you see?" Crow asked.

She clamped her mouth closed and turned her head away from the men. Fire burned in the wall sconces, and the damp, acrid smell of the chamber conjured the memory of the rabbit's blood, threatening to overwhelm her with nausea.

Dr. Frederic stood to retrieve the knife, but Orla closed her fingers around it. The blade cut into the flesh of her fingers. As the blood trickled from her hand, she glared at the doctor, wishing for the strength to wrench her arm free and plunge the knife into his throat.

Frederic grabbed the handle that protruded from her fist.

"I can pull it out," he whispered, leaning close so she smelled his hot, sour breath. "Imagine the sensation as it tears through your tender palm."

She released her fingers, and the knife fell to the floor. Her hand throbbed, and the warmth of her blood dripped into her palm.

"Tell us what you saw," Crow hissed. He could be mean, cruel. If she upset him, he might leave her strapped to the bed and drugged for days with no food, no shower, no human contact whatsoever.

"You butchered a rabbit," she spit at the man who'd picked up the bloody knife. "And you liked it."

The doctor chuckled and took a seat.

"I liked the rabbit pie my wife made. But let's not get carried away."

They left Orla in the chair, and huddled near a huge, leather-bound book propped on a pedestal.

"We're wasting time," Frederic said. "I vote you reveal her to the brotherhood at the next full moon meeting."

"That's less than a week away," Crow argued.

"She's ready," Frederic insisted.

"The others will be angry we've been meeting in secret," Knight cautioned.

Orla didn't look directly at the men. She didn't want them to know she was listening.

"Not when they witness what she can do," Crow said. "I'll write the others tonight."

26

Hazel

The first time Hazel saw the girl, she thought nothing of it. Orla had only been missing for hours, maybe she wasn't technically even missing yet. But Hazel had been a little drunk on sangria, leaning her head against Calvin's shoulder as they left Leone's after a late dinner. It was pouring rain, but the warm rain of summer. Calvin had grabbed her hand and twirled her away from him, pulling her back in for a long kiss. As she stepped away, the rain a shock after the warmth of his mouth, she glimpsed the girl across the street. She stood along the metal fence that ridged the parking lot, and she seemed to watch them.

Through the mist, Hazel made out blonde hair and what looked like a yellow shirt, though the darkness and the storm blurred the details. Had it not been for the streetlight, the girl would have been in a pocket of darkness, and Hazel would never have noticed her at all.

Calvin had picked Hazel up, and she shrieked in delight as he ran across the parking lot to his car. He dropped her into the passenger seat, and Hazel forgot the woman.

Hazel had not given her another thought until more than a week later, when she saw her for the second time.

Hazel sat in Milly's Bakery on Front Street, facing the river that ran behind the little shop. Docks ran the length of the river, huge wooden beams disappearing into the calm, dark water below. Two men sat side-by-side, fishing poles dipped in the water, ball caps blocking the sun's glare.

Hazel drank coffee and ate a lemon muffin. They had been her mother's favorite. As the anniversary of her death drew near, Hazel indulged more and more in the things her mother had loved. Later, she would go to the Cherry Bowl Drive-In to take in 'Aloha Bobby and Rose.' Her mother took Hazel to the drive-in nearly every weekend in the summer. They lay on the hood of her mother's blue Plymouth Satellite, radio turned loud to hear the show, watching the larger-than-life actors fall in love, escape from spies, and battle evil.

When her mother died, Hazel inherited the house. Her father had died when she was four. Though she was only seventeen when her mother passed, Hazel had already taken over the finances a year before, when her mother fell ill. She understood how to balance the checkbook, send in the mortgage payment, tend to the lawn and garden. Within a year of her mother's death, she'd filled three of the home's rooms with roommates. She'd moved into the master bedroom, her mother's room, and tried to imagine a life without her mom.

July was her mother's month. It was the month of her birth and the month of her death.

"And now it's the month Orla disappeared," Hazel murmured, picking at her muffin.

She returned her gaze to the window.

A girl stood on the dock now. She was a ways off from the fisherman, turned half-facing the river. A sheaf of blonde hair covered her face. Beneath her hair, Hazel studied her yellow t-shirt depicting bright red lips and a lolling tongue. As the girl shifted, facing the bakery full-on, Hazel gasped and stood. Her chair clattered to the floor.

Milly, the shop owner, looked up startled from the register.

"Is everything okay?" she asked, hurrying around the counter to right Hazel's chair.

Hazel stared, transfixed, until Milly brushed against her.

"Yes, I'm sorry." Hazel stammered.

As Milly swept back to the counter, Hazel gazed at the dock, but the girl had vanished.

be

Abe scanned the tips his editor had dropped off. There'd been reported sightings of Orla on the day she went missing. A man driving on Road 210 who saw her riding her yellow bicycle. A family in a van called in - they too saw a young woman with long, dark hair riding on Road 210. But not a single sighting after noon. It appeared she had been riding to the park they'd already searched. But no one observed her riding back.

As Abe studied the other disappearances and tried to find a connection, his gaze drifted back to Stuart's comment. The asylum was only a few miles away. He could put the issue to rest in under an hour. He gazed at his scattered papers, sighing as he shuffled them into a pile and stuffed them in his briefcase.

"Done for the day?" Mona asked, mopping up spilled soup on the booth behind his.

"No, I need to check something out. I'll see you later."

Abe had never been inside the asylum walls. The structures were huge, overwhelming, yet beautiful. He felt small and inconsequential. Gazing up at the stately buildings, he tried to imagine the madness within. He could imagine how someone might disappear within their rooms and hallways.

A small woman, with large spectacles propped on her pointed nose, sat at a reception desk within the yawning entrance.

"Hi. My name is Abe Sevett. I'm a reporter for Up North News."

She gazed up at him, unmoved.

He took out a picture of Orla. "I received a call that someone may have admitted this woman. She's a local girl and has been missing for more than a week."

The receptionist looked at the picture.

"I know who she is," she said. "A darn shame, but if you ask me, she probably jumped in a car and headed out west. She's sunning on a beach in California by now."

Abe frowned.

"Actually, we think that's very unlikely. So do the police. They're investigating this as serious missing person's case. A woman who is possibly in grave danger."

"Well, she's not here," the receptionist clipped. "We have a logbook of every patient who comes through these doors. The police contacted us days ago inquiring about the girl. She's never stepped foot in this hospital."

"What about a Jane Doe? A woman who didn't remember her name?"

The woman rolled her eyes.

"This isn't network television. We deal with real problems here. Schizophrenia, suicidal behaviors, manic depression. This girl isn't in the asylum. Whoever told you otherwise was pulling your leg."

Abe set the picture on the table.

"I'd like to leave this here. Maybe you could show it around. There's no tip too small."

"I'll give you a tip. Send someone to the beach in California."

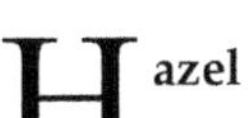

azel

Hazel found Miranda in the back room of the Moon Wisdom Bookstore.

"Knock, knock," Hazel called, shaking the beaded curtain as she stepped through.

"Hazel," Miranda bubbled, stepping away from the shelf to grab Hazel in a hug. "The anniversary of your mother's passing. I drew a card for you this morning. The four of swords, time for some rest and recuperation."

"Thanks, Miranda," Hazel told her. Miranda had known Hazel's mother, who'd visited her for tarot readings for years. Miranda had joined Hazel to stand vigil at her mother's deathbed three years before.

"How can I support you today, honey? Has there been any news on Orla?"

"Nothing on Orla, and I am here for help, but not about my mom."

"My pleasure, honey. Let's go to the tarot room."

Hazel followed Miranda into the store and through a heavy maroon curtain.

The small room was dimly lit, with a round table in the center butted by two chairs. A tarot deck lay on a silver scarf. On one side of the room, a long, narrow table contained a jumble of polished stones and porcelain figures of saints, goddesses, and even the horned figure of the Devil from the tarot deck.

Hazel sat down. Miranda lit several candles before dipping her fingers in a small basin of frankincense oil and brushing it along her temples and third eye.

"Tell me," Miranda said after she took a seat.

"I was in Milly's Bakery this morning, and I saw a woman on the docks." Hazel paused, remembering the girl's distinctive t-shirt. She'd looked at the Missing poster enough to recognize her face. "She's one of the missing women."

"One of the six?" Miranda asked. Since Abe's article, everyone in town knew about the missing women of summer.

Hazel nodded.

"You believe one of them is alive?"

Hazel shook her head.

"I hope Orla is still alive, but I saw Susan Miner."

"The girl from Petoskey?"

Hazel nodded.

"And I realized I saw her more than a week ago. It was late at night, after Calvin and I ate dinner at Leone's - the first night Orla didn't come home. I'm sure it was her, and now again today. She was there, and I sort of panicked, and when I looked again, she was gone."

"You've seen her spirit," Miranda murmured. She touched the

tarot deck, fanned the cards out, flipped one over. The Queen of Wands, and then a second card, the Moon.

"There is a woman," she said after gazing at the cards. "She has a connection to the dead."

"A connection?"

"She sees spirits. Her mother was a gifted medium, though not publicly. I believe she now denies the abilities, but her daughter remains… open."

Miranda stood and left the room. She returned a minute later with a Moon Wisdom business card. On the back, she'd written the name Hattie, and an address.

"Do you have a phone number?"

Miranda shook her head.

"It's best if you approach her directly. If you call, she might get spooked."

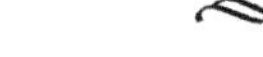

Abe

Abe walked to his car, gazing over the spacious grounds. The property looked more like an English boarding school than a haven for the mentally ill. Along the back of the property, hundreds of acres of dense state forest loomed as a picturesque backdrop to the magnificent hospital.

But Abe had heard stories. Anyone who lived in Traverse City for more than a few years was subject to frightening tales of life in the asylum. One reporter at Up North News had lived less than a mile from the asylum. Sometimes she awoke at night to the shrill asylum alarm, warning of an escaped patient.

Another of Abe's friends described picking up a man hitchhiking near the hospital. As he drove the man across town, he told a story of shooting his grandfather in the back when he was twelve years old. Abe's friend never picked up a hitchhiker again.

And then there were the strange stories told by those who loved to give a scare. Stories of weird inhuman experiments, haunted rooms, and sinister happenings in the woods around the hospital. Abe avoided such yarns. He didn't believe them, and he preferred not to spend time or energy on fictional monsters when the real ones were hiding in plain sight.

27

Abe

Abe looked up when the bell tinkled over the door at Grady's Diner. A big man in a plaid shirt, his stomach pushing out the fabric, lumbered in. A dark beard, spotted with gray, covered the lower half of his face.

When he stopped next to Abe's table, Abe looked up, surprised.

"Can I help you?" Abe asked, wondering if he'd taken over the guy's usual seat in the diner, and he was about to pull the macho move of demanding Abe pack up his shit and move along.

Instead, the man smiled, his dark blue eyes crinkling at the corners, and slid into the booth.

"I've got a story for you."

Abe sat back, folded his hands on the table, and surveyed the man.

"About one of the missing girls?"

"Yeah, Susie."

"Did you know her?"

The man shook his head, spotted the waitress and gave her a wave.

"Can I get a coffee, ma'am? One cream, two sugars."

"Pot's 'bout ready to pour. Give me a sec, hon," Mona told him.

He returned his gaze to Abe.

"Let me get this outta the way first. I ain't a liar. I don't take drugs, and I only drink a couple times a month on the weekends, when my wife permits it." He laughed and Abe joined him. "Lord, that woman is hard on me, but I love her anyway." He shook his head, but Abe could see real affection for the wife he spoke of.

"I have an open mind," Abe told him, careful not to lead the man by asking him a question.

"I drive for a livin'. Long-haul truckin'. Wife and kids are in Minnesota."

The man paused when his coffee arrived.

"Thanks, doll," he told Mona before taking a long drink and draining half the cup, which Abe imagined was a tad on the hot side. The man didn't seem to notice.

"Last summer, mid-August I reckon, I was heading up M-22 for Northport. You know the route?"

"Sure, yeah. On the east or west side of the peninsula?"

"West side, by the big lake."

Abe knew the journey; a beautiful, winding route that took in blowout views of Lake Michigan, towering sand dunes and dense wilderness.

"It was late, real late, after midnight. South of Leland in that dark stretch of forest where the trees crowd in, and you've got a hair-pin curve every half a mile; I come around one of those curves, and about bugged my eyes outta my head, 'cause a little blonde girl stood on the side of the road."

"A little girl?" Abe scrunched his brow.

"A young woman, you'd call her, but a little bitty thing. She didn't have a thumb out, but she watched me with eyes as big as saucers in my headlights, and I figured she needed help. I pulled right over and rolled my window down, told her to hop in. She did. I drove on a bit, asked her name. Susie, she told me. I asked what on God's earth had her wandering that road in the middle of the night, but..." He paused and leaned in. "She vanished."

"She vanished?"

The man stared at him hard now, no sign of laughter in his face. Something else had replaced his look - unease, edging towards fear.

"I looked at her seat so long, I about missed my next curve and sent that truck flying into a ravine."

"I'm sorry," Abe said. "Mr....?"

"Name's Jim."

"Okay, Jim. I don't know if you read the story about Susie, but she disappeared three years ago, in August 1972."

"Oh, I read it, all right. I spilled half a cup of coffee down myself." Jim held up his arm, where Abe spotted a shiny red welt on his wrist.

"But you believe you picked Susie up in your truck? Are you saying she's alive and well and hitchhiking the Leelanau Peninsula?"

"Didn't you listen to my story? She got in my truck and disappeared. She ain't alive and well."

Abe tried to erase the skepticism huddling at the back of his mind.

"You think it was her ghost?"

"I ain't no candy-ass, but I had goosebumps the size of golf balls that night. She had on a yellow t-shirt with a red mouth on it, dark shorts. My wife doesn't own those clothes, my kids don't either. If I imagined her, I'd sure as shit like to figure out how I came up with that weird shirt. And another thing, she was only wearing one shoe."

Abe frowned.

Susan's parents weren't sure what she'd been wearing, though Liz had insisted a yellow Rolling Stones t-shirt was missing from a stack of clean laundry she'd put in her room, as well as her white tennis shoes. Missing posters included the possibility of the yellow shirt and shorts, but not the missing shoe. Kids had discovered Susan's shoe in a wooded area near her home, four months after her disappearance.

"You've got a pretty good memory of what she wore." Abe's palms grew sweaty. If the man knew about the missing shoe, it implied something very sinister indeed. Some criminals confessed cryptically, and others liked to put themselves in the middle of an investigation. Was this their man?

"My headlights lit her up like a Christmas tree. Sure as eggs is eggs, I remember. I'd been looking at trees for hours and it was a dark night. That's not the kind of thing you forget. Especially a young girl missing a shoe."

"Did you tell anyone about the girl that night? Call the police?"

"Hell, no." Jim shook his head as if he could hardly believe the question. "Not five miles down the road, I pulled off and got a room. I'd been driving eighteen straight hours. I thought maybe..."

"Your mind was playing tricks on you?"

Jim nodded.

"But now, a year later, you're convinced you saw Susie?"

Jim put his large hands on the table and leaned in.

"I know it. You hear me, kid? It was her. I knew it the minute I laid eyes on her picture in the paper."

"Jim, can you tell me where you were on the day Susie disappeared, August 27th, 1972?"

Jim drained his coffee, slapped a dollar on the table and stood, not giving Abe a second look as he strode to the parking lot.

Abe studied the large hauler truck parked at the edge of the lot.

When Jim climbed into the cab, Abe hurried out the door, staying out of sight of Jim's mirrors. He wrote down the license plate number.

~

Abe listened to his messages, several tips with return call numbers. The fourth call made him stop cold.

"Hello? I'm calling for the reporter - Abraham Whatever. I just want to tell you that Susie girl isn't dead. I nearly hit her on M-22 - not two weeks ago, in the middle of the night. She was hitchhikin' like a nitwit. If I'd a known she was causin' all this grief, I would have picked her up and taken her to the cops." The woman rattled off her phone number and hung up.

Abe continued to play his messages, but scarcely listened.

He rewound back to the fourth call and played it a second time and then a third.

The woman answered on the third ring.

"Mullers' residence."

"Shannon Muller?"

"Yes!" She huffed.

In the background, Abe heard a small child crying.

"I'm sorry, am I calling at a bad time?"

"It's never a good time around here. Got both my grandkids clawing at each other like pack wolves over some nonsense toy from a cereal box. Who thought putting a toy in there to begin with was a good idea? Timothy," she barked. "You let go of your sister's hair this instant, or I'll paddle your bottom and throw that toy in the trash."

More crying, followed by a thump, and the line quieted. He waited, wondering if she'd hung up.

"Sorry. Shooed 'em out the door. My daughter's raising downright heathens."

"I'm calling because you left me a message, Mrs. Muller. I'm Abraham Sevett with Up North News."

"Yes, well, I'm not sure I can add more. Just figured you all should know the girl you're so worried about is hookin' her thumb on the peninsula. Probably doesn't wanna go home and do her chores."

Abe planted a hand on his table and imagined Liz Miner, her drawn face, the haunted look in her eyes.

"Can you describe the incident for me? The time and date, and what she was wearing?"

"Sure. It happened July 10th, a Sunday. I remember because I don't make a habit of drivin' after dark, but my sister in Thompsonville had a potluck. By the time we got the dishes washed, it was after ten p.m. I drove home real slow. My eyes don't work too well in the dark. I come around a curve, just past Sapphire Lane, and there she stood on the side of the road, wearing nothin' but a yellow t-shirt and shorts, and only one single shoe. If I hadn't been lookin' so hard, I'd'a run her right over."

"Why are you so sure it's Susie? There are a lot of young blonde women who live around there."

"Oh, I figured you'd say that. I knew because of that yellow t-shirt with the red lips and tongue stickin' out. Not somethin' I ever would have let my daughter out of the house in."

Abe jotted down her comments. Liz had told him Susie went to a Rolling Stones concert in Detroit during July 1972, a little over one month before her disappearance. She had bought the t-shirt there.

Liz had not been a fan of the shirt, but respected her daughter's right to wear what she wanted. Abe suspected Liz's dislike of the shirt helped her realize it was absent after Susie went missing.

"Is it possible that another young woman was wearing the same shirt?" He knew it was. Eyewitnesses were rarely reliable, but he didn't say so.

"I'm sure all kinds of young women wear that hideous shirt, but no. This was the same girl from the paper. I'd bet my life on it."

"Can you remember what else she wore?"

"Just what I told you. Blue shorts, and one sneaker. I thought she must have gone mad."

Abe stared at the words, the same description the trucker had given.

"Did you speak to her? Did she wave?"

"No. She likely had her thumb stuck out, but I had no intention of pickin' up a hitchhiker in the middle of the night. I drove on by."

"Did you see anyone pick her up after you passed her?"

"No. I looked back and didn't see her in the mirror, but it was dark, so I didn't expect I would."

28

Hazel

"My goodness," Liz smiled as she walked into Hazel's yard.

Tables crowded the yard, loaded with donated household items, clothes, tools, and even furniture.

"A lot of people donated." Hazel beamed. "Everyone loves Orla."

Liz smiled and picked up a glazed black and orange vase.

"That was my mother's," Hazel told her.

Liz frowned.

"You're selling it?"

Hazel nodded.

"The attic is filled with her stuff. Next week will mark three years since she died. It's time to let a few things go."

Liz stepped to Hazel and wrapped her arms around her.

"I'm approaching three years without Susan. I haven't parted with so much as a sock. You're a stronger woman than me."

Hazel hugged her back, resting her head on her shoulder.

"Weird, in a way," she murmured. "You lost a daughter three years ago, and I lost a mom."

Liz pulled back, studying Hazel's face.

"Perhaps that's why we've been brought together," Liz said. She sighed and gazed at Hazel's garden. "If only it could have been under happier circumstances."

She reached into her pocket and withdrew a small pearl bracelet.

"This was Susie's." She handed the bracelet to Hazel. "Can I ask why you want something that belonged to her?"

Hazel took the piece of jewelry, the fake pearls shining in the sun, and thought of the girl standing on the dock.

"I read the tarot. I wanted to do a reading about Susie, and it helps to use a memento. I promise I'll return it."

Liz gazed sadly at the bracelet.

"It has no value. Susan didn't wear much jewelry. Jerry bought it for her to wear with an Easter dress during grade school, and she took a liking to it. The last couple of years before she disappeared, she mostly wore it on her ankle."

"I'm partial to ankle bracelets myself," Hazel told her, tilting her leg so Liz could see the hemp anklet she wore beneath her long skirt.

Calvin pulled into the driveway and jumped from his car, followed by an explosion of yellow balloons. He held the ribbons clutched in his hand.

"Nearly lost the bunch of them in the parking lot," he announced.

"They're perfect," Hazel called. "I'll help you tie them."

Liz and Hazel took balloons and moved among the tables, tying the balloons to the legs.

"Orla's favorite color is yellow," Hazel confided.

"Susan's was green. Her graduation from high school was like a leprechaun's birthday party."

Hazel smiled.

She spotted Mr. Sullivan's pickup moving down the road. He parked at the curb and moved to the back, lifting out a cardboard box.

"Hi, Patrick," Liz said, offering to take the box.

He nodded at Liz, and then Hazel.

"Fiona and I really appreciate you putting all this together," he said. "There're clothes in that one. I've got tools and some other stuff."

When he returned with a small wooden rocking horse, Liz shook her head.

"Oh, no, Patrick. Don't give away Orla's rocking horse."

"It wasn't Orla's," he said.

Hazel glanced at Liz, but neither of them asked the question.

He answered anyway.

"Fiona and I lost our infant son."

"I'm sorry," Susan murmured.

"Me too," Hazel added.

She considered the three of them, such different people, experiencing such similar pain.

"Someone donated a first edition of *The Catcher in the Rye*! For a garage sale," Calvin yelled as he dug through a box. "Hazel, I'll give you twenty bucks for it right now."

Hazel rolled her eyes.

"He loves books," she explained. "Sure, Calvin. Put your money in the lockbox."

"Abe's article's been shaking things loose," he said. "Had three cops stop by my house in the last two days."

"No cops at mine," Liz sighed. "But half a dozen reporters. I try to remember there's no bad publicity, but Jerry's taken to sneaking across our neighbors' back lawn and borrowing their car if he needs to go to the store."

Patrick nodded grimly.

"Fiona's not one for the attention, either. She hasn't opened the store since the article came out."

"Did she read it?" Hazel asked.

He shook his head.

"Unlikely. She's hangin' by a thread. My sister Effie's coming for a visit this weekend. She has a way with Fiona, calms her."

"That's Liam's mom?" Hazel asked. Orla had told Hazel about her aunt, who she loved like her own parents. The woman drank beer and swore while knitting booties for Liam's baby daughter.

"That's her. She's a brute, though she barely reaches my shoulder. Used to thump me good as kids. She still keeps me in line. Orla and her are thick as thieves."

"Good," Liz murmured unpacking a box of coffee mugs. "It's

important to have support right now. The early days are the hardest."

Hazel saw tears welling in Patrick's eyes, and he turned away.

"Channel six news," Calvin announced, pointing at a news van pulling up across the street. "You guys ready to raise some reward money?"

By the end of the day, they'd raised over eight hundred dollars. Nearly everyone who purchased items from the sale donated an extra few dollars.

"My feet are killing me," Liz sighed, plopping into a patio chair on Hazel's porch.

"It's my lower back," Patrick complained. "Feels like somebody took a jackhammer to it."

"Lemonade, or if you're willing to wait a few minutes, Calvin is whipping up some margaritas," Hazel announced, setting a pitcher of lemonade on the table.

Patrick yawned and stretched his legs before standing up. He pounded his fists into his back a couple times.

"It's a bottle of Coors and a foot rub from my wife for me," he told them.

"A foot rub?" Hazel asked. "She must be devoted."

He grinned.

"Most likely she'll just wash my socks and demand I hose my feet in the backyard, but if I close my eyes, it almost feels like a foot rub."

Hazel gave him a hug and handed him the envelope of cash from the sale.

"I'll have to ask Abe to print the new reward amount," Patrick murmured, tucking the envelope in his back pocket.

"I'm surprised he wasn't here today," Hazel added.

"I'm not," Liz admitted. "That article has people talking. I'd say the cops, the families, and other reporters are after him, not to mention the tips. I always hope not to see Abe, because it means he's following a lead."

She hugged Patrick goodbye.

"Give Fiona our love," Liz told him.

He nodded and headed for his truck.

Calvin appeared on the porch with two margaritas. Bethany followed behind him with two more.

"Bethany, this is Liz Miner," Hazel told her roommate.

Bethany put a margarita before the woman, and then shook her hand.

"Great to meet you, Liz. I'm really sorry about your daughter."

Liz thanked her and sipped her drink.

Hazel noticed a little crease between Liz's eyebrows, and the way her eyes shifted back to Bethany's face again and again.

Hazel gazed at Bethany and realized why. She bore a striking resemblance to Susie Miner. Golden blonde hair in a cascade over her shoulder. Her eyes were green, her nose little and upturned, with a spray of freckles across the bridge.

Liz stood abruptly, leaving her glass half-full.

"Best get home," she said, her voice thick.

Hazel stood and reached to hug her, but Liz had already started down the steps.

She offered a half-wave as she hurried down the driveway to her car.

Abe

It was the third sighting that put Abe on edge. Something about that number three, as if two didn't quite validate the claim, but when you added the third…

The young man sat in the line of plastic visitor chairs just inside the office at Up North News. He held a cup of untouched water on the knee of his ripped jeans. He looked young, eighteen or nineteen, with long hair tied back by a piece of leather. His tanned face gave him a beach bum appearance, but when Abe glanced at his rough hands, he pegged the guy for an outdoor worker - lawn maintenance or construction.

"Mr. Sevett?" the young man asked as soon as Abe strode into the office.

Abe glanced toward his editor's office, but the door stood closed and his boss was on the phone.

"Yes, how can I help you?" Abe had an armload of paperwork, his briefcase clutched beneath his armpit.

"I have a… clue."

"A tip?" Abe asked, lifting an eyebrow.

"Yeah, yeah, a tip."

"Follow me." Abe led the young man to his desk and dumped his stuff on top.

The man glanced around. Other reporters sat at their desks, a stream of noise filtered from typewriters, the shuffling of papers, conversations. The guy fidgeted, shoving his hands in his pockets and shifting from one leg to the other.

"Shall we take a walk?" Abe asked.

"Yeah, sure. I could use a smoke."

Outside, the young man took a cigarette from behind his ear and lit it.

"I didn't catch your name," Abe told him. "Do you mind if I tape this?"

The man licked his lips and looked at the recorder.

"No, sure, yeah, that's fine."

Abe smiled, hit record, and they walked.

"My name's Ricky."

"Have a last name?"

"Palmer."

"Okay, Ricky Palmer. Fill me in."

He took another drag, licked his sunburned lips, and glanced sidelong at Abe.

He let out an uncomfortable laugh and inhaled again.

"I don't publish tips," Abe reassured him, "and even if I did, sources are anonymous. Understand? You won't see your name in the paper."

The man nodded, tugged on his ponytail, and dropped the butt of his cigarette. He pulled out a second.

"I saw a girl who looked like the Susan girl from your article."

"Looked like her, or was her?"

He croaked a shrill laugh.

A trickle of cold sweat slid down Abe's spine; the odd, familiar sense of déjà vu nipping at his heels as they walked.

"If I hadn't read your article and only looked at the picture, I would have said it was her, without a doubt."

"But the article makes you question that?"

Ricky nodded.

"Tell me about seeing her. Every detail you can remember, dates, times."

"It happened about a month ago, real late at night, about three a.m. My girl and I watched some boob tube, and then I hit the road. Joan's dad's real funny about me staying overnight. So long as I'm gone when the sun comes up, we're cool."

"Where does your girlfriend live?"

"Empire."

Abe clenched his jaw, bracing for the story to come.

"I was driving up M-22, south of Leland. That's where I'm staying with my cousin. We're working on a construction site in Northport."

Abe nodded, glancing at the little wheel turning in the tape deck.

"Dig it?"

"Yeah," Abe muttered.

"I was cruisin' pretty good, went peeling around a curve, and saw a girl standing on the side of the road."

Abe took his thumb and forefinger to the bridge of his nose and squeezed.

"I pulled off, leaned over the seat, and swung the passenger door out. My girl would'a bugged out, but I wasn't plannin' to tell her. This girl got in my car. She had on a rad shirt - one of those Rolling Stone's mouth shirts. Weird thing was, she had only one shoe on."

He looked at Abe and laughed.

"I said, 'That shirt's bitchin',' and started to ask her where she was headed, but…"

Ricky scratched his head, his eyes troubled. He took another drag on his cigarette, only to realize he'd smoked it down. He dropped it on the sidewalk, stared at as if it were a mysterious insect, and ground it beneath his boot.

"She wasn't there. The seat was empty. I was sitting on the side of the road, talking to air."

"And what do you make of that story?" Abe asked.

Ricky laughed, groped around behind his ears and came up empty.

"I didn't think much of it until my girlfriend showed up at the job site with a copy of your article."

"I thought you weren't going to tell your girlfriend?"

"I wasn't. But then I did a few days after I saw her. It was strange, man. One minute, we were eatin' Chinese food, and the next I'm spillin' the whole freaky-deaky story. Joan said 'you saw a ghost,' like any old thing."

"She said you saw a ghost?"

He bobbed his head up and down.

"She's into weird stuff, reads a lot of spooky books. I tried to laugh it off, but she told me some stories of her own, seeing things that shouldn't'a been there. Joan thinks Susan is dead. She's trying to reach out or somethin'."

Abe looked down the sidewalk. It sloped toward the bay. People sat on the grassy courtyard having picnics beneath colorful beach umbrellas. It seemed to be a regular summer day in northern Michigan. At least that's what appearances said, but on the inside, Abe felt pressure gathering, an avalanche preparing to wash an entire mountain into the sea. His left eye pulsed with the start of a headache, and he realized he'd forgone his cup of coffee at the office. He needed caffeine.

"And you believe the girl you saw matched Susan from the newspaper article?"

"Unless that girl has a twin."

"But you said yourself it was late, it was dark. How can you be sure?"

Ricky laughed, kicked at a weed poking up from the sidewalk.

"I wouldn't bet my mom's life on it, but when I saw that girl in the newspaper, I got a case of the willies like you ain't never seen. I tried to think maybe she ran off, was hitchin' that night, but…" He shook his head. "She disappeared, man. Up in smoke."

29

THE NORTHERN MICHIGAN ASYLUM FOR THE INSANE

Orla

"Jesus Christ, Benjamin, watch where you're going," Dr. Crow snapped, shoving the young man away the from the metal table he'd nearly walked into.

Benjamin shuffled away, standing near the wall and waiting for orders.

"I need the vials, now," Crow barked.

Benjamin hurried from the room and returned a moment later.

Orla's eyes appeared closed, but she peered through tiny slits.

Crow drew her blood, but she continued to feign sleep.

After Crow left, Benjamin began his usual ritual of cleaning the room, removing the bloody cotton balls, putting the doctor's tools in a washbasin.

"Ben?" Orla spoke the man's name, gazing at him.

He froze, as he'd done before when he she spoke to him, but this time he looked up.

"It's better if you don't talk to me," he whispered, stealing a glance toward the door.

"He's gone," she said. "He won't be back today."

Orla had learned Crow's movements. He administered his drugs in the morning, returned in the evening to sedate her, but she never saw him overnight. She would not have known the time, except that Crow wore a watch, and Orla stared at it whenever he entered the room, allowing her to piece together a timeline of his comings and goings.

"I'm here against my will, Ben. I'm not a patient. I'm-"

"I know," he said, allowing his hair to fall back over his eye.

"Then help me," she pleaded.

He shook his head.

"Why? Please," she begged. "My family must be terrified. My parents, Ben. My friends. There are people who love me, who are desperate to find me."

"I can't help you," he muttered. "I know you don't understand, but I can't."

"Because he'd hurt you?"

Ben looked away.

"I don't have anyone else. Okay? This is my life. If I let you go… I just can't, okay?"

Orla needed something, a way in. Crow had put gloves on her hands before he left. She rubbed her hand against the bed, allowing one glove to slide off.

"Could I have a drink of water? Please? My throat is so dry."

He glanced at her, his dark eyes searching. Finally, he nodded and left.

He returned a moment later with a glass of water and moved to her bedside. He trembled as he held the water to her lips.

She reached toward him with her bare hand, touching his shirt.

Gulping the water, she searched the images that rose in her mind, reaching deeper to ferret out some clue that might get him to open up.

"Lemon," she murmured.

He jumped when she spoke and spilled water on her face.

"Sorry," he said, grabbing a towel and wiping the water from her cheek.

"You had a dog named Lemon."

He stared at her mistrustfully.

"How do you know that?"

She twittered her fingers, the nude glove resting beside them.

"You saw her?"

Orla nodded.

"Why did you name her Lemon?" Though she already knew the answer. She had seen the dog happily carrying a lemon around in her white-and-brown speckled muzzle.

He smiled sadly.

"She played with them, carried them in her mouth, even buried them in the yard."

"Where did you get her?"

A wistful expression transformed his face.

"Here at the asylum. A patient came in with a puppy in his bag. He shoved her at me and said, 'she's yours.' And she was."

"Until Dr. Crow killed her."

He backed away, smacked into the metal tray with the doctor's tools. They went crashing to the floor so loud that even Orla expected Crow to reappear in the doorway. He didn't.

"It was an accident," Ben whispered.

Orla shook her head.

"It wasn't. He hated your dog. He backed over her with his car. He saw her in his side-view mirror and hit the gas."

Ben shook his head, brown eyes tormented.

He didn't run from the room, but he stopped looking at her and didn't speak. He moved slowly as if heavy with the burden of her words. He didn't leave until he'd cleaned the room and carried all the supplies away.

When he walked out, he avoided her eyes, flicking off the lights and leaving her in darkness.

30

Hazel

Hazel touched the crumbling banister that flanked the old house. Moss-streaked gargoyles sat at either end of the rotting wooden staircase. Grass and weeds, even a few flowers, poked through the sagging planks. Shuttered windows closed the interior from prying eyes.

Time had weathered the house and given free rein to the vegetation, jungle-like, that surrounded the aged walls - once white, now chipped and peeled. Delicate clusters of yellow blooms speckled the moonseed vines climbing up the exterior.

When Hazel lifted the knocker, she feared the door beneath the brass ring would chip away. It didn't. She heard the loud bang echoing through the house.

A woman opened the door, her eyes a dazzling opaque blue, her hair long and golden.

"Hi," Hazel stammered, unnerved by the beautiful woman like a fairytale princess dropped into a haunted old mansion.

"Are you here for Mrs. Cooper?" the woman asked in a soft, lyrical voice.

"Mrs. Cooper?" Hazel asked, trying to get her bearings. The

house loomed deep and bottomless. White candles flickered from tables in the dusky interior.

"She lives here," the woman continued.

"Umm, yes, maybe." Hazel laughed. "I'm not sure. My friend Miranda told me to come here for Hattie. I need help."

The woman's smile faltered, but she stepped back, allowing Hazel to enter.

Hazel walked into the stifling foyer. Despite the house's size, it felt oddly claustrophobic and too warm.

They passed a great room with a fireplace crackling in a stone hearth, despite the hot summer day.

"Mrs. Copper is ninety-seven years old," the woman told her. "She chills easily."

Hazel saw another room, the floor covered in white sheets and splashed with paint. Canvases, stacked several deep, lined the walls.

"Is she a painter?" Hazel asked.

The woman glanced back at her with a smile.

"No, I am the painter. I care for Mrs. Cooper, so she offered me a room to paint while I'm here."

"You're not her daughter, then? Or granddaughter?"

The woman shook her head, pushed open a swinging door into a brightly lit kitchen. This room differed from the rest of the house. Sun streaked through tall windows, revealing the tangled woods behind the house.

The kitchen counters were clean, the table empty except for a bowl of fruit.

"I know Miranda," the woman said, gesturing toward a chair. "And I am Hattie."

"Oh, I'm sorry. She didn't say an age. I just assumed…"

The woman nodded.

"I rarely involve myself in such matters."

"What matters?" Hazel asked.

Hattie let her delicate hands rest on the table. Hazel could see bits of paint in her cuticles.

"The dead. That's why you're here, I assume?"

Hazel blinked at her, unnerved by her directness.

"Yes, but…"

"Seeing the dead is a terrible burden. It nearly destroyed my life, and my mother's as well. My mother vowed to never speak of her gift again. I have been foolish with my own. You see, when the dead appear, there is always a reason. They are persistent. If you allow them, they will consume your life. Their messages will never cease, their appearances never falter. To live a life free of their influence has to be a conscious choice again and again, until they fade."

Hazel frowned.

"But you could do so much good. People are suffering, searching for their loves ones…"

Hattie smiled.

"And that is why I did not close the door in your face. But I am not as open as I once was. I may not be able to help you."

Hazel studied the woman's unlined face, her gentle eyes. If she had to describe her in a word, she'd say angelic.

"Thank you, Hattie." Hazel tried to think where to begin. "A woman disappeared in 1973. Her name was Susan, or is Susan, I guess. She is part of a series of women who have vanished. Do you read Up North News?"

Hattie shook her head.

"I don't read the news, nor do I watch television, other than an occasional movie."

"Okay, well, six women have disappeared in the last four years. I believe the ghost of one of them has appeared to me. I've seen her twice."

Hattie nodded.

"Do you have something that belonged to her?"

"Yes."

Hazel pulled out the fake pearl bracelet Liz had given her.

Hattie took the bracelet and held it in her hand. She closed her eyes, lashes fluttering.

"Hattie?" an old woman's strained voice drifted in.

Hattie opened her eyes, slipped the bracelet over her wrist, and stood.

"I'll be back soon," she promised.

Hazel watched her go, her long blonde hair swishing along her narrow waist.

Minutes clicked by, and Hazel grew restless. She wandered from the kitchen, pausing at a closed door when she heard voices.

"There, there, Claudette. Lie back and rest. Oh look, Chester has come to join us. Can you feel him, Claudette? Chester is here with you."

"Chester?" the old woman croaked. "Oh, my love, my heart. Hattie, ask him to tell you about our trip to Paris in 1921. We stayed at the Hotel d'Angleterre."

Hattie laughed.

"Chester says you spilled your espresso in the lap of Ernest Hemingway and fell into the Seine."

When the voices died in the room, Hazel returned to the kitchen. She paused at a window, gazing into the dense yard.

"I'm sorry," Hattie spoke, startling her.

The woman, as quiet as a ghost, had drifted into the kitchen and stood just behind Hazel.

Hazel managed not to jump, but her heart hammered in her chest.

Hattie handed her the bracelet.

"Susan is filled with purpose," Hattie said, brow furrowed. "I cannot understand her. I believe she seeks justice, but more so an end to the pain of those who mourn her."

"She's dead?"

Hattie nodded. "I'm sorry. A violent death, and there were others."

Hazel swallowed and drew a scarf from her bag that belonged to Orla.

Hattie eyed the scarf for several seconds, and then took it. She took a big breath in and closed her eyes.

"Nothing," Hattie said, handing the scarf back.

"Does that mean she's alive?" Hazel asked, hopeful.

Hattie shook her head.

"It means she's not available to me. I don't know if she's alive."

"Can you tell me anything, Hattie? Anything about who did this?"

Hattie shook her head.

"He was a stranger to the girl with the bracelet. But she keeps showing me a number: 3-1-1."

~

Abe

Abe sat on a tree stump and stared across the street at the empty field where the boy had found the bike. Elder Park was unremarkable. An open space surrounded by trees, crisscrossed with trails that circled back to the entrance. He'd found a few discarded beer cans and the remnants of an old fire pit. The State of Michigan owned the land, and it was located on the complete opposite side of town from the park Hazel believed Orla had ridden to the day she disappeared.

Could Hazel have been wrong? Maybe Orla had ridden west instead of east. What if they'd been looking in the wrong place all along? But then, there'd been tips, multiple sightings of Orla that Sunday morning on Road 210, the road which led to Birch Park.

As Abe watched, a green pickup truck pulled into the grassy parking lot.

A young man stepped out. Dark hair to his chin concealed much of his face. He wore black pants and a black shirt. He drew a paper sack from the cab and walked to the rear of the truck, folding down the tailgate. He slid onto the back and took a sandwich from his bag. As he chewed, he gazed toward the trees.

Abe studied the man, likely in his mid-twenties with watchful eyes and hunched shoulders. He looked like a loner, the guy in high school who sat alone during lunch, reading a horror novel and avoiding eye contact.

Luke Dixon had described a pickup truck to Deputy Waller - a green pickup truck, with a rusted bumper. An identical truck to the one before him.

Abe waited until the man finished his lunch and climbed behind the wheel.

He squinted toward the back of the truck, writing the license plate number in his notebook. Abe waited several seconds after the truck pulled from the park, and then he followed him. The man turned onto Division and wound back around the bay, taking 131 south. Two turns later, Abe knew where the man was headed: the asylum.

The man parked in an employee parking lot and lumbered toward an entrance tucked into an alcove at the base of the enormous building.

31

Hazel

"Abe just wants a story," Hazel exploded, after they'd hit another dead end. "Frankly, I'm sick of feeling guilty because he's running around town like a lunatic. It's his job, and he has unlimited time to devote to searching."

Abe had received a tip from a woman convinced that Orla was being forced to work at a topless club in Cadillac. Liz had picked up Hazel, and they'd driven together to Cadillac spotting the woman as she walked in for her shift. She had long black hair, and the resemblance ended there. Her lined face was haggard; her eyes brown, not blue; and when she saw them staring, she flipped them her middle finger.

"Hazel," Liz said quietly.

Hazel looked at Liz, her face warming as guilt rushed over her.

"I'm sorry, Liz. I didn't mean that. I-"

Liz interrupted her.

"Do you know why Abe became a reporter?"

Hazel propped her bag in her lap, digging for her sunglasses.

"No."

Liz nodded, merging onto the highway.

"It's not my story to tell, and I probably shouldn't, but when Abe first started investigating Susan's disappearance, I had a reaction similar to yours. The man was a journalist, he dredged up painful stories for a living, he exploited people's suffering. It's not true, though. Read any of his pieces. He's a compassionate man, a man driven not by ambition, but justice."

Hazel bit her lip, embarrassed at her outbursts.

"I think you should know why he does it," Liz continued. "When Abe was eighteen, the summer after he graduated from high school, his girlfriend, Dawn, vanished."

Hazel regarded Liz with surprise.

"Vanished?"

"Yes, but it's more complicated than that. After work, she called him from a pay phone at a convenience store in town to see if he wanted snacks before she drove to his house. During their conversation, a man pulled up. She told Abe the guy gave her the creeps. A minute later, Abe heard her scream. He jumped in his car and raced to the parking lot of the store. The truck passed Abe, and he saw Dawn inside. Abe chased them. He followed the truck on back roads, and then he ran out of gas."

"He ran out of gas?" Hazel blurted. "Oh my God. And the guy got away?"

Liz nodded.

"They never found her. They released a sketch based on her description from Abe, and the image of the man's truck, but… nothing. Abe searched for years. I'm sure he's still searching."

~

They met Abe at his apartment. Coffee mugs littered every surface, coffee mugs and notes, notes with coffee stains.

"I'm sensing a theme here," Hazel murmured, gathering half-empty mugs and carrying them to the sink.

Liz seemed oblivious to the mess and joined Abe at a desk beneath a corkboard filled with pictures of the missing girls.

"The topless bar was a dead end," Liz told him.

Abe pulled a Post-It note from the corkboard, crumpled it, and dropped it in the trash.

"I figured as much. I appreciate you both going to check it out."

"Anything that gets us closer," Liz said.

Hazel set about washing dishes, ashamed of her outburst in the car with Liz. She glanced at him from the corner of her eye, imagining him on a dark street long ago, watching the taillights of a truck disappear.

"What's this?" Liz asked.

Hazel set the dishes on a towel and moved back to the corkboard.

Liz pointed at a note that read 'M-22 just past Sapphire Lane' with several names listed beneath it.

Abe didn't look at her, but he pulled the note down.

"A few sightings in that area. Lots of false sightings when the article first comes out, that kind of thing."

Liz nodded and continued browsing his notes, but Hazel saw an expression of guilt cross Abe's features.

"And this is where the boy found Orla's bike?" Liz asked, pointing to a map of Birch Park.

"Yeah. I've driven out there once, but I'm going to stake it out over the next few days. Dixon saw a pickup truck there the day Orla's bike showed up."

"You think it's connected?" Liz asked.

Hazel sighed and shifted her attention to Abe's apartment. The space was small, sparsely furnished, and buried in an explosion of paper and books. He devoted one corner of his living room to the missing girls. Corkboards flooded with their images, stacks of flyers on his desk, newspaper clippings about each girl. A couch sat in the center of the room facing a small TV. Otherwise, there were few furnishings.

The scene made Hazel anxious. She wanted to scoop pages up and file them.

She walked to the window and pushed some books aside to sit on the little bay seat extended over the backyard. A flowering dogwood tree dropped a blanket of white petals on the grassy courtyard that edged the parking lot.

Hazel remembered the summer after she met Orla. They drove up Old Michigan Peninsula in the spring and ran through the blossoming cherry trees; lying beneath one and gazing at the opulence of pink petals. The memory caused an ache beneath Hazel's ribs, and she pressed her head against the window, wondering if she would ever hear Orla's laugh again.

Liz and Abe seemed right at home in the chaos.

"Have you found any connection between that Spencer guy and the girls? Any evidence that the girls ever met him, knew him somehow?" Liz asked.

"No," Abe admitted. "But I'm not ready to dismiss him. And I got a tip yesterday morning. A woman vacationing here last summer saw a gold sports car near Platte River, the beach they suspected Rita went to the day she disappeared. Spencer Crow drives a gold Corvette. It's a very nice car."

"And a hard car to miss. Is it possible he's abducting girls in a gold sports car, and no one notices?" Hazel asked.

"A lot of girls would get in a car like that," Liz murmured, gazing toward the wall of pretty girls.

After Abe filled them in on a few more tips, Hazel took a walk outside. The apartment seemed to be closing in on her.

They joined her several minutes later.

"I've got to get home. I told Jerry I'd pick up Chinese takeout. Can I give you a ride?" she asked Hazel.

"I'll take her," Abe said.

Hazel hugged Liz goodbye, and Abe gave her a quick peck on the cheek.

They drove the first few minutes in silence.

When Abe finally spoke, his words surprised Hazel.

"Liz told you about Dawn," Abe said.

Hazel nodded.

"She wasn't trying to go behind your back. I got frustrated about the girl at the strip club and vented."

"About me?"

"You seemed like the easiest target."

"I get it," he admitted. "I know that anger. I remember it well."

"Can you talk about her? Dawn?"

Hazel watched him consider her question.

"I couldn't for a long time. It's easier now, in a way. The rawness of it is gone, but I'm not sure you ever move on. Especially when you don't know, when their fate is a mystery. I met Dawn my sophomore year at Juniper High in Spokane. I was a new kid, still reeling from my parents' divorce. New city, new house, a new life. I struggled for the first few months, and then I met Dawn."

"What was she like?"

"Like her name, as corny as that sounds. Light and fresh and always smiling. She played tennis, and ran track, and dreamed of owning a farm and having seven kids."

"Seven?"

He laughed.

"Yeah. I told her I'd commit to three, and we could reevaluate."

"You guys were serious, then? A farm and seven kids didn't scare you off?"

"I'd never given a lot of thought to my future. Once my parents' marriage fell apart, I lost interest in the future. I worked on the school newspaper. I'd always been into that. She said I would be a novelist. I'd be like Thoreau writing about borrowing an ax from my neighbor so I could chop a tree for firewood. I could pen long, boring novels about tending the pastures and people would love them because it would remind them of simpler days. There was something romantic in her future for us. I fell in love with her dream. I joined the 4-H club and learned about farm animals." He laughed, as if still astounded by the choices of his younger self.

"It was a lovely dream."

"Yeah. I saved money to buy a ring. I planned to ask her at Christmas the following winter. We both attended the community college. Her parents owned a big farm, and they'd help us get a piece of land to build a house."

He stared in puzzlement through the windshield.

"On Saturday, June 11th, 1966, Dawn finished work at Patty's Ice Cream Shop at nine p.m. She'd planned to come over and watch a movie, but stopped at a pay phone near Daryl's Convenience Store to ask if she should bring snacks."

Abe parked on the street in front of Hazel's house, but neither of them got out.

"A man pulled into the parking lot next to her car. He had a beard and dark glasses on. He spooked her. I told her to ask him if he needed the phone. She asked him. He didn't respond, but shook his head no, which was weird. He'd parked his truck between the phone booth and her car. She wanted to run to her car, but she felt foolish and also scared. I stood in my kitchen, my mom watching ABC Scope in the other room, and I didn't realize the magnitude of that moment. I would regret it, sitting there, talking. I could have been to that store in the length of time we talked on the phone."

Hazel wanted to say something to erase the tormented look on his face.

"Dawn whispered, 'He's getting out of the truck,' and then she screamed and dropped the phone. I yelled her name and bolted. Ran to my car, jumped in, drove like a madman to get to the store, and as I got there, the truck passed me. I saw her inside screaming and fighting with the guy. I whipped my car around and chased them. He drove fast, and I kept trying to pull up beside him, force him off the road, but his truck was faster. I drove an old station wagon. I chased him for miles on back country roads. And then..."

He stopped, his face bone-white at the memory.

"I ran out of gas." He looked up and stared at Hazel with such confusion. "Remember when I asked you if you believe in fate? I think that was the moment for me, the instant that question became like a looming force in my life. I ran out of gas, and I watched that truck disappear into the night. The headlights smaller and smaller. I had gotten out and started running down the road, panting, screaming. Eventually, I stopped. I had to stop. They were gone, long gone."

He closed his eyes and leaned his head back on the seat, but continued talking.

"I started to walk back to town and, a half-hour later, someone drove by. I flagged them down. They weren't going to stop. I threw myself in front of their car. Luckily, there was a man and a woman inside. If it had been a single woman, she probably would have sped off scared. They picked me up, and I screamed we had to get to the police. I must have told them the story, though I don't remember it now. That night, everything that happened after that guy's taillights vanishing is like a murky nightmare with bits of faces and words all jumbled together. The cops were suspicious. It took hours before they sent someone to look for that truck. They never found it, and they never found Dawn."

He opened his eyes and tilted his head.

Hazel reached a tentative hand to Abe's and held it.

He squeezed, and then pulled his hand away, returning it to the steering wheel.

"That's my story."

"Were there ever any suspects?"

He shook his head.

"Never. They had evidence from the scene, a button that may have been ripped from the guy's shirt. They found scuff marks on the side of the phone booth. Dawn fought back, probably kicked the booth. Nothing that pointed them toward a specific person."

"I think I should tell you something as well," Hazel said. "I've seen Susan." She had not expected to feel so nervous relaying the tale, but found that her hands shook and her nerves seemed frayed. She bunched them in her skirt and gazed at her garden. The flowers soothed her, their tranquil blossoms shivering in the afternoon sun.

Abe didn't speak for a long time. When he did, they were not the words Hazel expected.

"On M-22?"

"M-22? The road? No, the first time happened the night Orla vanished. I was leaving Leone's Restaurant with Calvin. I saw her across the street, barely visible in the rain and dark, though now I think more visible than a regular person would have been, almost as if she were lit from within. The second time was a few days ago at Milly's Bakery. She was standing on a dock in a yellow t-shirt with a big mouth on it, wearing one shoe. When I looked back a second later, she had disappeared."

Abe said nothing, but Hazel saw the creases in his forehead as he mulled over her story.

"Why did you ask about M-22?" she asked.

Abe hesitated. "I've received some bizarre tips the last couple of days."

Hazel waited.

"Three separate people have told me they saw Susie hitchhiking M-22 near Sapphire Lane."

"What? Have you told Liz?"

Abe shook his head.

"Their stories mirror yours. She's there, and then she disappears. Yellow t-shirt with the red mouth, and one shoe."

"Unreal," she murmured.

"Yeah, I wanted to think so, but now…" He waved a hand towards her.

"Yesterday, I visited someone who…" Hazel searched for the right words. "Who communes with spirits, I guess."

Abe pressed a hand to the side of his head, as if it hurt his brain to hear her.

"She told me Susie is dead. That a man killed her, it was violent, and there were others."

"She could have read my article and inferred those things."

Hazel shook her head.

"She doesn't read or watch the news, Abe. But she said one more thing."

"What's that?"

"She said Susie kept showing her the number 3-1-1."

32

THE NORTHERN MICHIGAN ASYLUM FOR THE INSANE

Orla

Cold, stiff fingers brushed across Orla's cheek. She opened her eyes and stared into darkness.

The drugs blurred the lines between dream and reality. She turned her head to the side, searching for the source of the sensation, but the black room offered no clues.

"Is someone there?" she whispered hoarsely. The sedative also made her mouth dry. When she woke in the night, she thirsted as if she'd walked in a desert for days.

She heard the soft rush of a man's breath, and froze.

"Ben?" she whispered.

"Is Ben your lover? Or is it your daddy you call out for in the dark?"

She bristled at the sound of Dr. Frederic's voice. The sharp sound of a match striking wood split the silence, and she watched the flame light his awful smile.

He lit a candle and held it before him, stepping closer to her, sliding the candle along the length of her body, scanning her. She could not see his eyes fixed on her body, but she sensed them. The thin nightgown that covered her breasts and thighs left her exposed, vulnerable.

"You are luscious, aren't you?" he murmured.

The candle tipped, and a bud of hot wax struck Orla's knee.

She hissed and bit her teeth together.

"I'll tell Crow," she seethed.

Frederic laughed, lifting the candle to his face.

"Do you think he would mind, Orla? You are an experiment, an object for dissection. I could strip you naked, rape you, beat you, and Crow would care only that I didn't damage your precious hands." Frederic rubbed his fingers over Orla's gloved hand.

She swallowed bile rising into her throat, desperately searching for a way to stop him.

"Please," she whispered. "I can help you. Bring me anything. I'll give you answers."

Frederic leaned close to her face, not near enough for her to clamp her teeth upon his cheek, though the thought crossed her mind.

"I could take you and demand answers, Orla - steal you from this place and keep you forever, my little pet. Look at the color flushing your pale face," he whispered. He shifted lower, and his mouth brushed her nipple.

"Stop," she shrieked.

He stood abruptly and stuffed a hand over her mouth. He'd left the door open to her room, and he glanced toward it as if concerned someone might come.

"He's clearly not giving you enough medicine."

Frederic produced a syringe from his coat.

"Please, no," she muttered, but he had already slipped the needle into her arm.

The warmth of the liquid rushed through her bicep, and a moment later, he blew the candle out.

33

Abe

Abe picked up his phone, punching in the number and the extension for Deputy Waller at the Grand Traverse Police.

"Deputy Waller speaking," the man said.

"Jeremy, it's Abe."

"Oh, hey." His voice dropped, and Abe knew Waller didn't want anyone to know who he spoke with.

"Sorry, you guys are probably under a lot of heat."

Jeremy laughed.

"You could say that."

"Any prints lifted off the bike?"

"Yeah, nothing in the system, but we've got four sets of prints."

"Good, that's good," Abe murmured. "I'm looking for another favor."

Jeremy sighed.

"You know, Detective Moore would chew my ass if he knew about all these favors."

"I know, man. I do, but that same detective will be eating humble pie when we nail this guy."

"With a side of shit soup, I hope," Jeremy mumbled.

Abe laughed.

"Remember the guy I asked you to run the background check on?"

"Yep."

"He's been going to school in Ann Arbor for the last four years. I'm hoping you could call the local cops down there and see if they've ever picked him up for anything."

"Good grief, man. Can't you find someone else to do your grunt work?"

"I only want the best, Waller. You know that."

"Yeah, okay. But you owe me, man," Waller told him.

"Since I owe you, I need one more thing."

Waller sputtered.

"Just a quick license plate check." Abe rattled off the license plate of the green pickup from Elder Park.

"You'd best tell your dad the next time he's trout fishing, the biggest one goes to his favorite deputy."

"A fish fry is in you near future, Wallace. I swear it," Abe promised, hanging up the phone.

~

That evening, Abe played his phone messages.

"Abe, it's Jeremy. It took a bit of digging, but Spencer Crow was questioned four years ago about a young woman found murdered in Ypsilanti. Apparently, he was the last person to see her alive. Looks mighty suspicious. The officer who questioned him told me he wanted the guy for this girl's murder, but his mother provided him with an alibi. He also had a lawyer within hours of getting picked up. The license plate you asked about connects to Benjamin Stoops. Address is 12 Misty Lane, Lake Leelanau."

"Another guy from Leelanau," Abe muttered, listening to the message a second time to make sure he'd gotten the address right.

~

"Hey, Dad." Abe pushed into his father's house, a pizza balanced on one hand.

His father reclined in his easy chair watching a baseball game. Several beer cans lay haphazardly on his TV tray.

"'Bout time you showed your face around here," his dad called out. "Your mom has phoned me three times this week. She seems to think you're ignoring her."

Abe sat the pizza on the kitchen table and pulled plates from the cupboard. The kitchen was clean except for a few dishes stacked in the sink. His dad's cat, Flea, stood on the counter, paws on the window ledge over the sink, watching birds picking at the feeder on the back porch.

Abe scratched Flea's head. The cat leaned into him but kept his gaze fixed on the birds.

"I'll call her soon. I've been busy."

"I noticed." His dad gestured to the newspaper next to his chair. The girls' faces peered out from the black-and-white pages.

Abe felt a little tug in his gut. He hadn't taken a break from the case since he learned of Orla's disappearance. He usually took dinner to his dad twice a week and called his mother every other day. He'd neglected both of his parents.

"Your mom wants to come for a visit," his dad said, taking his plate and settling it on his lap.

He muted the television.

"Really?" Abe asked, surprised. His mother hadn't been back to Michigan in a decade. Once her mother had died, she had insisted Michigan held nothing for her but bad memories. A divorce, dead parents, why go back?

Abe and his younger sister had moved with his mother after the divorce to Spokane, Washington. When his girlfriend vanished, he adopted an attitude not unlike his mother's. He wanted to escape the bad memories. He stayed for a few years, finished school, and searched for Dawn, but eventually he moved back to Michigan to live with his dad.

"She figures if she ever wants to see her only son again, she has to come back."

Abe took a bite of pizza, forced it down. He wasn't hungry, only aided by an additional helping of guilt. He'd promised his mother he'd visit her that summer, yet August was fast approaching and he hadn't set a date, asked for a week off work, or called about flights.

"I know you're busy, son. And it's important work you're doing, but take it from a man who's learned the hard way - you have to put time into the people you love. It's hard to believe at the moment, but someday you'll realize there was never anything more important."

"Yeah, I know, Dad," Abe sighed.

"No, you don't. Unfortunately, you've got a lot of your old man in you. But listen to me, anyhow. Call your mom tonight. And not to beat a dead horse, but she also mentioned her nonexistent grandchildren and daughter-in-law."

"Okay, now I need a beer," Abe grumbled, standing and shuffling back to the kitchen.

"Make it two," his dad said.

They drank their beer, and each ate two pieces of pizza. Abe barely tasted his but didn't want the 'you need to eat' lecture. His dad put the leftover pizza in the fridge and returned to the living room.

"Tell me what you've got," he said, sitting on his chair, but not reclining.

Abe's father had been a prosecutor for thirty years. Two years earlier, he'd retired to pursue fishing and getting reacquainted with American sports. He also jokingly referred to himself as Abe's private counsel.

"The cops have formed a task force. They're finally communicating between jurisdictions. But they still don't have a suspect."

"They don't, but you do?" his dad asked, a knowing look on his face.

"Maybe. I saw a guy at the park where Orla Sullivan vanished. I did a background check based on a hunch and came up empty. Then Deputy Waller dug deeper. The guy attends University of Michigan. Four years ago, Ann Arbor police questioned him about the murder of a young woman. He was the last to see her alive."

His dad nodded, swept the crumbs from his TV tray and dropped them in the waste basket next to his chair.

"Have the police questioned him in connection with any of these girls?"

"Not that I'm aware of. I've asked every officer who's still speaking to me, and none of them have ever heard of him."

"So, he's either very clever, or innocent."

"He's not innocent," Abe grumbled. "He may not be guilty of these murders, but he's not innocent. There was something…"

"Off about him?"

"Yeah.

"You gotta trust your gut. In all my years of practicing law, it never steered me wrong. When I was in the room with a murderer, my body sensed it, even if my mind tried to remain unbiased. The hair on my arms would stand on end. I'd release adrenaline like I might have to fight for my life. What tips have come out of this?" He picked up the article.

Abe sighed. He told his father about the sightings of a girl who looked like Susie hitchhiking late at night on the Leelanau Peninsula before vanishing without a trace.

His dad pulled a toothpick from his pocket and balanced it on his lips.

"Now that is a strange tale, if there ever was one. What makes you link those stories to this perp?"

"He lives a few miles from that stretch of road."

His dad frowned, poked at his teeth with the toothpick.

"You don't think it's bogus?" Abe asked.

His dad pulled the toothpick out and gazed at it thoughtfully.

"Your mom believed in ghosts. She told me she lived in a haunted house when she was a little girl."

"A haunted house?" Abe couldn't hide his skepticism.

"She said they used to hear a woman singing in the night. Her own mother had a priest come out and bless the house, but it didn't matter. They moved when your mom was eight, but the memories of that house stuck with her. In her twenties, your mom went back to that town and spoke with the sheriff. You can see where you picked up your journalistic leanings." He winked at Abe. "The sheriff told her someone had murdered a woman in that house five years before your mom's family moved in. The local police thought the husband killed her, but they never proved it."

"Are you saying I should believe this girl is haunting that stretch of road?"

Abe's father leaned back and steepled his fingers on his belly.

"Your mother was convinced the woman from her childhood home had a story to tell. She believes ghosts have unfinished business. If this girl is dead, but is showing up out there, maybe there's a reason. Tell me about this young man's family. Does he have parents?"

"I met the mother. Not a warm woman, by any means."

"What's her name?"

"Virginia Crow."

Abe's father stood, brushed the crumbs from his pants. He ambled over to his phone.

"Jack, it's Martin Sevett. Retirement's good. Catching up on all the sleep I missed over the last few decades. Yeah, yeah. Listen, I'm calling about a woman." Martin laughed. "Hardly, Jack. My days of womanizing are long gone. Her name's Virginia Crow. Sure, yeah. Divorced? She's widowed, okay."

Abe watched his father scribble onto a little note pad next to his phone. He talked for several more minutes.

"Have time to chat with my son this week?" Martin continued. He mouthed 'tomorrow' at Abe, and Abe nodded. "Yep, tomorrow works."

"Jack Miller's been on the Board of the Leelanau Historical Society for years. He's a long-time resident of Glen Arbor, and he's also a cartographer. He's a man in the know, so to speak."

"And he knows Virginia?"

"According to Jack, she's not an easy woman to know. Widowed over twenty years ago, never remarried, though rumors flew about the dead husband's brother, also named Crow. He's a doctor at the sanitarium."

"The asylum?"

"Yep. Virginia has one son, Spencer. The whole family puts on airs, according to Jack. Her kid was homeschooled, has attended the University of Michigan for the last four years, and works summers for Dr. Marlou in Suttons Bay. The husband died in his sleep, a young man under thirty years old at the time, strange circumstances according to Jack, but that's just talk."

"Man, that guy is in the know."

Martin ripped the sheet of paper from the notepad and handed it to Abe.

Abe looked at the neat, bulleted list of points written in perfect block writing. His father had perfected note-taking during his previous life as an attorney.

"Jack's number is there at the bottom. He's at the Historical Museum tomorrow from noon to four. If he doesn't have the answer, he'll know who does," Martin explained.

"Does he know how to talk to ghosts?"

Martin smiled and nodded.

"Wouldn't put it past him."

34

Abe

"Jack?" Abe asked, approaching the souvenir counter at the Leelanau Historical Museum.

"Jack's my name, history's my game," the man said sticking out his hand. "You must be Martin's boy. You've got that fierce, lawyerly look in your eye, though I hear you're a newsman."

"Yeah, I would have opted for a profession raising hairless rats before I spent half a decade in law school."

Jack chuckled.

"We all must forge our own way. I'd imagine both your parents would have found hairless rats a difficult career to accept from their only son."

Abe grinned.

"My little sister's in medical school. She'd have made up for my inadequacies."

Jack guffawed and walked around the counter.

"I've got three daughters myself. A schoolteacher, a mom of six, and a nurse. I love 'em all just the same."

"Any sons?"

Jack nodded.

"Two. One followed after me and became a cartographer, the other works as an electrician."

"Five kids," Abe wondered. "My house felt crowded with my sister."

"A house can feel crowded if you're sitting alone," Jack told him with a wink. He stopped beside his counter and pulled a rolled map from a canvas bag, spreading it out on the counter before picking up a pair of tiny spectacles and perching them on his wide nose. He was a big man, the type who played football in college, and his largeness seemed out of place in the small museum. "We keep maps of the entire peninsula in the back. I pulled Sapphire Road this morning so you could take a peek at the Crow property."

Jack placed several Leelanau sand dune paperweights along the edges and picked up a stack of 'Leelanau is Groovy' pencils. He put the pencils end-to-end in a large square from Sapphire Road to M-22.

"Technically this property is divided. Half belongs to Mrs. Virginia Crow. The other half belongs to her brother-in-law, Dr. Byron Crow."

"She owns forty acres?" Abe leaned over the map, staring at the property lines. The back of the property ran right up to M-22. A particular stretch of road along M-22 where people had seen a young woman hitchhiking late at night.

"Yep," Jack said, tapping his finger along the print. "Mighty fine piece of land right there. I know more than a handful of folks have tried to buy a parcel or two. Used to have lumber kilns out there in the late 1800s."

"But she won't sell?"

"No way, no how. Claims her son hunts the property, and she likes her privacy. Don't dare show up selling vacuum cleaners, she'll run you off so fast the rubber on your shoes will burn up."

"Wait." Abe leaned over the property, following the line of pencils to the road on the north side of the estate. He leaned closer and read. "Misty Lane?"

"Yep." Jack ran his finger down the road. "Runs near-parallel with Sapphire - as much as any road can run parallel out here. When you've got woods and hills and sand dunes to contend with, roads get rather twisty. This property here," Jack pointed to a driveway marked on the north side, "belongs to Dr. Crow."

"12 Misty Lane?" Abe asked, incredulous. "Does he have a son?"

"No children and no wife. Though I've seen a young man around there over the years. He's a gangly fellow, all arms and legs, long hair in his face. Not too friendly."

"And Virginia Crow's husband died?"

"Sure did. Twenty-some odd years ago now. Nice man, too. Hector Crow. He and his wife had barely lived on the Peninsula five years when he passed. Byron already lived there. You see, the Crow boys grew up in Chicago, but visited Leelanau in the summer with their parents. Their father, Troy Crow, bought that piece of land intending to build a summer house, but then he stroked and died before they ever broke ground. The mother split the land between her boys. She couldn't bear to return, apparently. Byron Crow built his house on Misty Lane fresh out of medical school and took a job at the asylum. Hector lived in Chicago until he got married. Then he packed up and moved north to Leelanau. Hector hung out his shingle as a dentist. He had a little practice in Leelanau, and also performed dental visits at the asylum. Never went to him myself, but townsfolk spoke highly of him."

Abe continued to study the map, trying to make sense of the connections. *Connections, not coincidences,* his dad used to tell him when too many seemingly unrelated parts kept appearing together. The shaggy man from the park, Ben, lived on the same piece of property as Spencer with the gold car. Spencer had visited the park Orla disappeared from. Ben was spotted in Elder Park where Orla's bike was found.

"A duo?" Abe wondered aloud.

"A duo?" Jack repeated back to him.

"Sorry, thinking out loud." He tapped a finger on his head. "I'm curious about Spencer Crow. Ever heard anything about him? Has he got into trouble? That kind of thing?"

Jack grinned.

"Gossip says he's broken a few hearts - what with that shiny gold car and those big blue eyes - but nothing unusual. He's studying to be a psychiatrist like his good ol' Uncle Byron, so he spends the school year in Ann Arbor."

"Have any names that go with those broken hearts?"

Jack grinned. "You are tenacious like your father, Abe Sevett." He rolled the map and returned it to his bag. "I know the name of one girl because her mother works here at the museum, but if you speak with her, keep me out of the conversation. Last thing I need is Patty's mom in here giving me the evil eye all week."

"Patty?"

"Patty Janik. She works at the Frosty Cone in Suttons Bay. Bright green eyes, long blonde hair, you can't miss her. And remember, you didn't hear about her from me."

~

Hazel

"I'd like a strawberry ice cream cone, please," Hazel told the pretty blonde girl through the window at Frosty Cone.

"That will be twenty-six cents," the girl said, handing Hazel the cone.

Hazel gave her the change, and then glanced behind her. No other customers stood in line for ice cream.

"Are you Patty Janik?" Hazel asked.

The girl smiled.

"Sure am. And you are?"

"My name's Brenda," Hazel lied. "And this probably seems far out, but my best friend has just started dating a guy and I heard you used to go out with him."

Patty frowned.

"Bret?"

Hazel shook her head.

"His name is Spencer."

Patty scowled.

"Bummer for her. He's a total phony." Patty whipped her hair over one shoulder.

"Really? I wondered," Hazel murmured. "Any chance you have a couple minutes to tell me about him."

Patty nodded.

"Wendy, I'm taking a break."

Patty emerged from a side door in the little ice cream shop.

"There's a bench over there." Patty pointed to a park bench across the street. "I went out with Spencer for two months last summer," Patty started, before she'd even sat down. "He seemed nice at first, and it didn't hurt he drives that beautiful car."

"The gold one?" Hazel asked.

Patty nodded.

"Anyway, after a month, he started acting weird, not showing up for dates, missing on Friday and Saturday nights. I mean, seriously, what's the point of having a boyfriend who's not around on Friday and Saturday nights?"

"Agreed. If my boyfriend didn't show up on Friday night, I'd tell him to get lost."

"Exactly. After a few weeks, I told him to forget my number. I'd warn your friend to stay away from him."

"Anything else? Was he mean or anything?"

Patty shook her head.

"Not mean, but..." Patty laughed. "I used to joke to my girlfriend, Annie, he was like having a cardboard boyfriend. Half the time I'd be telling him a story, and he'd give me this blank look like he hadn't listened to a word I said." Patty kicked her legs out in front of her and lifted one long, tanned leg, admiring her purple toenail polish. "And another strange thing? He cut my hair one time."

"He cut your hair?" Hazel asked.

"It was bizarre. He must have thought I was sleeping. The sound of the scissors cutting startled me, and I opened my eyes to find him holding a piece of my hair. He got up real quick and threw it away. Or said he threw it away. He claimed there was gum in it."

"But you didn't believe him?"

Patty reached for her hair, running her fingers through it and examining the long strands.

Hazel noticed a striking resemblance between Patty and the missing girls.

"I did at the time, but later... I don't know. It bugged me when I thought about it."

35

THE NORTHERN MICHIGAN ASYLUM FOR THE INSANE

Orla

Orla's body ached, and when Ben pulled back the sheet to wash her, he gasped and stumbled back.

She couldn't see the bruises, but she felt them. Her throat ached as if the man had strangled her.

Ben swallowed, visibly shaken, and stepped back to her bedside.

"Who?" he started, glancing fearfully at the door.

"Dr. Frederic," she mumbled, tears sliding over her sore cheeks.

Ben put his head in his hands and shook his head for a moment.

"Please unstrap me," she whispered. "I promise I won't try to escape. I just need. I need..." But the sobs had begun, and she could no longer speak. As she cried and tried to force air beneath her bruised ribs, Ben hastily undid the straps on her forearms and ankles. He put his hands behind her back and helped her up to sitting. She ached between her legs. And when she sat, she saw bite marks on her thighs. The tears flooded and pooled in her lap. Ben held her awkwardly, a hand pressed against her back.

"There's a room down the hall with a bathtub. I washed it out a few days ago. I can take you there, but please, please don't run away," he pleaded.

Orla nodded, not sure if she could stand, let alone run away.

When she put weight on her feet, they stung. She'd only walked a few times since Crow had brought her to the asylum. Her muscles groaned in protest.

She put most of her weight on Ben, and he held her around the waist, supporting her to a cold, sterile room with a bathtub in the center.

She sat on a hard wooden chair and watched as he filled the bathtub with steaming water. He produced a bar of soap and a washcloth from a bag.

When she settled into the water, the bite marks stung, but she sank deeper.

She had no memory of the assault. She'd lost consciousness seconds after Frederic extinguished the candle, but her body remembered.

She soaked until the water turned cold. Ben sat in the chair, facing away from her and reading a book.

"What are you reading?" she asked him.

He lifted his head but didn't turn.

"'The Hobbit'," he said, holding up the book.

Orla smiled.

She and Liam had read The Hobbit together. Well, not together, but simultaneously. They'd spoken on the phone after each chapter, gushing about the giant spiders of Mirkwood, and later about the hideous wargs. They plotted their own hobbit-style adventures in the days before Liam met Erin and shifted his focus to building a family.

"I love that book," she said.

He turned, saw her nakedness, and quickly twisted away.

"Really? I've read it five times," he admitted.

"Can you help me out of the bath?" she asked.

He set the book on his chair and moved to the tub. He tilted his face away, his cheeks red as he touched her slippery body. She grimaced at the pain but gritted her teeth and limped back to the room.

Ben looked at his watch.

"Crow will be here in two hours. Please, don't tell him about the bath."

"I won't," she assured him.

He offered her a clean nightgown and underwear. When she lay back on the bed, he left the straps undone.

"I'll have to secure them, but I'll wait another hour, okay?"

"Thank you," she murmured. "What will he do?" she asked, nodding at her beaten body.

Ben frowned.

"I don't know."

But when Crow arrived, he did nothing. He paused, gazed at the bruises distastefully, and then went about his usual work administering truth serum, drilling her with questions, and then forcing her to touch a variety of objects. He wrote down his observations.

In the hall outside the room as the doctor left, Ben stopped him.

"Dr. Frederic raped her," Ben said, his voice rising.

"And what proof do you have of that?" Crow hissed.

"Didn't you see her body? The bruises?"

"Doctor Frederic is an esteemed colleague, a highly accomplished doctor, and a value to this institution. I suggest you keep your outlandish accusations to yourself."

"But-" Ben started.

"Enough," Crow barked.

Orla heard the sounds of his steps fading down the hall.

Orla woke that night disoriented, but sure of one thing: no straps held her bound to the bed.

She fumbled her blanket away, but the gloves made getting her bearings more complicated. She forced them off, clutching the mattress and swinging her legs to the floor.

Orla stumbled into the dark hall. Her legs, weak, wobbled beneath her. She huffed, unable to catch her breath, and forged on despite the dizziness pulling her sideways.

Pausing, she pressed a hand against a wall.

Screams, sobs, the faces of a dozen people in various states of despair exploded in her mind. She reeled away, turned, pushed her hands out to keep from falling. This time her hand caught on the back of a wheelchair abandoned in the hall. Its last occupant reared up in her vision. A young woman who fought with her husband, who went into the asylum with big dreams, a wild spirit, but emerged catatonic and compliant.

"No more," Orla mumbled, curling her hands against her chest. She was in the bowels of the asylum, in a dark place, a forgotten place. Crow had hidden her there, knowing they would not find her.

"Have to get out," she cried. Tears streamed down her cheeks. Her leg buckled, and she fell to one knee. Pain exploded in her kneecap and her arms swung out for a safehold. She found nothing and hit the ground with a thwack, smacking her face on the cement floor. Another explosion of pain in her chin and jaw.

The drugs were too powerful, impossible to hold on to consciousness.

She lay her cheek on the cold, hard ground, legs splayed out behind her. A mass of sticky warmth spread out from her face, a bloody nose, she thought. The darkness crept toward her, softening the edges, pulling her gently away from awareness.

Ben's face hovered above her. His brow wrinkled, his hands moving quickly as he wiped her face.

Orla had a vague memory of the previous night. Somehow, she'd gotten loose, fled into the hallway. She had not escaped.

"I shouldn't have undone the straps. I didn't think you'd try to escape. I just wanted you to be able to defend yourself. That was stupid," Ben fretted, hurriedly lifting her from the floor.

She whimpered and bit back the pain.

"I'm sorry, I'm sorry, we don't have much time." He carried her back to the bed, hoisting her on top.

He strapped her to the bed, and seconds later, Dr. Crow strode in, Dr. Frederic behind him.

36

Liz

Liz found Hazel and Abe in Grady's Diner, hunched over a map.

"He cut a piece of her hair," Hazel said. "Who does that?"

"But she never saw him act violent? He never tried to hurt her?"

"No, and she wouldn't have lied. She wasn't protecting him."

"Hi!" Liz said.

They both looked up, surprised. Abe glanced down at the map.

"I left you a message yesterday, Abe. You never called me back."

Hazel scooted over, and Liz slid into the booth beside her.

Abe brushed a hand through his hair and sighed.

"I'm sorry, Liz. My brain has been hijacked by tips since that article came out."

"Who cut whose hair?" Liz asked.

"Remember the guy with the gold sports car?" Hazel asked.

"Spencer," Liz stated. She remembered. Did either of them believe she did anything except think about the cases, wonder who stole her daughter, who ended her bright, beautiful life full of promise?

"I spoke with a girl yesterday who dated him last summer. He cut a piece of her hair."

"Why?"

"He claimed she had gum in it, but she clearly didn't believe him. It creeped her out."

"What did she look like?" Liz asked.

Hazel's eyes darted to Abe.

"Long blonde hair, green eyes, very pretty," Hazel admitted.

Liz bit her lip. Susie had long blonde hair and green eyes. Jerry sometime called her his green-eyed beauty.

"Did Susan have any connection to the Leelanau Peninsula?" Abe questioned Liz.

She frowned and shook her head.

"What kind of connection? She liked to go to the beach out there. All the kids did, because of the sand dunes. She never dated anyone who lived there. Spencer is a name I would not have forgotten."

Abe nodded.

"Family out there? Close friends?"

Liz shook her head.

"We took her to the Polka Fest in Cedar when she was younger. We camped once in a while, but no, nothing that sticks out."

Liza gazed at the hand-drawn map. A road ran along the side, M-22, with two additional roads leading away from it. She read Misty Lane and Sapphire Lane.

"Those sounds like the cobbled streets of Disney World," she murmured.

"If you're heading to the haunted mansion, maybe," Abe muttered, almost too low for Liz to hear.

"Explain the map," Liz insisted.

Her companions didn't speak and Liz slapped her hand on the table.

"Abe!"

Abe lifted his coffee and drank it down.

"Ben Stoops? That name ring any bells?"

Again, Liz shook her head.

"I saw him at the park where Orla's bike was found," Abe explained. "He's got a look. 'The guy police love to hate,' my dad would call him. He's unkempt, withdrawn, and he drives the truck that boy saw in the park the day Orla's bike disappeared."

Liz blinked at him.

"That's gotta be him, then. Right?" A rush of exhilaration made her want to fling Abe's papers in the air. "You've got his name? And an address?"

Abe sighed. "It's more complicated than that. This guy, Stoops, lives on the same piece of property as Spencer Crow. They live in the same stretch of woods." Abe pointed to the map he and Hazel had been looking at.

Liz glanced down at the map. She had spent little time on the Peninsula and wasn't familiar with Sapphire or Misty Lane.

"What does that mean?"

"It could mean they're working together. It could mean it's one of them, or it's neither of them." He threw up his hands. "I don't know what it means."

~

Hazel

"Should we have told Liz?" Hazel asked, settling into Abe's passenger seat. "About the sightings?"

He seemed to consider her question for a long time, maneuvering his car away from the bustle of Traverse City to the shrouded forests of the Leelanau Peninsula.

When he spoke, he sounded weary and uncertain.

"Not yet. Since I met Liz, she's had one desire - to bring Susan home. She knows Susan is dead. If I tell her about sightings, she might start to hope again."

"And that's a bad thing?"

He glanced at her.

"I don't know, Hazel. But yeah, I think hope could derail her. She told me about the first year after Susan vanished. She couldn't get out of bed for days, and she lost twenty pounds - stopped eating. Jerry had to call a doctor to the house. I'm sure it was worse than she ever let on. Searching for the truth, she has a purpose again. These sightings are... a complication, in a way."

"A complication?" Hazel protested. "Susan is trying to tell us what happened to her. Don't you see?"

"I need to concentrate," he snapped. "Can we just drop this for now?"

Hazel didn't add more, and Abe regretted bringing her. He'd allowed her to ride along mostly because he knew his own disbelief might cause him to miss something. He preferred to work alone. The more minds, the more theories, the more sleepless nights.

They didn't speak until they pulled into a driveway to pick up Ricky, the young man who'd spotted Susie on that dark stretch of road.

Ricky climbed in the backseat.

Hazel twisted around and stuck out her hand.

"I'm Hazel," she said.

"Ricky," he told her. "Sorry about the dirt."

She shook his hand anyway, seemingly unfazed by his dirty hands. They'd picked him up from his job site. Dark sweat stains circled beneath his armpits. A layer of dirt coated his arm and face, giving him a bronzed look.

As they drove up the peninsula, Ricky leaned forward between the seats.

"Slow down as you come up on this curve," he said.

They'd just passed Sapphire Lane.

"Just up here."

Abe slowed the car to a crawl. In summer, the forest road was dense with trees, especially in this area. At various points along the road, they glimpsed spacious views of climbing hills, an occasional hint of Lake Michigan sparkling in the sun, but in this area, the trees were so thick the eye couldn't penetrate their leafy branches.

Abe pulled off on the shoulder, and all three stepped from the car.

Ricky walked toward the trees, turned and walked back a few paces.

"Right around here," he said. "It was night, so I can't give you an exact location."

Hazel stood in the spot, closed her eyes. She squatted down and rested a hand in the dirt.

Abe watched her and felt mildly foolish.

"It happened at night," Ricky started. "I mean, my girlfriend thinks she only appears at night."

Abe sighed. What had he expected? Susie's ghost to step from the trees and lead them to her killer?

A car came around the curve, and Abe hustled them all back.

The orange sports car flew by, hugging the curves and spitting dust in Abe's face. He watched the car disappear around the next curve.

"We better go," he blurted, sensing another car rolling their way. As they piled into Abe's car and drove down M-22, they passed a green pickup truck driving the other way. Ben Stoops was behind the wheel.

~

Abe

Abe scrolled through microfiche, reading all the obituaries during the week of October 1951. Hector Crow's death notice included a brief snippet about his being a well-respected dentist, survived by his wife Virginia, his son Spencer, and his brother Byron.

It took some digging, but Abe tracked down the police officer who'd responded to a call of death at 311 Sapphire. The man had retired three years earlier, but Abe found his phone number and an address in Suttons Bay, Michigan. Abe called the man, and the retired deputy agreed to meet with him.

The retired officer lived in a small Cape Cod at the end of a dirt road. A wrought-iron fence contained an overweight, yellow Labrador retriever asleep next to a pile of chew toys.

When Abe stepped from his car, the man emerged through the front door.

"Officer Brewer?" he asked.

"Come on up," the man called. "Clementine won't hurt a fly."

Clementine barely batted an eye when Abe passed. He stepped

onto the porch, where the man sat in one of two plastic lawn chairs. He waved his hand that Abe should sit.

"Thanks for agreeing to meet with me, Officer Brewer," Abe told him, shaking the man's soft, age-spotted hand.

"You're digging into some awfully old history for such a young man," Officer Brewer told him. "My name's Dan. I haven't been an officer for three years, and I rather enjoy going by simple old Dan now."

"Okay, Dan. I have a few questions about Hector Crow, and I'll be out of your hair."

"What hair?" Dan laughed and patted his bald head.

Abe smiled.

"You responded to the call of a death at 311 Sapphire Lane on October 5th, 1949?"

"Sure did. It was a pretty straightforward call. A man had died in his sleep."

"But the man was only twenty-nine years old?"

Dan shrugged. "Heart attack, brain aneurysm. People die in their sleep, son."

"What did the coroner say?"

"Couldn't find a cause of death. He labelled it natural causes. His wife buried him three days later. Uneventful, the whole thing."

"What was Hector's wife like? Virginia Crow?"

"Real cool," the man told Abe. "She stood there and watched as we loaded him on the stretcher and carried him off. For all she reacted, she could'a been watching us carry a slab of meat from the freezer out of her house. Dry-eyed and not a sniffle out of her."

"Did you see her son, Spencer Crow? He would have been little, not even two years old."

Dan nodded.

"Caught a glimpse of him sitting in the kitchen when we carried out the boy's daddy. He didn't make a sound, just sat in a chair staring at the table. A quiet little guy. I remember feeling real bad for him and his mama, though she was a card, I'm sure."

"The mother didn't console him?"

"Not in front of us," Dan said. "One thing I remember bein' a little strange."

"What was that?"

"I saw that woman about six months later, walking down to her mailbox. Belly out to here." Dan held his hand two feet out from his stomach.

"She was pregnant?"

"Sure looked it, though she never mentioned it when the husband died. I ran into her a few years later at a store in town, asked about her children. She told me she had one child, and he was fine. Then she turned and walked away as if I'd insulted her. Strange woman, indeed."

"You have no idea what happened to the second child?"

He shook his head.

"None of my business. Might'a lost it, maybe gave it up because her husband was dead. Impossible to say."

"Not impossible," Abe said.

37

Abe

Abe sat at his desk at Up North News.

He had missing girls' tips to follow up on, he still hadn't called his mom, and he'd told his dad he'd stop by again for dinner. Instead, he'd spent hours calling hospitals, inquiring about records for Mrs. Virginia Crow. He scoured birth records but found nothing. He'd left messages with a handful of connections. Finally, he got a hit.

"I'm looking through midwife records from 1963," the woman who worked for Leelanau County Health said. "A birth that happened at 311 Sapphire. A midwife assisted."

"So, she had the baby. A boy or a girl?"

"A boy."

"Got a name?"

"No name on record."

"How about a name for the midwife?" Abe asked.

"Rosie Hyde."

Abe's editor stopped at his desk.

"I was hoping for a follow-up story, Abe. Some leads, at least. Not to mention you promised me a work-up on each girl. Instead, I'm looking at a blank basket in my office with your name on it."

Abe held up a finger, finished scribbling the address for Rosie Hyde, and stood.

"I'm on it, Barney."

"You're on what? I need a pitch. Wait, where are you going?"

Abe grabbed his keys, walked backwards toward the door.

"You're not a detective, Abe. You're supposed to write the story. You..."

But Abe had already pushed open the door and was running down the hallway.

~

Hazel

Hazel turned onto Sapphire Lane, driving at a creep while studying mailboxes. Many of the houses stood far off the road, invisible behind the wall of trees and foliage. The few Hazel observed were grand estates surrounded by sprawling yards with gardens, flowering shrubs, and several elaborate fountains displaying kissing children or chiseled saints.

She slowed at the mailbox marked three-eleven, staring into the thick forest. The stone driveway disappeared into the woods, concealing the house and its inhabitants.

She pulled onto the shoulder, gazing in her rearview mirror at the mailbox for 311 Sapphire Lane.

What would it hurt to get out and look around?

"If he's a murderer, it could hurt a lot," she grumbled, opening her door.

Bird song and crickets greeted her. It was peaceful. She loved her house in town, but sometimes the traffic and neighbors made her garden feel as if she lived in Chicago instead of northern Michigan. She enjoyed the sounds of nature and the quiet, the deep penetrating quiet, beneath them. Except as she slipped into the woods, the quiet grew unnerving. Her feet crunched over twigs and leaves so loud, she paused every few feet to listen. Had someone heard her?

An acorn fell from a tree overhead, and she sprang back when it landed in the leaves in front of her.

"Where are you going?" a woman's sharp voice sliced through the stillness, and Hazel froze, caught.

And then another voice, a man's voice, answered the woman's question.

"Out," the man said.

"Out where?" The woman's shrill tone made Hazel's ears ring.

She crept forward until she spied them through the trees. A man and a woman, facing off in the stone driveway of 311 Sapphire.

"What's the problem, Mother?"

The woman stomped her foot and stabbed the air with a finger.

"The problem?" she shrilled. "It's not safe."

The man didn't respond. He'd turned and started away, but the woman lunged forward, stopping just behind the man. He shrugged her off.

"Spencer!" the woman wailed, but the man got into his gold sports car and pulled down the driveway.

Hazel turned and sprinted back to her car. She waited until Spencer turned on Sapphire Lane, and then she jumped behind the wheel and followed him.

When she reached M-22, the car had disappeared.

"Damn," she cursed.

She turned south, hoping the man in the gold car was heading for Traverse City, but she'd lost him.

"It's not safe," she said out loud. What had the woman meant?

~

Abe

"Hi, are you Rosie Hyde?"

The woman had frizzy red hair pulled into a white scarf. She sat on a huge tire half-buried in the sand. Kids ran around the yard, screaming, blowing bubbles, crawling over an iron jungle gym.

"That's the name my father gave me," she said with a big, joyful smile. She beamed at the kids as if they were all her own.

Abe jumped to the side as two little boys raced by with squirt guns, shrieking and spraying water in long, sparkling streams.

"Michael and Andy, watch where you're aiming those things," Rosie called.

Abe stopped near Rosie and held out his hand.

"I'm Abraham Levett. I called about the Crow baby."

Rosie frowned and leaned sideways, grabbing his hand and giving it a little shake. She looked soft and warm, like a grandmother who baked cookies and sampled every batch.

"Such a sordid tale for a sunny day as this," Rosie told him. "But I've suspected ever since that dark day in that big, drafty mansion that someone would come calling."

Abe climbed onto a matching tire, propping his feet in the grooves to keep from falling off.

"Why did you believe someone would come calling?"

Rosie slid from the tire, her large, soft bottom swishing as she walked to a bucket and pulled out a big wand. She blew a stream of bubbles into the air. The kids screamed with delight and set about chasing the bubbles through the grass.

"Children are the light of the world," she said, returning with a smile and moving deftly back onto the tire. "I became a midwife because I love children, and I love mothers. I have four children myself, grown and scattered now like seedlings from a cottonwood tree."

Rosie lifted a locket from her large bosom and opened it toward Abe.

"Amanda and Matthew," she said, revealing two tiny, smiling faces. "My first grandbabies. There will be more to come out of my first three children, but the fourth one is a wild child who will never settle down."

Abe smiled, thinking of his own mother's insistent questions about grandchildren. Neither he nor his sister had produced grandchildren, much to his mother's dismay, but his sister, Lisa, had just gotten engaged and hoped to start a family after medical school.

"They're sweet," he said.

She smiled, proud.

"Sweet as strawberry pie. The little boy on Sapphire was a different sort of child. He might have been sweet, given another mother, another life."

"Spencer?"

"Yes. I remember him well. Empty dark eyes, skin the color of rotten turnips. Poor, sad child."

"Was he ill?" Abe tried to reconcile the handsome man in the gold car with this memory of a sick child.

"Unwell, yes, but from a disease or from abuse, I can't say."

"Abuse?"

Rosie nodded, touched her locket again.

"Midwives have a responsibility to the children, but to the mothers as well. We're chosen because we do not adhere to the laws of man. We are ruled by women." Her mouth grew pinched as she spoke, and the lines of her age deepened in her face. "In the end, I spoke with a friend in Social Services. They visited the house and reported a doting mother, an ill toddler, and a healthy newborn baby. I tried to visit Virginia three more times to provide after-care for her and the new baby, but found the gate locked. She didn't return my calls or respond to my letters. I never saw her or the children again."

"Today, she only has one son," Abe told her. "Spencer. I'm curious, though, you said dark eyes. Do you mean brown eyes?"

"The sickly child had brown eyes, almost black."

Abe frowned.

"Spencer has blue eyes. Could illness have made his eyes look a different color?"

Rosie lifted an eyebrow.

"Never heard of a disease that changes eye color," she murmured, "but I'll tell you this. That second baby had the brightest blue eyes you've ever seen. Blue as the name of his street, Sapphire."

Abe remembered Spencer's glittering blue eyes. They were an uncanny blue, icy.

"What did she name the baby?"

"She didn't. She refused to name him, insisted she wanted to wait, though as far as I knew, the baby's daddy was dead. Though…"

"What?"

"Another man was there. The children's uncle. A strange man, with eyes like the new baby."

"But don't most babies have blue eyes?"

"Yes, they do, but I've seen enough babies to know whose eyes will change and whose eyes will stay blue. That baby's eyes were unique. I'd bet they look the same today."

Abe watched the children and tried to make sense of the woman's story.

"Did she mention putting the second baby up for adoption?"

Rosie shook her head.

"She looked at that baby like... like he was a rare jewel. Not the way of most mothers, overflowing with love, but her own kind of curiosity and desire. A greedy look in her eyes. I helped that baby out of her body, and then she clutched him like he might disappear from her arms. I didn't hold him again. I tried to weigh him, and she snarled at me like a rabid possum."

"How old was the sick child?"

"No more than two. He barely walked, sort of lurched around. He didn't speak."

"Spencer is twenty-five, according to his driver's license," Abe thought out loud.

"Well, the second baby was born twenty-three years ago, so that's the right age for the older child. But that child did not have blue eyes."

"Blonde hair?" Abe asked.

"Black as a bad luck cat."

"His hair was black?" Abe asked, incredulous. Eye color was one thing, but black hair to blonde? "This doesn't make sense."

"If I had to describe the older boy in a phrase, I'd call him steps from the grave."

"You think he died?"

"Unless something remarkable happened, I suspect he was dead within a year."

"But Spencer's the name of her son."

Rosie shrugged.

"Women sometimes call on midwives because they have secrets to keep."

38

THE NORTHERN MICHIGAN ASYLUM FOR THE INSANE

Orla

"Ben," Orla said.

Ben looked up from his mop and offered her a half-smile.

"You're neglecting your pants." Unable to lift a hand and point, she nodded in the direction of his jeans.

He glanced down, and she watched him frown at the tear along the seam of his pants, growing larger every day.

He shrugged.

"I'll fix it sometime," he said.

"Like you did on that side?" She saw where he'd crudely sewn black thread into a split on the opposite side of his pants.

He blushed and shrugged.

"Bring me a needle and thread, and I'll have those pants looking good as new," she told him. "I'm a seamstress. Did you know that?"

He nodded.

"I read it in the paper."

"You read about me?" she asked, her pulse quickening.

He nodded, setting his mop down and shuffling over to his bag on the floor.

She expected him to pull out the newspaper; instead, he drew out an apple.

"I brought this for you. Are you hungry?" he asked.

"Yes, please." The apple was red and smooth. Crow gave her a piece of fruit only when she performed for him. The fruit always tasted overripe, bordering on rotten.

Ben pulled a chair next to her bed and pulled out a small knife.

"How does he keep me hidden?" Orla asked. "The hospital is huge. There have to be hundreds of patients and doctors..."

"There are," Ben murmured. "But this wing was closed after an outbreak of influenza a few months ago. After they clean it, the hall has to remain empty for three months. It will open in five weeks."

"So, he could keep me here for five more weeks?"

"Yeah," Ben confessed.

He cut a slice of apple.

"Thank you," Orla whispered, leaning forward and opening her mouth.

Ben popped the apple into her mouth and cut another piece.

It tasted crisp and sweet, and she closed her eyes, savoring the fruit.

When she opened them, she gazed at the knife, but knew even if she managed to free a hand, she could never hurt him. She'd gleaned bits from touching Ben, little glimpses of his past. Somehow, Crow had become his guardian. The man used him as a servant, belittled him constantly.

"How old are you?" Orla asked, studying his downcast eyes.

He pursed his lips and shook his head.

"I'm not sure. In my twenties, I think."

"You don't know?" she asked.

He fed her another piece of apple.

"I've never celebrated a birthday. I asked Dr. Crow a few times, but he claims not to know either. He took me in. I was an orphan, and he raised me."

"He's a terrible man, Ben. You deserve better."

Ben gave her the last bite of apple and returned the core to his bag.

"I don't," he murmured.

He left before she could ask more.

39

Abe

Abe had been watching the green pickup truck for an hour when Ben Stoops hurried from the asylum. Dark shaggy hair and dark eyes, sickly-looking - all the characteristics the midwife had attributed to Virginia Crow's older child.

Abe waited until the man was halfway to his truck.

"Excuse me," he said, stepping out from the shadow of trees and holding up a hand.

The man stumbled and nearly dropped the box he carried. He looked at Abe with wide, startled eyes.

"Hi." Abe strode up to him and stuck out his hand. He looked at the guy's box and laughed. "Maybe a handshake's not the best plan. Can I open your door? Or help you?" He nodded at the box.

The man shook his head.

"No, thanks," he mumbled, picking up his pace.

"Have time for a few questions, Ben? It is Ben, right? Or Benjamin?"

The man's shoulder's stiffened at the mention of Benjamin.

"Ben," he said.

He hoisted the box into the bed of the truck.

Abe gazed into the bed and noticed a shovel flecked with fresh dirt.

"Do you work at the asylum, Ben?" Abe asked.

Ben shook his head.

"I work for Dr. Crow."

"What kind of work, Ben?" Abe continued, stepping closer to the man. "Do some digging for him?" He gestured at the shovel.

Ben sidled along the truck toward the door.

Abe fought the urge to put a hand on the driver's door to prevent him leaving.

"Have you seen this woman?"

Abe thrust a picture of Orla in front of him.

Ben's eyes bulged and he turned, smacking into the truck. He fumbled with the door handle.

"No," he whispered.

"I'm sorry, what did you say."

"No, I haven't seen her."

Ben swung open the door and practically dove into the truck. He started it up, but Abe noted his trembling hands as he gripped the wheel. He drove off, leaving Abe in a plume of dust.

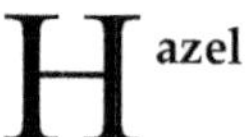

Hazel

Hazel gazed at Abe across the table. His cheekbones looked hollowed, his eyes sunken. He'd undoubtedly been over-doing it, though she had the sense Abe operated at maximum capacity for most of his life.

"What happens after you find resolution? Do you crash?"

He looked up, eyes distant. When they cleared, he nodded.

"Something like that. Although resolution is an optimistic word. I'm not even sure what a resolution would look like."

"Orla sitting in the chair beside me," Hazel offered.

"That's not much resolution for Liz or the other families."

Hazel sighed, glanced at the clock over the kitchen sink. It was after eleven. Her eyes felt crusty and her neck ached. She longed for bed, and yet the feverish gleam in Abe's eyes, the way he pored over the material, left her unable to drag herself up to bed. She had to fight for Orla. He was fighting for all the women, but Orla needed a voice, an advocate.

"The midwife said the older child appeared sickly. He looked nothing like Spencer with his blue eyes and blond hair," Abe continued.

He'd told her about the adjoining property of Dr. Crow and Virginia Crow, and the mysterious second child.

"What happened to Virginia's husband?" Hazel asked.

Abe rolled his eyes.

"He reportedly died of natural causes."

"And then his brother was at the birth of his son. And that guy is a doctor at the asylum?"

Abe nodded.

"A doctor at the asylum would have access to powerful drugs. If her husband did die of mysterious causes…"

"Exactly. And Hector, her husband, died before her pregnancy showed. Were they trying to hide an affair? And a pregnancy?"

"So, you think the second son was Dr. Crow's. And this Ben person lives with Crow. Why can't he be the second son?"

"For starters, his last name is Stoops. But the interesting thing is that Ben matches the description of the older son, the sickly son."

"Whose name is Spencer?"

"His name was Spencer."

"You think what, they gave his name to the second child?"

Abe shuffled some papers, eyes flicking between them.

"I'm leaning toward that, but I don't understand why they'd do it. Why not just give the second child his own name? And why would the first child suddenly become Ben Stoops?" he asked.

Hazel stood and folded in half, allowing her upper body to dangle, hands brushing her feet.

"My back feels like somebody's crunched it in a vice."

She stood back up, swayed from side to side a few times, and stretched her arms overhead.

"Coffee?" she asked.

"Yeah, that'd be great." He thumbed through his notes from the midwife, brow furrowed.

Hazel made a pot of coffee, casting another yearning glance toward the stairway. Calvin had gone to bed hours earlier. He had to work early in the morning. Hazel wished she was in bed next to him, listening to the rhythmic sound of his breath. She bent her legs and jogged in place for a moment.

"Tired?" Abe asked, not looking up.

"Yes, but I want to see this through."

He laughed.

"It's okay to sleep, Hazel. I'll let myself out. You can stay up all night and you won't have seen this through."

Hazel sighed.

"I will, but... I'm not ready yet. I'll go up soon."

She poured each of them a cup of coffee and returned to the table.

"Is there any chance you're chasing a dead end here?"

He grabbed his coffee, took a long drink.

"Yeah, there's always that possibility. But it's gotten under my skin. I can't shake it until I understand why it's piqued my interest."

"Maybe it's jealousy."

He cocked an eyebrow.

"How so?"

"Well, you said Spencer is handsome, and drives a nice car. Maybe you want him to be the bad guy. He just happened to be at the wrong place at the wrong time, taking a pee, just as he claimed."

Abe shook his head.

"I wish it were that simple. It's not. There was something off about this guy. Did he abduct Orla? That, I don't know, but there's something...."

"And this other child plays a part in that?"

"You're asking my own questions back to me. Until we have the whole picture, it's just a bunch of pieces. Maybe they're connected, maybe they're not."

"Have you tried talking to Spencer? Questioning him?"

Abe shook his head.

"I don't want him to realize I'm interested in him. He might run, destroy evidence."

"Assuming there's evidence to destroy."

"The guy was at the park Orla went missing from, his house is miles from the sightings of Susie, his uncle works at the asylum, and I received a tip about Orla being there. He was also questioned about the murder of a nineteen-year-old girl four years ago in Ann Arbor. He was the last person to see her alive. This other guy, Ben, was at the park where the kid found Orla's bike. He lives on the same property as Spencer. That's too many coincidences. One or two, fine, but..."

Hazel frowned.

"But why would Orla be at the asylum? I mean, they'd turn her over to the police. Right? They wouldn't keep her when her face and name are all over the news."

Abe frowned, pushed the papers away.

"I don't know. That tip makes little sense."

"So maybe it's bogus."

Abe closed his eyes.

"Yeah, maybe."

"Which knocks one from your coincidences."

"Still leaving far too many to call them coincidences. Connections, not coincidences. I have to look at them that way."

"But I still don't get why they'd lie. Why call the second baby Spencer and change the first baby's name to Ben? That deception travels back twenty years. The girls have been disappearing for four."

Abe took a piece of paper and drew a line down the center. He wrote Spencer's name on one side and Ben's on the other, detailing in bullet points what they knew about each man, which was far less on Ben's side.

"I'm not concerned about whether Virginia Crow and Byron Crow were involved. I wonder if we have two deeply disturbed men, because of whatever mischief Virginia and Byron were up to twenty years ago."

"You think their neglect created murderers?"

He leveled his gaze at her.

"What do you think a murderer is, Hazel? A monster who crawls out of the sewer? He's a man with a family, sometimes with a wife and a white picket fence. Let me tell you what I've learned about studying murderers. They don't grow up in families like the Brady Bunch.

"A weird, blended family where everyone is smiling and there's too many kids to keep track of?"

He didn't smile.

"In a happy, balanced, healthy household. They're often beaten, sometimes sexually abused. Those things might not create killers, but they tip the scales. This backstory on Ben and Spencer reads like the biography of a killer. Their mom is cheating with her husband's brother who lives on the other side of the woods, and their father dies mysteriously. The kids are neglected, possibly abused."

"How do you know the kids were neglected and abused?" Hazel thought of the woman from 311 Sapphire, likely Spencer's mother. Had she seemed negligent? No, the opposite, actually. She came across as protective, even possessive. She hadn't mentioned her little trip to Abe, fearing his response.

"A retired cop and a midwife both told me the older child looked neglected. No one can read people like a cop, and I know less about midwives, but I'm guessing they're even better judges of character, especially when it concerns mothers and children. They both mentioned a cold mother and a sick, strange child. The midwife called Social Services."

Hazel sighed. She didn't want to feel sympathy for the man or men who abducted Orla, but as she studied the two mens' names, she imagined babies, small children raised in a home of fear and lies. Did their mother hug them? Tell them she loved them? Hazel's own mother had doted on her, adored her. Hazel knew nothing except love and safety in the presence of her mother. Who would she have become if her mother was cruel and withheld affection?

"Where do we go from here?" Hazel asked.

Abe tugged on his beard and tapped his foot beneath the table.

"It's time to talk to Spencer."

40

Abe

"Spencer? Hey, wait up," Abe called, hurrying to catch up with Spencer as he left his job at Dr. Marlou's office, blazer slung over one shoulder and smiling as if he didn't have a care in the world.

He faltered when he spotted Abe and stopped, covering his momentary disquiet with indifference.

"Do I know you?" he asked.

"Not in the flesh, but you might have seen me in the paper. I write for Up North News." Abe stuck out his hand.

Spencer eyed it for several seconds before offering his in return.

Abe shook Spencer's hand, squeezing harder than necessary. The man pulled his hand away and fished in his pocket for his keys.

"Did you need something?" Spencer asked when Abe followed him to his car.

"Just following up on a tip about a gold sports car."

Spencer halted, glancing at his gold Corvette but not walking over to it.

"What kind of tip?" he asked.

"Well, to give you some context, I've been investigating a series of disappearances in northern Michigan. Six young women have vanished in the last four years."

Spencer gazed at him, face hard, eyes expressionless.

"Have you heard about them?"

Spencer shook his head.

"Nope, but I make it a point only to read The Detroit Free Press. Most of these northern papers are a bunch of stories about farm disputes and prized heifers."

Abe grinned and nodded.

"Prefer your news a little edgier? Violent, even?"

Spencer's face darkened.

"I've gotta jet. Was that all, or…?"

"Oh sure, sure. I just wondered if the police had talked to you yet? What with your driving that beauty over there, and multiple sightings of a gold sports car in the vicinity where the women disappeared."

Spencer's eyes flicked a second time to his car.

"No, they haven't. And I'm sure they'd be wasting their time."

Spencer didn't wait to see more. He walked briskly away and climbed into his car.

Abe shifted in bed, kicking the covers off, squirming in the heat. The fan whirred lazily overhead, doing little to circulate the muggy air. He flipped onto his belly, and then his side. He needed to sleep. Gazing between and beyond his legs, he squinted toward the clock over the microwave but couldn't make out the neon green numbers. Near the foot of the bed, his comforter shifted as if someone had brushed it aside.

Abe stared at the crumpled blanket and the white sheet beneath it. As he watched, something slid over the edge of the bed. It moved toward his foot, and as he puzzled at the thing, it came into focus: a hand. A hand streaked with mud, fingernails torn and bloody, reached toward his leg.

Abe sat up abruptly, kicking out his legs and scrambling off the bed. He stood next to the mattress, heaving for breath, awake now. It had been a dream: the insomnia, the hand - a nightmare too real, except the heat of the dream had been replaced by bitter cold. He shivered, standing naked, gooseflesh covering his body.

Across the room, the clock blinked 3:11 a.m.

Bleary-eyed, he lurched into the kitchenette, filled a glass of water, and gulped it down. He drank a second before pulling on a sweatshirt and pants and brewing a pot of coffee. He filled a mug, slipped on sandals, and left the apartment.

Traverse City slept. In the halo of streetlights, he walked. The veil of fog gradually lifted from his mind, chased away by the coffee, his breath, and the starry sky overhead. Far off, an ambulance siren wailed. Abe listened to it and wondered at the source. A homicide, a fight outside a bar, an old man falling from a bed. Every second, another tragedy befell someone. No one escaped the ravenous clutches of death.

He thought of Dawn with her boisterous laugh, despite her soft, feminine voice. He remembered the first time he'd heard her laugh as she sat on the edge of her desk in high school English, gazing at her friend's caricature of the devil in Dante's Inferno. The friend had depicted the beast with long, stringy hair filled with bows and Christmas ornaments before scrawling above her drawing: *Hell is Christmas in July*. The laugh had caught Abe off guard, such a deep, soul-shaking sound, and when she'd noticed him staring at her, she winked and smiled. In the months after her disappearance, he dreamed of her laughter, and woke sick and filled with dread every morning when he faced another sunrise without Dawn.

He swallowed the last of his coffee, dumped the dredges in the grass, and made his way to the lake. Hands planted on the iron railing that flanked the water edge of Grand Traverse Bay, he stared into the shifting waters. The metallic dark of sky and lake varied only by the spray of stars overhead.

As he gripped the metal rail, a shuffle sounded behind him. Abe froze, wondering if someone stood in the darkness, having spotted an easy victim to snatch a wallet from. Not that he was weak - at over six feet, and thin but wiry, Abe knew how to take care of himself. However, desperate men were apt to fight a bull if they could sell the hide for a buck. He'd covered enough stories to know the void of night called a certain kind of someone into the empty streets. Pity the person who stumbled upon them.

He turned slowly, fists clenched, but the sidewalk remained empty, the road beyond as quiet as a tomb.

The curse of your calling, his dad once told him, in reference to Abe's tendency to see every situation as a crime unfolding or barely thwarted.

Abe sighed and grabbed his coffee mug from where he'd left it on the grass. He started for home, walking a block before turning back to gaze a final time at the lake.

There, in the sphere of light from a post near the water, stood Susan Miner. She half-faced him, her hair unperturbed by the breeze rolling toward the shore. Face tilted toward the great expanse of Lake Michigan, her body angled so he could see the yellow t-shirt with the red mouth. As his eyes shifted down, he took in the dark shorts, bare legs, and a single bare foot.

The sound of his coffee cup shattering on the pavement shocked him from his daze. He jumped, glanced toward the bits of white ceramic, and then immediately back to her. But Susie had disappeared.

41

THE NORTHERN MICHIGAN ASYLUM FOR THE INSANE

Orla

Ben drew out a small sewing kit and two pairs of pants.

"Do you mind?" he asked.

Orla grinned.

"Do I mind? I'm elated. My hands have been desperate for a needle and thread."

His eyes darted to the sewing kit.

"Not to attack you with. I promise."

He released her arms from the straps, and she lifted her hands, numb and tingling. She rolled her wrists back and forth and removed her gloves.

"No, wait," he said, reaching out to stop her.

"It's okay. I sew without gloves all the time. I can turn it off. I don't have to see things."

He paused, watching her, and then carried over the pants and sewing kit. He retreated to the other side of the room and watched her from his chair.

She lifted the sewing kit, having no intention of stifling the visions. The sensation was brief. He'd purchased it that morning. A kind woman with dark eyes and curly gray hair commented how lovely it was to see a man who sewed.

He'd recently laundered, but when she brushed her finger over the button on the second pair, she glimpsed Dr. Crow ripping the pants from Ben's body and whipping the young man in the back with them. He lashed the stiff fabric against Ben's bare back and legs until red welts glared from his pale skin.

She shuddered, lifted the needle, and gingerly slipped the thread through.

"Do you know why I'm here, Ben? How I got here?" She thought back to that morning, the tooth in the stones. But Spencer's mother couldn't have known what Orla saw, so why did she attack her?

"Mrs. Crow sent for the doctor. I accompanied him. You were in the woods, unconscious. We put you in the truck and brought you here."

"But why? She injected me with something. It doesn't make sense."

"She told the doctor you were dangerous. You'd found something. She saw you. She needed him to erase your memory."

"I'm sorry, what? Erase my memory?"

He shifted in his chair, balling his hands in his lap.

"It's called electro-shock therapy. A lot of the doctors here use it. They say it helps with mental problems, but it also affects short-term memory. Some patients lose days, even weeks of memory."

Orla closed her eyes, resting the pants on her stomach.

"Why hasn't he done it yet?"

Ben blinked at her hands.

"Because he discovered your gift."

Orla took a breath and slid the needle back into the fabric. For several minutes, she didn't speak. The rhythm of the needle gliding in and out of the pants slowed her heart rate. She relaxed into the sensation, almost forgetting she was trapped in an asylum in a nightmare she never seemed to wake up from.

"Why do you do it, Ben? Help Dr. Crow?"

Ben stood and picked up a mop resting in a bucket by the door. He swept it in ever-widening circles across the cement floor.

"He's all I have," Ben whispered.

"But why? Where's your family?"

Ben's mouth turned down.

"My mom gave me up when I was a baby. I grew up here at the

hospital. During holidays, Dr. Crow took me home. I don't have a family, just the doctor."

Orla frowned.

"Do you live with him?"

"I have a room here at the asylum, and a room in Dr. Crow's garage."

"A garage?" Orla scowled.

"It's okay," he continued.

"I spent the night with a man named Spencer," Orla started, thinking back to that night. It seemed a lifetime ago. "Is he Dr. Crow's son?"

Ben's face darkened.

"He's the doctor's nephew. His father died a long time ago."

"That's what he told me," Orla murmured. "I wondered if he'd lied. Does he know I'm here?"

"I don't think so," Ben murmured.

"What is that weird room they took me to? In the woods?"

"The chamber," Ben said. "I've only been inside a few times." He shivered.

"What's the chamber?"

"It's a secret place for a group the doctor is part of."

Ben looked away. His eyes had taken on a look she'd grown familiar with. He looked like a rabbit sitting in an open field with a pack of wolves surrounding him. If she didn't tread carefully, he would leave.

"I won't ever tell him," Orla whispered.

Ben cracked a sardonic smile.

"If he suspected, you wouldn't have a choice. Neither would I. He's given you the truth serum. He has ways of discovering people's secrets. He could bring in other patients, a patient who sees like you do."

"There are others?"

Ben nodded.

"They're all different. He tells me about them sometimes. There was a woman here who could see the dead. She escaped. There have been so many others. There's a brotherhood…" He shut his mouth, eyes darting toward the door.

"He won't come back today. He never does," Orla murmured.

"Dr. Crow's unpredictable," Ben corrected her. "He wants you to get used to his schedule so he can catch you off guard."

Orla frowned. She finished one pair of pants and held them up.

"Look at that gorgeous seam, Ben."

He smiled shyly.

"Thank you," he told her.

"Will you tell me about the brotherhood?" she asked, starting on the second pair of pants.

He sighed and leaned against the mop.

"I don't ask him questions. The brotherhood is a secret. If he suspected I was curious, he might get paranoid."

"But you've picked things up?"

Ben nodded.

"The doctors come from all over the country. There are other asylums with secret meeting places, though I don't know which ones. Dr. Crow travels a few times a year to meetings in other sanitariums. They study patients who are special, like you. Some of them can predict the future, others see energy, or auras, they call them. Dr. Crow told me about a woman who could do astral projection. If you gave her an item that belonged to a person, she could project herself to that person psychically. She could give exact details about what they were doing and saying. Dr. Crow found her very intriguing."

"What happened to her?"

Ben shrugged.

"I don't know what happens to any of them," he said sadly.

"He's not going to let me go, is he?" Orla asked, fighting tears.

Ben stopped mopping, his expression pained.

"No. He won't ever let you go."

Orla clutched the needle and thread and tried not to scream. As she sewed, she felt her mother next to her guiding the needle, pointing out mistakes, teaching her to make it cleaner, better.

Orla stopped, hanging her head and allowing her tears to fall on Ben's pants.

They didn't speak. He mopped, and she sewed. When she finished, she handed him the needle and thread and lay back on the bed. He fastened the straps and gazed at her for a long time.

"Thank you," he murmured, before slipping from the room.

42

Hazel

"There's been another one." Hazel stood, and her book fell to the floor.

Early American Gardens by Ann Leighton lay forgotten on the rug, pages splayed, as she stared at the television.

"What do you mean?" Bethany asked from a couch on the opposite side of the room.

"Turn it up," Hazel said, already striding to the TV and adjusting the volume.

A reporter stood in front of a little wooden sign reading *Welcome to Mancelona.*

"Amber Hill, twenty-one years old, was last seen here at four p.m. yesterday afternoon. She was walking her dog, Chester, a small cocker spaniel. Chester returned to the family home, less than a mile away, after dusk. Amber has not been seen or heard from since."

"Oh no," Bethany breathed.

"I have to call Abe." Hazel hurried to the kitchen and dialed his home number. It rang and rang. Next she tried the newspaper, but the woman who answered said he hadn't been in the office.

"I'm going to look for him."

Hazel got in her car and drove to the diner.

No Abe.

When she arrived at his apartment, Liz sat on the cement steps outside. She stood when Hazel arrived.

"Have you heard from him?" Liz asked, her face pinched with worry.

"No, I tried to call him."

A hopeful gleam rose in Liz's eyes.

"Abe's already on the story. I know it. Maybe we will get him this time."

Hazel swallowed.

If the man had abducted another girl, what did that mean for Orla? That he'd killed her? That she was never coming back?

Hazel's breath hitched in her throat, and she cried. A terrible sob ripped from her chest, and she sank down.

Liz stepped into her, wrapped a supporting arm around her waist, and lowered with her to the steps.

She didn't murmur 'it's okay' or 'everything is all right,' but tightened her hold, as if to keep Hazel from following her grief into the cracks of the pavement beneath them.

Hazel cried until she soaked Liz's shoulder. When she pulled away, her face felt raw and sticky.

Liz pulled a handkerchief from her purse and handed it to her.

"Let's go to the diner. I'll leave Abe a message to come find us there when he gets home."

~

Abe

When Abe arrived at the missing girl's house, he was surprised to see three squad cars parked on the small city street. The lawn in front of a two-story blue house, with white shutters and a red door, crawled with officers.

Abe spotted the parents easily.

Amber Hill's mother leaned against her husband, her eyes dark where her makeup had run. The father stood tall, shoulders braced like a football player preparing to get tackled by the oncoming team. His face was stony, his eyes haunted.

Neighbors lingered in their yards, watching. The couple next door to the Hill's spoke with an officer, while several more walked up and down the street, asking questions.

Abe spotted Deputy Beeker, a man he'd worked with a year earlier on a case involving a husband who'd murdered his wife. Abe jogged over to him.

"Beeker," he said.

The deputy looked up, blinked at him in confusion, and then seemed to recognize him.

"Abe." He offered him a curt nod.

"Got a scoop for me?" Abe asked.

Beeker's mouth turned down, and he shook his head.

"You realize I can't talk to you, right? You're a stand-up guy, but the task force assembled around these disappearances has issued a gag order. If I so much as slip that she was wearing a pink tank top, the chief will pound me."

"Was she?" Abe asked.

Beeker rolled his eyes.

"You're going to release what she was wearing," Abe said. "How else will people know what they're looking for? This is off the record, Beeker. I want to help. I've got a file on these girls as tall as that tree, and I'm not operating on the chief's orders or your budget. Give me a break."

Beeker walked a few paces away, and waved back some gawkers who'd trickled into the Hills' yard.

"Please step back, people. This is someone's home. Give the family some space. We'll be down to question everyone in the neighborhood shortly."

Beeker ambled back to Abe.

"I'm not lead on this. She went missing yesterday afternoon. Took the dog for a walk and never came home. The neighbor brought the dog back around nine last night. That's all I've got."

"Did the leash come back with the dog?"

"No leash. Now bug off. If the chief shows up…." Beeker trailed off.

Abe gave him a nod and backed up. He moved closer to a group of people talking.

"Which way did she walk?" one woman asked.

"Down that-away," replied an older man, leaning heavily on a cane.

"Toward Fountain Park?" another man asked.

"Yep," the man replied.

Abe sauntered off, got in his car, and drove away.

When he spotted Fountain Park, he hopped out. A single squad car blocked the entrance.

"Trails are closed today," the officer barked, eyeing him suspiciously.

Abe returned to his car and followed the road around the park. It was more than a park. Like Birch Park where Orla disappeared, Fountain Park bordered state land. Abe drove half a mile and discovered another unmarked dirt parking lot with a trail disappearing into the woods.

He pulled onto the side of the road, grabbed his camera, and jumped out.

There were multiple sets of tire tracks intersected with bike tracks, but one set was predominant, clearly the most recent. The tracks appeared as if someone had stopped at the mouth of the trail - or backed up to it.

Abe took close-up pictures. He snapped a picture of the trailhead, before moving into the shadow of the trees. The heavy vegetation muted any sound beyond the forest. A squirrel snapped its head up when he passed before returning to its foraging.

Abe studied the grassy trail, but could not distinguish footprints. A few feet further, he stopped. The tall grass on either side of the path had been trampled, and someone had snapped a branch of a maple sapling. He took more pictures. He imagined a struggle, a woman reaching for something to cling to and snapping off the flimsy branch.

Squatting close to the ground, Abe saw a rounded divot that pushed into the dirt. He imagined it was the imprint of a bare knee.

Further down the trail, he heard voices and knew the police were moving toward him. He took a final picture, and trotted back to his car.

~

Abe found Hazel and Liz waiting for him at the diner. They sat before plates of untouched apple pie.

Liz stood when she saw him, knocking over her water glass and sending a rush of lukewarm water into Hazel's lap. Hazel jumped up and waved her skirt. Liz didn't seem to notice.

"I'm coming with rags," Mona called.

"Anything?" Liz asked.

Abe shook his head, and Liz's face fell.

"But the cops are combing the scene. They're taking it seriously, which is a good thing. Plus, people are paying attention. If Spencer's gold sports car or Ben's green truck was anywhere near Fountain Park, someone will report it."

"Fountain Park?" Hazel asked.

"It's a big, wooded area, just like the others," Abe admitted.

"Which means no witnesses," Liz fumed.

"It's different this time, Liz. None of the other girls had this kind of coverage. There are police, news teams, and people on the look-out. This is the case that will shake him loose. I can feel it."

Mona leaned over the table, sopping up water.

"Thank God for you, Abraham. You're a good boy. Piece of pie on the house. Tell me your flavor?"

He smiled, not hungry, though he hadn't eaten since breakfast.

"Have any rhubarb?"

"Sure do," she exclaimed. "Baked it fresh this morning."

43

THE NORTHERN MICHIGAN ASYLUM FOR THE INSANE

Orla

Orla woke in the grip of a nightmare. A man had been dragging her through the woods. Her head bounced over roots and twigs caught in her hair. He wore a black hooded shirt and, in the hand not clutching her ankle, he held a shovel dripping blood.

She moaned and opened her eyes - not to darkness, but the flicker of a candle.

"No, please," she begged, cringing away and lifting her arms, shocked to find them free from their straps.

"It's okay," Ben's voice rose from beside her. "It's me."

He stepped into her line of sight, his face lit by the flame.

She blinked at him, breath still clenched in her chest, the remnants of the dream streaming away like black smoke.

"I was dreaming," she whispered. "Horrible. A man, and…" she trailed off.

Ben held up a glass of water.

"Would you like a drink?"

She gazed at the glass, parched, but hesitated. Why had he come? Had he put something in the water?

When she took it, her hands shook, and a low throbbing pulsed in her head.

She drank and handed the glass back, falling heavily onto the sweaty pillow beneath her.

"Why are you here, Ben?"

He put the glass down and pulled a chair to her bedside.

"I heard Dr. Crow on the phone last night. You're scheduled for a presentation in the chamber tomorrow. The brotherhood is gathering to witness your," he pointed at her hands, "abilities."

The small flame lit Ben's dark eyes and made him appear ominous, like the dark figure in her dream.

"What will they do?" Orla sat back up, wrapping her arms across her chest, a small comfort she'd rarely experienced since entering the asylum.

"Crow has something special in mind, but he didn't mention it on the phone. Afterward, he's going to perform the electro-shock therapy, and then he plans to send you with a doctor who is the director at an asylum in Pennsylvania."

"Pennsylvania?" The chill of the room moved into her body and settled low in her belly. A cramp took root, and she hunched over, suddenly questioning the contents of the water glass.

"I won't let them," he told her, his voice cold and hard.

She looked at him for a long time, and the pain in her abdomen softened, drifted away.

"What are you going to do?"

Ben pulled at his dark shirt, as if it felt too tight.

"I've got a plan," he said.

"Why can't we go tonight, Ben? Right now?" Orla begged.

He shook his head.

"Orderlies monitor the halls at night. The hallway beyond this one," he gestured toward her door, "is a violent men's ward. The orderlies would never let us past without an explanation. They'd call Crow immediately, assuming a patient didn't see us first."

Orla shuddered, remembering her near-escape as she plummeted down that dark hallway. What would have happened if she'd made it through the curtains into the hall beyond?

"Crow will transfer you to the chamber first thing in the morning, when the hospital is quiet," Ben assured her.

"No," she whimpered, wanting to curl into a ball on her side and weep.

"Please, Orla. Trust me. This is the only way. The best thing you can do is go along with him tomorrow. It will make everything easier."

Ben strapped her arms back to the bed and slipped out the door.

Orla stared into the black room and knew she would not sleep.

44

Hazel

"What are we going to say? Excuse me, Mrs. Crow, can we take a quick peek in your garage?" Hazel asked, pulling her knees up on the passenger seat and wrapping her arms over her shins. She was nervous and already wishing she'd kept her mouth shut when Abe mentioned his spy mission to the Crow and Crow residences. She could have stayed home, finished her book, and waited for his phone call.

He looked at her sidelong.

"I don't plan to say a word to her. I want to get a look at the other cars, that's it. I tipped Spencer off about sightings of his gold car, and guess what? A guy jogging near Fountain Park where Amber was abducted saw a blue Lincoln Continental. Virginia Crow drives a black Eldorado. I'd like to know if there's a Continental in the driveway."

"I thought you were afraid he'd destroy evidence?"

"I am, but I needed to push him and see what he'd do."

"And have you considered, what he did was abduct another girl?"

Abe cringed away as if she'd spit at him. He didn't respond, and she regretted her words.

"I'm sorry. That was out of line."

"If Spencer's the guy, he was already hunting. He didn't abduct someone because I pushed him. He drove a different car, changed his M.O. to reduce his chance of getting caught," Abe told her, glaring through the windshield.

"Why would they have three cars?"

"Because they're the type, believe me."

"Okay, let's say they do. What if they park the third car in the garage?"

"Then I check out the garage. You sit in the car as the lookout. Somebody comes along, honk the horn."

Abe parked down the road from Spencer's house.

He disappeared into the woods, and Hazel craned backwards in her seat watching the road, counting the minutes, and wondering what she'd do if he didn't return.

When someone tapped on the window, she screamed and dove toward the driver's seat.

Abe gazed at her, an amused expression on his face.

He walked around and climbed in.

"Sorry. I didn't mean to spook you. It was satisfying, but I genuinely didn't intend it."

"Maybe I deserved it," she grumbled. "No Continental?"

"No third car in the garage at all," he admitted.

"Now what?" she asked.

"Ben's house."

"Is this legal? Or ethical?" she asked.

"Legal? No. Ethical...?" Abe considered as they turned onto Misty Lane. "It depends. If the guy is involved, then we're under a moral obligation. Plus, she could be there, this newest girl, Amber. She could be there right now. And if that car is there, it confirms we're on the right track."

"I want to go too," Hazel murmured. "You said they're both working at the asylum, right? Ben and the doctor?"

"They were an hour ago," he said.

He drove past the house on Misty Lane. Like the house at 311 Sapphire, trees surrounded Dr. Crow's home. Abe pulled onto the shoulder, and they got out.

Hazel took a deep breath and stuffed the paranoia trying to overwhelm her. She followed Abe through the woods, lifting her long skirt to avoid branches poking up from the dense foliage.

"Watch out for the nettles," she told him as they neared a spiky green plant.

He dodged around them, and they waded through high grass into a clearing.

A large Tudor-style house sat in the center of a vibrant green lawn. A circular driveway curved in front of the house. Behind it, Hazel saw a large garage.

They walked the exterior of the house, peeking in windows and rattling doorknobs, but they found every door locked. When they reached the garage, Abe looked in the window.

"Gotcha," he whispered.

"What?" Hazel ran to the window and looked in. A dark blue Lincoln Continental filled one side of the garage.

They found an open door and slipped inside.

"Whatever you do, don't touch the car. Here." He pulled a pair of disposable gloves from his pocket and handed her one, sliding the other over his left hand.

"You brought these with you?"

"If you're going to think like the bad guys, you have to act like them sometimes too," he murmured, drawing back a curtain that ran down the center of the garage.

The other half of the garage contained a bedroom of sorts.

"Do you think he lives here?" Hazel murmured, trying not to imagine what the room felt like in February when snow piled to the little prison-like windows encased in the concrete walls.

A thin mattress sat on a plain, metal frame covered by a thread-bare brown blanket. A scarred wooden desk stood along a cement wall, stacked with books. Clothes hung from hangers attached to a metal beam in the ceiling, and a stack of clean laundry sat on top of an over-turned crate.

"I figured as much," Abe confessed.

"What?" Hazel whispered.

"I assumed Ben didn't live in the doctor's house."

"Why?" Hazel asked.

"Because the guy looks like an outsider, like he's been rejected most of his life."

"But if he's the older son, why would Virginia Crow allow this?"

Abe bent down to examine a pair of hiking boots near the back door to the garage. He kicked them, and fresh mud broke off in clumps.

"I told you what the midwife said about the older son. She saw an abused kid. For all we know, the doctor offered him a room in his garage because it was safer than living with his mother."

Abe wandered to a closed door.

"This door is locked," he mumbled.

He shook the handle a second time.

"Here." Hazel pulled a credit card from the bag slung over her shoulder. She slid it along the door frame, and after a bit of wiggling, they heard a pop.

He cocked an eyebrow.

Hazel shrugged. "You're not the only one with bad guy skills."

Abe pushed open the door.

"It's a records room," he exclaimed, striding to a series of tall, gray filing cabinets.

"And it would take a century to sift through it," Hazel said.

"It's labeled." Abe pointed at the little cardboard face cards with dates.

Hazel gazed in overwhelm at the records. She couldn't imagine gleaning anything important in the short time they had.

"Go watch the driveway," Abe told her.

Hazel moved to the door of the garage, surveying the quiet yard. When a crow burst from the trees, she sprang back, letting out a shaky laugh when she spotted the bird.

"They're both at work," she reminded herself.

Hazel walked along the perimeter of the sparse room. A few odds and ends had been stacked on the cement ledge beneath the window. As her eyes roved over the contents, she stopped cold.

One of Orla's yellow crystal earrings lay on the gray block. Hazel's fingers trembled as she reached for the piece of jewelry. They were distinctive earrings with a bronze cone base. Orla wore them often, and Hazel was sure she had been wearing them the day she disappeared.

"Abe," Hazel whispered.

He didn't respond.

"Abe," she shouted.

"What? Is somebody coming?" He peeked his head from the doorway, his arms filled with folders.

"This is Orla's earring."

He walked across the room and squinted at the earring, oddly placed amongst the other items. A pencil also lay on the shelf, along with a small glass figure of a bear, a set of reading glasses, two keys, and a vanilla-flavored Charleston Chew.

Hazel reached up to take the earring.

"A souvenir," Abe breathed. "No, don't touch it. I'm going to take a picture. Let me grab my camera."

He started toward the door, but stopped.

Hazel heard tires in the gravel driveway.

"Shit," he whispered. "Out the back."

They hurried through the back door, Abe's arms stuffed with folders.

"But she might still be alive. We have to confront him," Hazel whispered.

"Quiet," he hissed.

They stood with their backs against the garage, listening.

A door opened, and then closed. Minutes ticked by. The late July sun beat down on Hazel's face, and she grew lightheaded. She wanted to slide down the brick and sit in the grass.

Dense forest stretched behind the garage, so thick in the peak of summer that some areas were impenetrable.

After several minutes, the truck started, and they heard it backing down the driveway.

Hazel started around the garage, but Abe shook his head.

Moments later the truck returned, the engine idling as a door again slammed as if the person had left something behind.

When it left the second time, they waited several minutes before hurrying around the house and running to the road.

. . .

Abe sat on Hazel's porch, reading, long after dusk. Hazel had gone to bed, but his eyes devoured the pages of notes.

Crow had been conducting strange experiments at the Northern Michigan Asylum for more than twenty-five years. Some of the material seemed standard - potential diagnoses coupled with the varying amounts of medicine, and then notes on the perceived response. Crow had written about drug interactions, effective versus non-effective therapies, and interesting results regarding placebo affect.

But other folders contained bizarre case studies of patients who predicted the future or read minds. These patients were subjected to a range of disturbing treatments including psychedelic drugs, isolation, and even torture.

In Crow's garage, Abe had spotted a cabinet drawer labelled Spencer Crow, and he taken several of the folders. He expected standard stuff - birth records, hospital visits, and the like. Instead, he discovered detailed notes about experimentation on the child.

Abe read:

After an extensive inquiry, including detailed case studies highlighted in the Enchiridion, and personal interactions with patients exhibiting psychic abilities and enhanced sensory abilities, it is my hypothesis that individuals develop psychic abilities after extreme trauma or illness during the postnatal years. Experiences of near death have been reported by more than seventy-five percent of patients with heightened psychic capacities.

The paper listed a dozen examples of patients with psychic abilities and their so-called near-death experiences.

To test this hypothesis, we have chosen Subject X (Spencer Arnold Crow) as the focus of analysis.

As Abe read, he sat up straighter, his eyes boring into the words, shaking his head at the cruelty detailed.

The doctor had been experimenting on Subject X - beginning at only six weeks old. The trials included immersion in water until he turned blue, long periods of blackout confinement with no extrasensory sights or sounds of any kind, and a list of drugs.

Each trial listed Subject X's before and after blood pressure, heart rate, body temperature, and observed physical, mental, and emotional changes in the days following the experimentation.

As Abe read, he witnessed the downslide of young Crow's health. His skin, noted at the start of the experiments as pink, was later recorded as yellow, and finally gray. The whites of his eyes were documented as bloodshot and cloudy. His behavior shifted from alert and playful to subdued and lethargic.

In a second file, Abe found a letter addressed to Byron Crow.

Byron,

I thought it prudent to write you a letter, as Hector's increasing suspicions finds him home more and more, monitoring the telephone and my comings and goings. He is preoccupied with Spencer's ill health and angry at my refusal to take him to a physician. I fear, my darling, that the time has come to take the next steps. How can I explain to my small-minded husband, the gravity of your work, our work? I leave it to you to secure the appropriate remedy. I shall do my best to bring Spencer to the sanitarium by week's end, but I fear Hector will become inflamed and refuse my use of the car. If so, I will prepare Hector's favorite meal for our family dinner on Sunday. I will rely on you to bring the special ingredient.

All my love,

V.C.

Abe studied the initials.

"Virginia Crow," he murmured.

In the same file, Abe found a prescription for arsenic. A hand written note taped to the page stated: *Lethal dose: 180 mg.*

"Why is that in this file?" he asked, setting the paper aside, but as he gazed at the prescription, he understood.

Arsenic was the special ingredient for Virginia Crow's family dinner.

45

Abe

"She killed her husband, and experimented on her own son?" Hazel repeated the story back to Abe, her mouth hanging open.

"It appears that way," he admitted.

"Let's call the police," Hazel insisted. "We found Orla's earring. The Continental was in the garage. Ben is the guy. Maybe the Crows are in on it. What are we waiting for?"

Abe paced around the kitchen. He'd slept less than two hours the previous night, falling asleep at one a.m. only to awaken at three-eleven.

"It's not enough."

"Jesus, Abe! What do you need? A body in the back of Ben's truck? I'm calling the police."

"Wait," Abe held up a hand. "I saw a shovel in Ben's truck, and muddy boots in his room. I want to go to Elder Park and look around."

"What? Why? You've already searched Elder Park, you-"

But he cut her off.

"When I saw that shovel, I knew he buried something there, Hazel. I knew it. We need something tangible for the police. That earring is not proof, and guess what? We found it by breaking and entering. In court, it would be inadmissible. The cops can't pick Ben up based on an earring that might not be Orla's, and a car one person spotted near the last abduction sight. Get it? We need more."

"Fine!" Hazel huffed.

Calvin sat at the table, drinking his coffee and watching his angry girlfriend. Smartly, he didn't intervene.

Bethany, too, watched the scene unfold from the doorway.

"You found Orla's earring?" she asked in a small voice.

"I think so," Hazel murmured.

"Exactly," Abe exclaimed. "You think so. I'm going."

Hazel started to follow him. Calvin stood and grabbed Hazel in a hug.

"Maybe you shouldn't, honey."

Hazel hugged Calvin hard, tucking her head beneath his chin.

"I have to, for Orla," she whispered.

He pulled her away and kissed her.

"Do you want something for protection, Hazel? If this guy's as bad as you two think..."

Abe waited impatiently but didn't argue.

"Don't give her anything that will get us into trouble," Abe snapped.

"No, Calvin. I'll be okay. Whether or not we find anything, we're calling the police." She didn't look at Abe but spoke loud enough for him to hear.

She kissed Calvin a second time, gave Bethany a hug, and followed Abe out the door.

~

Hazel

"What are we looking for, Abe?" Hazel asked, following him on the trail at Elder Park.

"I want to see if there's disturbed dirt..."

"Like what? A fresh grave?" Hazel asked, horrified, and also irritated with Abe's insistence on searching.

Abe glanced back but offered nothing to reassure her.

They scoured the woods for an hour. Abe stopped every time he noticed a bare spot in the grass or a decaying log.

"Abe, there's nothing," Hazel said.

She watched him digging, his hands deep in the muddy earth, sweat speckling his forehead. He looked frantic, his eyes intent on the hole.

"Abe!"

"There might be," he muttered, not looking at her.

"Abe, it's time to stop."

He grabbed a handful of mud and flung it back down hard. It splattered his face and clothes. When he glanced at her, she saw his eyes glistening, as if he'd been on the verge of tears. He replaced the look with a scowl and stood, brushing off his pants, which only smeared the mud across his thighs.

"I don't need your help, Hazel. Here." He dug his keys from his pocket and tossed them to her.

She didn't catch them, and they landed on the ground near her feet.

He returned to his knees and reached deep into the hole flinging the mud away.

"Fine," she said. She picked up the keys and walked angrily back down the trail.

In her mind, she argued with him, unleashed her opinions on his dogged searching. Why hadn't they called the police? What could they do if they found something?

Gazing at the trail, she skimmed over the grass, the weeds rising on either side.

She almost missed it - a ridge in the otherwise untroubled earth. She scrutinized the ground, walking closer. A pattern emerged, a rough circle, as if someone had dug up a piece of the grass and then dropped it back in place.

"Abe," she called. When he didn't respond, she yelled louder.

"Abe!"

He appeared on the trailhead, wiping his hands together and shaking off the dirt.

He didn't ask why she called for him, but jogged to where she stood and squatted in the grass. He pushed his fingers along the ridge and lifted. A large chunk of intact earth pulled away revealing, recently tamped soil.

Abe reached into the loose dirt.

Hazel stepped back, breath catching as she watched him pull something loose, an edge of familiar fabric - a pair of red and orange floral-patterned shorts. Orla's shorts.

"No," she murmured, turning away into a web of branches. She screamed as the branches caught in her hair. She fought them away, a sob erupting in her throat.

"Whoa, it's okay. Stop moving." Abe braced a hand on her shoulder. With his other hand, he untangled her hair. "Maybe you should go to the car."

"Is she in there? Is Orla in there?" Hazel pleaded.

He shook his head.

"I don't think so. I need a pair of gloves and my camera. I want a closer look, and then we need to call it in."

"Call it in?"

"The police."

She tried to follow his words, but beyond him, Orla's shorts lay crumpled and dirty. Her stomach rolled and cramped.

"I think I might be sick."

Abe glanced behind him, and then stepped into Hazel's view, blocking the clothes. He steered her back toward the car, one hand resting on her back.

Images swarmed in her mind. Orla in those shorts the last morning Hazel saw her, smiling, long black hair like a silky stallion's mane down her back. Why hadn't Hazel grabbed her friend and asked where she was going, given her a hug, suggested they sit together and have coffee instead?

The image was accompanied by visions of her mother those final days. Her mother's sunken, feverish eyes, and hands more like claws gripping Hazel as if she might hold on and not be pulled from the world. Hazel remembered, in her sleeplessness and grief, a momentary terror that her mother would grasp so hard she'd take Hazel with her, down and down into the darkness.

I can't, she thought. I can't go through this again, and yet she was. *Death comes for us all,* her mother had said days after the initial diagnosis of stage four cancer. *But still, we never know his face.*

"Hazel," Abe spoke her name.

Hazel snapped her head up, realizing she'd stopped on the trail. "Just a few more steps."

He settled her into the car and started the engine.

"I'll be back soon," he told her, grabbing his camera and disappearing into the woods.

~

Abe

Abe left Hazel in the car, air conditioner blasting, though she looked more cold than hot.

He returned to the woods, snapping pictures along the way. He took shots around the perimeter of the hole and of the clothes themselves.

Wearing gloves, he dug deeper, but found no other evidence, no clumped dirt that might imply blood, no tangles of hair or bits of bone. He patted the clothes and reached his fingers into Orla's pockets. In the left pocket, his finger struck something hard, and he pulled the object out. At first, he thought he held a tiny stone, but when he lifted it closer, he realized he was staring at a tooth.

"Damn," he grumbled, shaking his head.

The tooth did not bode well for Orla's fate.

46

THE NORTHERN MICHIGAN ASYLUM FOR THE INSANE

Orla

"I have good news, Orla," Crow announced when he swept into the room.

He held a bag of oranges in one hand and a pair of women's jeans and a t-shirt in the other.

"You're going home."

She swallowed and glanced toward Ben, who stood in the corner avoiding her eyes.

"What do you mean?" she asked.

Crow arched his dark eyebrows and smiled.

"Jaded, are we? I understand. People with mental illness rarely believe it when good things come their way. We have one final journey together. Remember that neat little place in the woods? I need you to walk there with me. No funny business, okay? Today is a very important day. You can eat as many of these as you'd like, and this afternoon, after a few other doctors witness your extraordinary abilities, you get to put on these brand-new clothes and go home to your family."

"How can I trust you? After everything you've done to me..."

He laughed and shook his head, as if she'd made preposterous claims.

"What I've done to you. I've merely been treating you, my dear. But let's not waste our last few hours together arguing semantics. I have a very special object for you today. I want you in tip-top shape for the presentation. Benjamin, help me unstrap her."

Before Ben could move to the table, Crow stuck his hand out, catching him in the chest.

"On second thought, let's wait a few more minutes. Dr. Frederic is joining us. He'll accompany us to the chamber to ensure we don't have any problems. But we won't, will we, Orla?" He stared at her.

She thought of Ben's words from the night before - *go along with it*. But what if she went along with it, and Ben couldn't save her? They'd do the electro-shock and whisk her to another asylum, and perhaps another after that. How many were there? Could they keep her in captivity forever if they chose?

The forest was muggy, and Orla fought the urge to break free and run. Her eyes were blindfolded, her arms strapped to her body. Ben held her on one side, Crow on the other, and Dr. Frederic moved along behind them. Orla felt his eyes on her back, on her body.

The blindfold slipped down. She glimpsed a towering Willow tree and woods in every direction.

"The key, please?" Frederic said.

Crow jerked Orla to as stop, and she stumbled, steadied by Ben's hand on her back.

She tried to see the entrance to the chamber, but Frederic appeared to be reaching into a large bush.

Suddenly, she was moving again, being pushed through leafy branches into the damp quiet of a tunnel.

The coolness of the chamber was a relief, though Orla would have preferred the humid forest to the dank stone room.

Crow thrust her into a wooden chair, removing her blindfold.

"Strap her," he commanded Ben, who quickly knelt by the chair and secured leather straps to Orla's wrists and ankles.

Crow gazed at her proudly, as if he'd accomplished some great feat and expected heaps of praise for his efforts. She glared at him.

"I'd like an orange now," she told him.

He shook his head.

"After the presentation," Crow stated, checking his watch. "Dr. Frederic, I have two patients to see, and then I'll return. Ben will prepare the room for the brotherhood. If you could keep an eye on our patient."

"My pleasure," Frederic told him, scooting a chair close to Orla.

Ben opened a black leather bag and took out a small metal safe. He set it on a bench, and then removed a series of unrelated items - a stethoscope, a bottle of pop, a book.

Frederic's fingers brushed Orla's knee, and she cringed away from him.

"Pity you won't be with us anymore," Frederic whispered, leaning close to Orla's ear so his breath moved hot against her skin. "Though I visit the sanitarium in Pennsylvania regularly."

Orla looked up, desperate, and saw Ben watching them. He quickly looked away, taking something else from the bag. He shuffled behind them and Orla could no longer see him.

Frederic stood and Orla saw his eyes flicker to Ben.

"What are you doing?" he snapped.

"Dr. Crow asked me to sweep before the meeting," Ben stammered.

Frederic sneered and slid a syringe from his pocket.

"A little sleep in preparation for your debut," Frederic murmured, sliding a needle into Orla's neck.

"Ben," she cried out, and Frederic's eyes widened in surprise as Ben smashed the handle of the broom into his temple. Frederic pitched forward, but stayed on his feet. The doctor stared at Ben, shocked, with a fury in his eyes that chilled Orla. If Frederic got the upper hand, Ben would die.

Helpless within her restraints, Orla rocked the chair, pounding her feet into the stone floor and bucking backwards. Ben took another swing at Frederic and missed. The doctor lunged, and Ben jumped out of the way, but Frederic caught the collar of his shirt and ripped him backwards off his feet. Ben landed on his back with a thud. Frederic spit on the floor, and Orla saw blood and something small and white, a tooth. He took a step toward Ben, but the impact against his head was catching up with him. Orla noticed a trickle of blood from his ear.

Ben didn't wait. He rolled to the side and kicked the doctor's legs out from under him. The man crumpled to the ground, head smacking the earth, and lay still.

Ben bent down and put his fingers on the man's neck.

"He's still alive," he told Orla, relieved.

Orla stared at the doctor, unmoved.

"Ben, he gave me a sedative. There's not much time."

Ben stood, a confused expression on his face.

"We're almost there, Ben," she asserted. "Unstrap me."

He gazed at Frederic for another moment before turning to Orla and fumbling the straps from her arms and ankles.

"This way," he said, gesturing to the dark tunnel at the mouth of the room. They hurried into the corridor lit by flickering torches. As they neared the entrance, a shaft of light suddenly split the darkness.

Ben's arm shot out, plastering Orla against the stone wall.

Voices floated in from the entrance door.

"Dr. Crow, hold on," a man said.

"What is it?" Crow asked his voice impatient.

Orla's heart beat against her ribs. She felt Ben trembling beside her.

"Your patient on Floor Five is having a seizure. The nurse is asking for you."

"Right now?" Crow spat. "Fine, fine. There's still time."

The door swung closed, the light vanishing. Their voices grew smaller, quieter, until Orla and Ben were left with only their breath.

"Oh God," Ben mumbled.

Orla heard the fear in voice. He was questioning his choice.

"Ben," she said, grabbing his hand. "Please, please help me."

His hand shook, and he didn't move. Finally, heavily, he turned and pulled her toward the opening.

Thick, dark clouds marred the brightness of the day. Rain was coming.

Orla's legs buckled as she stepped into the shady forest.

"Ben," she mumbled.

He was walking ahead, starting to run.

She dropped to her knees, her head swimming. He turned back as she fell forward onto her hands, straining to focus on the grass beneath her, but it blurred.

"It's hitting me," she mumbled, and her eyes drifted closed.

47

Abe

Abe stood on the sidelines as police searched the park. They'd cordoned off the trails and blocked the parking lot. They hurried in and out of the woods like ants compiling rations for winter.

Abe snagged Deputy Waller as he walked by.

"This is your guy," Abe told him, thrusting a sheet of paper with Ben Stoops' name on it.

"The guy with the truck?" Waller asked, folding the sheet and sliding it into his pocket. "How do you know?"

"A car that was just spotted at the latest abduction is literally in the guy's bedroom. I've also seen him at this park multiple times, and -" Abe dropped his voice to a whisper, "Orla's roommate saw one of her earrings through a window at Ben's house. This is the guy. If you want any chance of finding the latest girl alive, I suggest you nail him now. Not in an hour. Right now."

"An earring isn't a body, Abe. You understand if I haul him in and he's innocent-"

"He's not innocent. You saw those clothes in the woods, right? Those are Orla's clothes. Look in the pockets of the shorts."

Waller sighed, flicking the holster on his gun opened and closed.

"Save me the shock and tell me what I'll find."

"A tooth."

Waller grimaced.

"Okay. I'm going to bring him in. Hopefully, he'll spit the whole story out, and no one will ask about probable cause."

Abe took a quick step away as Detective Moore pulled up, jumping from his unmarked car.

"Get him, Waller," he murmured, and slipped behind a row of squad cars.

~

Abe dropped a tearful Hazel at home and stopped at a payphone to leave a message for his dad. His nerves were frayed, muscles jumping beneath his skin.

He got in his car and drove to the diner, but pulled back out. He couldn't stomach another cup of coffee.

Back on the road, he decided he'd go up the Peninsula. What could it hurt? If Ben had the girl captive, perhaps Abe could find her.

As he pulled from the diner, a black-and-white turned onto the road behind him. The police car approached fast before slowing down, on his tail. The red and blue lights flicked on.

~

Hazel

Hazel opened her door to Liz bouncing on the balls of her feet.

"Did they get him?" she asked.

Hazel looked beyond Liz into the street, expecting the world outside to reflect her turmoil. But cars ambled by, kids raced on bikes, birds continued their antics in the sky, and Orla… Orla, what? Hazel saw the vision of her friend hovering at the edge of an abyss. She feared to look deeply at what had become of Orla.

Hazel shook her head.

"I don't know. The news is on. Abe sent a deputy to pick up Ben. There's a reporter at Elder Park, but nothing new." She didn't say more, but backed into the house.

Liz followed her to the sitting room, where Calvin waited on the couch.

He opened his arms to Hazel, who snuggled back into his side.

Hazel turned up the volume, and they listened to a reporter comment on possible clues related to the missing women while gesturing at the caution tape strung along the trailhead.

"Abe said you found Orla's clothes?" Liz started. "How did you know where to look?"

Hazel ran a shaky hand through her hair and gazed at the yellow tape sagging as officers stepped back and forth over the flimsy barrier.

"Abe saw a shovel in Ben Stoops' truck. He-"

"Ben Stoops?" Calvin asked, surprised.

Hazel turned to him.

"Do you know him?"

Calvin nodded.

"Yeah, he comes into the bookstore all the time. He's a nice guy, quiet, but nice. Are you telling me he's the guy?"

The disbelief in Calvin's face made Hazel squirm away.

"We found Orla's earring in his room," she murmured.

"How did you get into his room?" Calvin demanded.

"It's a garage. It wasn't hard," she snapped, looking to Liz for backup.

"Calvin, Ben Stoops was at the park where Orla's bike was found. He obviously buried her clothes. He had her earring," Liz offered.

Calvin frowned and glanced at the television.

"He came into the store one time with an injured chipmunk in his coat. Its leg was broken, and he nursed it back to health. He sat and read his book and fed that chipmunk sunflower seeds for two hours."

"What are you trying to say, Calvin? Because he took pity on a chipmunk, he couldn't have killed Orla or Susie or any of the other missing girls? His being in those places with Orla's stuff is a complete coincidence?" Hazel's voice had grown shrill.

Calvin reached out and took her hand, but she jerked it away.

"Hazel, I'm not disregarding what you've found. Maybe I'm wrong, but... genuinely caring for a living thing is hard to fake. He seemed like a compassionate guy."

"For animals, perhaps. Then again, he might have taken the chipmunk home and crushed it with a hammer."

Fighting tears, she stood and rushed from the room onto the porch. She strode down the stairs and into her garden, but that too did not bring peace. An overwhelming desire to stamp the flowers beneath her sandaled feet washed over her. Before she lashed out, she jogged to her car and jumped behind the wheel. As she pulled out, Liz and Calvin stepped onto the porch.

She drove away, refusing to watch them in her rearview mirror.

~

Abe

Abe sat in the interrogation room, glaring at the two-way mirror.

Time ticked by. There was no clock, an intentional move by the police to disorient their suspects.

Eventually, Detective Moore pushed into the room, a thick folder clutched in his hands. He dropped it on the table with a thud and sat across from Abe.

"Why am I here?" Abe demanded.

"Why are you here?" Moore sneered, opening the file. "This afternoon, you called in a burial site containing Orla Sullivan's clothes, which interestingly also contained a tooth. We have an officer who spotted you at the purported scene of the abduction of Amber Hill. A second eyewitness who saw you getting into your car just outside the Fountain Park entrance. I've also received a very interesting police report faxed in from Spokane, Washington, about your potential involvement in the disappearance of a young woman, Dawn Piper, in 1966."

Abe bristled, hands that he'd been relaxing in his lap instantly turned to fists.

He said nothing, but stared at Detective Moore with such ferocity he thought he might burst a blood vessel in his eye.

Moore cocked his head to the side.

"Blood pressure jump? A lie detector would give us a good idea of how you're feeling right about now. Figured we'd never find out about her, huh? Dawn Piper. Awfully suspicious when the prime suspect in the disappearance and suspected murder of an eighteen-year-old girl moves across the country, where conveniently a slew of other young women start vanishing without a trace."

Abe swallowed the lump of rage forming in his throat. Hearing Dawn's name on this man's lips, the injustice of the accusation, tensed every muscle in his body. It took all of his will to remain in the chair when he wanted to shove the table aside and grab the detective around the throat.

"You piece of shit," he hissed. "You low-life piece of shit."

The detective narrowed his eyes.

"You best watch your mouth, young man."

Abe flicked his eyes to the mirror. Other men would be observing the interview, a videotape might be running. Abe had to calm down. He understood his rights. This wasn't an arrest. Legally, they couldn't hold him.

"If you have questions, you can talk to my lawyer. You're familiar with him, I'm sure, former prosecutor Martin Levett. I know my rights, Detective Moore. If you hold me for another fucking minute, I will sue this police department, and I will broadcast your misconduct from here to the moon. As for Dawn Piper, I'm guessing your little fax also contained verification of my story. As for your other bullshit claims, let me put it to you this way. I'm a reporter. Usually, I just write the stories. That is until the lead detective in a series of disappearances sits on his thumbs and watches the birds instead of investigating. Frankly, I'm not that kind of guy. That's why I was at Fountain Park, and that's how I found about Orla's clothes - good old-fashioned investigating. Have you heard of it, Detective Moore?"

Abe glanced at the mirror.

The detective's face flushed red, and his hands, previously resting on the table top, now gripped the edge.

Abe dropped his voice. "If I'm not walking out that door in ten minutes, you're going to be headline news."

It wasn't ten minutes, more like twenty-five, and by the time a deputy told Abe he was free to opened the interrogation room door and told Abe he was free, he felt sick to his stomach.

Moore had left his folder open on the desk, pictures of Dawn staring up at him.

48

Orla

Orla pitched forward. It was dark, wooded. Branches grabbed at her hair, scratched her face. As she ran, a figure stepped from the trees. A shadow man, eyes black, hands raised to catch her. Orla turned and plunged the other way, but again the man loomed before her. No matter which direction she turned, he was there.

"No," Orla whispered.

She mumbled, raising her arms to fight off her attacker, lunging away.

Suddenly she was falling. Her eyes flew open as she thudded onto the floor, gasping for breath. She sprang to her feet, backed into the couch she'd been laying on, and fell landing on the armrest. She blinked the room into a focus.

The shadow man had been a dream.

She put a hand on her chest, her heart racing, and tried to get her bearings.

Two candles on a wooden table illuminated a small kitchen and living area with a wood burning stove and threadbare rugs. Dark curtains hung over the windows.

Trembling, Orla crept to the table. Her hands shook as she pulled out a note tucked beneath a candle.

I brought you somewhere safe. It's over, Orla. I'll be back before dawn. -Ben

Orla sighed, a low, throbbing pulsed in her head, as she sat heavily in one of the wooden chairs.

After several minutes, she stood and pulled back the curtain. Night had fallen. It was pitch black and pouring rain. Through the storm, she glimpsed thick woods.

The cabin had the hot stuffiness of late summer.

Orla opened the door, and a warm, wet breeze blew into the room.

In the distance, lightning lit the sky through the canopy of trees. A loud clap of thunder followed. She jumped and hauled the door closed. She trembled as she leaned against it.

She moved through the cabin quickly, searching for a phone. There was none. One door, likely to a bedroom, was locked. She rattled the knob, but it didn't turn.

~

Abe

As Abe stepped into the hallway, he heard a voice.

"It's not me," the man insisted.

Abe gazed into the interrogation room across the hall as a detective slipped through the door. He saw Ben Stoops seated at a table, hands clasped at his mouth as if in prayer as he pleaded with the detective who faced him.

"I was trying to protect her..."

The door closed, but Abe had not missed his words.

The man denied it. Of course, he did, and yet... Something niggled at Abe. He thought about the folder stuffed with experiments, the midwife's comment about the health of that first child, and then there'd only been one child. It shouldn't matter. They'd found Orla's clothing, and Ben had buried it.

Abe imagined the very first tipster at the diner, the man who'd insisted he saw Orla in the asylum.

He couldn't shake the sense that he'd gotten it all wrong.

He ran into the rain-swept night.

Orla

Orla paced around the cabin. The sedative had not completely worn off. She turned on the faucet in the kitchen sink and splashed cold water on her face. She wanted to go home, but there was no phone in the cottage, no driveway even. The place stood in the middle of a dark forest. She half-considered running into the rainy night, but the terror of her dreams, of the previous weeks, made her legs feel weak at the thought.

She found a paperback copy of Carrie by Stephen King. She'd never read the book, though Liam loved Stephen King. She sat down on the couch, gazing again at the rain-spotted window, and tried to read. She'd barely read the first paragraph when the door burst open.

She jumped up, expecting Ben. Instead, it was Spencer who stood dripping in the doorway.

He looked at her, surprised.

"Orla?" he said, as if he couldn't believe his eyes.

"Spencer?" She lifted a hand to her throat, realizing she still wore her nightgown from the hospital. Self-consciously, she tugged the hem toward her knees.

"Where have you been?" he asked. "I was worried sick. You've been all over the news. You disappeared that morning." He stepped into the cabin, shrugging off his raincoat.

His blond hair was dry thanks to his hood, and he studied her with a mixture of surprise and intrigue.

"I've been held hostage in the Northern Michigan Asylum. It's been..., I don't even know how long it has been. What's the date?"

"It's July 25th."

Orla shivered and rubbed her hands up and down her bare arms.

"Would you like some clothes?" he asked. "Here." He slipped across the room and pulled a heavy trunk from a closet, flipping back the lid. He drew out a gray University of Michigan sweatshirt and a pair of sweatpants, stained with dark patches.

"These might be a little small," he told her.

She took them, grateful, and slipped into the pants. They ended at mid-calf, more like pedal pushers than full pants. She slipped the sweatshirt over her head. Her fingers brushed against her ribs, and she realized she must have lost weight in the hospital. Her bones felt sharp and close to the surface.

She touched her face, feeling the hollows of her cheeks and eye sockets.

"Were you sick, Orla?" he asked.

She shook her head. How did she tell this man that his mother had injected her with something, that his uncle had forced her into the asylum and spent weeks experimenting on her?

"Did Ben tell you I was here?" she asked, hoping to push the confessions off a bit further.

"No." Spencer shook his head. "I was out for a walk and saw lights, figured I'd come check it out. How do you know Ben?"

"Where are we?" she asked, ignoring his question.

He looked at her funny.

"In a cabin behind my house, and behind my uncle's house. My mom and uncle live across the woods from each other."

"And Ben lives with your uncle, Dr. Crow?"

Spencer gazed at her and nodded.

"I'm on Sapphire, and Ben's on Misty Lane. This cabin is somewhere in the middle. We used to play in here when we were boys."

Orla's tried to focus, but her thoughts lay jumbled in her mind.

She yawned and rubbed her eyes.

The rain grew louder, beating against the roof and the trees outside.

Beneath the rain, an odd sound emerged, like muffled crying.

"Do you hear that?" she whispered, putting her feet on the ground and standing.

Spencer shook his head.

"What?"

Orla walked to the locked door. She pressed her ear against it. The sound was clear: a woman crying and calling out.

"Oh my God." She backed away, staring in horror at Spencer. "There's someone in there! A girl."

Spencer stared at her, confused. He turned the door handle, but it didn't budge. He too pressed his ear against the wood, his eyes growing wide.

"But why…?" he murmured.

"Ben," she breathed. "Ben must have killed the girl with the tooth. Her name was Susan." Orla's legs quaked beneath her. "Is that why he brought me here?"

Spencer stepped back from the door, horrified.

"Ben…" he muttered. "I always knew he was screwed up."

"He's going to come back at any moment," Orla stammered. "We have to help her. We have to get out of here."

"Let me find something to jimmy this door open."

Orla watched Spencer move into the little kitchen, opening and closing drawers.

As he rifled through the contents of a drawer, Orla glanced back at the room, no longer hearing the girl inside.

Odd, she thought, that Spencer would have been out walking in the rain.

She looked down at her sweatpants, at the dark stains marring the fabric.

Without making a sound, she slipped off one of her gloves and touched a finger to the stained fabric.

The vision jolted her. She saw a girl in the sweatshirt and sweatpants, smiling at Spencer, his arm in a sling. She was helping carry his books to the gold sports car. As she stepped out of the streetlight into a patch of darkness, he struck her. The blow caved in the back of her skull, and she fell to her knees.

Orla wrenched her hand away from her leg, her eyes bulging as the room around her refocused.

Spencer watched her strangely.

"What's wrong?" he asked, gazing at her bare hand hovering above the stained pants.

Orla swallowed and stepped behind the couch, putting a barrier between them.

"Nothing. They drugged me at the hospital. I'm nauseous. I think I need some air."

She started around the couch, walking quickly toward the door, but Spencer's hand shot out and caught her wrist. He held her arm, his eyes probing hers.

The truth hovered between them, evident on both their faces.

49

Abe

The gate at 311 Sapphire stood open, and he screeched into the driveway, sliding to a halt in front of the wide steps that led to the front door.

The house was dark except for a single light in a first-floor window.

Abe held his jacket over his head as he sprinted to the front door, protected from the rain by a second-floor balcony. He pounded on the door.

When no one answered, he beat harder with both fists.

Virginia Crow opened the door, looking irritated but well put together. Dark eyes stared out from her powdered face. She wore a black sweater over black slacks, a string of pearls resting on her chest.

"I'm here to see your son, Spencer."

The woman's eyes darted behind him, and Abe whirled around, expecting to find the man creeping up behind him. Through the rain, he saw only darkness.

"He's not here," the woman said, trying to close the door in his face.

Abe pushed the woman out of the way and stormed into the

house.

"Where is she?" he shouted.

He ran down the hallway, shoving through doors, looking wildly around each room. The rooms were dark, and he fumbled for light switches, blinking at the bright glare only to find furniture, clean and shining, stinking of furniture polish, and beneath everything the scent of bleach.

When Abe returned to the foyer, the woman had vanished, which unnerved him. But he stormed up the stairs, taking them three at a time, yelling Amber's and Orla's names.

~

Orla

"I always had this fantasy that one day I would meet someone, a woman, and this…" he paused, furrowed his brow, "compulsion would die. Whoosh, gone. It was like a fairytale. Young girls imagine their knight in shining armor, and I'm dreaming of a sorceress who has the power to make me stop wanting to kill."

Spencer had tied Orla to a stiff-backed wooden chair. He sat in a matching chair, facing her.

"I've never talked about this before. I sensed I could talk to you in the park that day." He chuckled. "When you disappeared, I racked my brain for days." He leaned toward her, hands balanced on his knees. "I thought I might have killed you and forgotten. I searched the woods for two days in a panic."

"Has that happened before? You killed someone and forgot?"

He shook his head slowly.

"I don't think so." He laughed. "Sometimes I'm wasted. The last hours get a little foggy. I remember, but… the memories are different from day-to-day things. I never realized how difficult it would be to articulate all this. Maye I'll write a fiction book someday. I could put it all down, and no one would be the wiser."

"Does your mother take part in the killings?"

Spencer recoiled as if Orla had slapped him.

"Of course not. Why would ask that?"

"The morning after I spent the night with you, your mother approached me in the driveway and stuck a needle in my neck," Orla told him.

He looked momentarily embarrassed, as if they were on a date and Orla had told Spencer that his mother insulted her shoes.

"She's very protective," he explained.

"Protective?" Orla couldn't keep the sarcasm from her voice.

He leaned back and rested his hands in his lap.

"I don't want to talk about my mother."

Orla studied his haunted blue eyes. This man intended to kill her. He'd bound her to a wooden chair, duct tape biting into the raw flesh of her wrists and ankles. Her only hope was to keep him talking until Ben returned.

"Does Ben know?" Orla nodded her head toward the closed door of the bedroom.

Spencer's lips curled away from his teeth.

"That square? He's the type who'd kill himself before he'd take a life. He's a virgin, you know? Unless you and he…"

Anger bubbled within Orla at his words.

Don't provoke him, she thought.

"No, he helped me. He's a good man."

Spencer scoffed and touched the handle of a long, serrated knife he'd set on the table.

Orla shifted her wrist back and forth, subtly, imperceptibly, feeling the tape catch on a splinter on the chair.

"When did it start? The desire to kill?" she asked.

He squinted, cocked his head.

"I don't know. My earliest memory is my mother sitting me inside this box. It was thick metal, soundproof, light proof. I saw her face disappear as she closed the lid and left me in the darkness. I don't remember ever coming out of that box. Almost like the good Spencer went in and never came back out. Later, when I started to think about girls, and sex, I always thought of that box. I didn't want to date. I wanted a girl I could keep in that box. Crazy, right?" He lifted the knife and pressed his finger against the point.

"There was no pivotal moment. I fantasized about girls like any young guy does but in my fantasies…" He paused and looked up.

His eyes were so dark, not the eyes she'd seen that first day in the park. "The girls were bound, they cried and screamed. I liked it. It aroused me."

Spencer's hand moved to his leg. He squeezed his thigh, as if an uncontrollable urge had begun to roll over him. Orla realized she'd made a mistake in probing. He'd begun with honesty, but the telling of the fantasy had ignited something.

From the other room, Orla heard the girl whimper.

Spencer darted his eyes toward the sound. She saw the color rising into his neck, and then his face. His breathing shifted, becoming shorter and faster.

"Please, Spencer," Orla said. She pushed against the restraints, searching for the words that would calm him. "Spencer," she said again, louder. She wiggled her arm back and forth, and heard the rip as the tape started to pull apart.

He looked back at her blankly as if he didn't know who she was.

"You don't have to do this. Let me help you."

He had stopped listening, and he had not heard the tape. He stood, eyes vacant, and picked up the knife.

"No," Orla shouted. "Stop!"

He didn't stop. From the other room, the girl cried out.

Orla scraped her wrist faster and jerked it up, breaking the frayed tape free. She fumbled, sweat making her hands slip as she removed the tape from her other wrist and her ankles. She stood and heard the woman begging for her life.

"Spencer!" Orla screamed.

She picked up the chair, she'd been taped to, and threw it towards the door. It hit the doorframe and sent a spray of wood splintering to the floor.

As Spencer emerged from the room, dazed, a wild look in his eyes; Orla wrenched open the front door of the cabin and raced into the storm.

**be**

. . .

The girls did not respond as Abe rushed down the hallway calling their names.

A huge picture, lit by an eerie pale light, caught his eye. He gazed at an aerial view of the Crows' property. He saw the house of Mrs. Crow. At the opposite end of the property stood the doctor's house, and in the center, nestled deep in the thick woods, he saw a small cabin, a ring of smoke curling from the tiny chimney. He blinked at it, followed it to M-22, to that special curve in the road.

He turned toward the stairs and the woman was there, her stance wide and solid. Something gleamed in her claw-like hand. A knife… no, a syringe. His mind flashed to that long-ago prescription for arsenic and her dead husband. He shook his head in vague disbelief. This woman with her made-up face and her string of pearls gazing at him with the eyes of a killer.

It seemed unreal that he could find himself in this moment, in this house of horrors.

He ran toward her, and she lunged at him. He tried to dodge the needle, but she sunk it into his shoulder. Before she could depress the syringe, he grabbed her arms and wrench her back, lifting her from the ground. She shrieked, her colorless eyes blazing, and swung the needle wildly, nearly sinking it into his cheek. He threw her toward the wall. She smacked into it and landed awkwardly, crying out as her ankle twisted. Her head thudded backwards. Not hard enough to knock her unconscious. But she looked dazed as she toppled sideways onto the hall rug.

Abe ran down the stairs and out the door.

Rain poured through the trees. The leaves, heavy and dripping, provided little respite. For the first several minutes he sprinted blindly through the storm, slipping on wet leaves, catching his foot on a root and sprawling on his face. He stood up, tried to get his bearings.

The cabin was located north, somewhere between the doctor's house and Virginia's.

As he fumbled through the dark, he glimpsed a light. He started to run, keeping his hands out to protect his face from the branches. As he neared the cabin, the door swung open and a woman fled into the night. He glimpsed her through the rain, and her long black hair streaming out behind her was unmistakable: Orla. Seconds later, a man emerged through the doorway and followed her.

Abe paused, gazing at the cabin. He took a step closer and then turned, rushing in the direction Orla had run.

50

Orla

Thunder cracked the night and lightning split the sky above her. For a dazzling instant, Orla saw Spencer behind her, barreling through the trees, and then it was black once more.

She hurled forward, blind in the rain, her feet crying out as she stepped on fallen branches and tried not slip. Her muscles shrieked as if she'd set them on fire. She clutched trees and heaved for breath but knew she could not stop. Her life, and the life of the woman in the cabin, depended on her escape.

A dark mass rose before her, and she nearly ran into it headfirst. She skidded to a stop and pushed her face closer, finding a rusted metal door to an old kiln. She dragged the door open and climbed inside, pulling it closed. Inside the kiln, she heard nothing. The instant the sound died, she regretted her choice. She was trapped.

The fine ash beneath her stuck to her wet hands and legs. She crawled deeper into the kiln, to the far back. The ash billowed when she moved and she struggled to breathe. It caught in her nose and throat. She needed to cough, but couldn't. Didn't dare.

Within the ash, hard things poked and shifted beneath her. She reached down and followed the outline of a long, thin object, like a stick, but no… As she grasped it, she realized it was a long bone, rounded and knobby at either end. If she took off her gloves, she could discover who the bones belonged to. She didn't, but she lifted the bone in her hand, ready to wield it as a weapon if Spencer opened the door.

"Please," she murmured to the silence. "Please don't let me die in here."

The door creaked open. It brought no light, but a rush of cool, wet air swept into the kiln swirling the ash up around Orla. She clenched her hand on the bone, biting back a scream.

"Orla?" a man whispered.

She did not recognize the voice.

She wanted to call out, scream for help, but maybe it was Spencer – somehow, he'd disguised his voice and hoped to trick her.

She stayed quiet and pressed her back against the cement wall.

Lightning lit the forest, and Orla glimpsed the stranger for an instant, his eyes peering into the kiln.

Worse, she observed the man who stood behind him: Spencer, a hammer in his raised hand.

"Watch out!" she screamed, but the bolt of lightning had vanished, and she stared into the black. Sounds drifted into the kiln, grunts and thuds.

Was Spencer killing the man? Would he soon crawl into the kiln to finish her, too?

She didn't wait to find out. She fumbled over ash and bones, leapt onto the slick forest floor, rain washing the grit from her face and arms. She spotted a dark mass rolling on the ground. She wanted to help, needed to help, but could not make out one man from another.

She fled back to the cabin, bolting the door behind her. In the now-open bedroom, Spencer had left his knife on the floor by the bed. The girl in the bed, arms and legs tied, stared at her panic-stricken, one eye bruised and bloodshot. Her blonde hair fell across her face.

Orla grabbed the knife and hacked at the ropes. When the girl's arm was free, she ripped the gag from her mouth. Red welts marked the creases of her mouth. She cried and blundered off the bed.

~

Abe

Abe ducked sideways as Spencer brought the hammer toward his skull. He landed hard on his shoulder, and already the man was striking again, arm raised, the clawed end pointing down. Abe rolled across the wet leaves, and kicked his legs out. His foot connected with Spencer's shin. He grunted, but didn't drop the hammer.

Abe scrambled with his hands, found a thick branch and whipped it toward Spencer's form but the rain and dark obscured him.

He stood, squinted into the downpour, and perceived the hammer too late as it crashed into the side of his head.

~

Orla

"Run," Orla bellowed, pushing the girl ahead of her into the blustery night.

The trees howled in the storm and dropped their leaves and branches as the girls tore through thick underbrush.

"I can't see," the girl cried to Orla.

"Just don't stop," Orla shouted, shoving her forward when she slowed.

Orla ached. A cramp in her right abdomen crept higher, and she hunched sideways to relieve the clenched tissue.

The blonde girl slipped, her feet sliding back to connect with Orla's ankles, and both women fell. Orla landed hard on the girl's back and heard her grunt. Rolling to the side, Orla reached for her knee, which had twisted in the fall, and winced. The blonde girl climbed onto her hands and knees. Her shoulders rose and fell as she sobbed and struggled for breath, her clothes and hair mud-splattered.

Orla reached out, found the woman's slippery hand, and drew her close. They held each other for several seconds, the rain pelting their heads. Lightning streaked and lit the forest, and Orla saw him - Spencer, hammer in hand, only feet from where the girls lay.

Orla stiffened, and for a few seconds time seemed to exist in a parallel world. She slipped into her long-ago self, a little girl lost in the sand dunes as a thunderstorm rocked the sky. As Orla cowered behind a gnarled, bone-white tree, she gazed in horror at a man holding a hammer and stumbling through the sand towards her.

A boom of thunder split the earth.

There was no time to warn the girl. Orla stood, jerked the other woman to her feet, and dragged her into the woods.

She tried to run, but her knee buckled, and she went down, hand slipping from the blonde woman's grasp. The woman lunged backwards, sprawling in the sodden leaves and narrowly dodging the hammer Spencer had swung at her head.

Orla crawled toward her, but Spencer's hand clamped on her leg, gripping through her sweatpants to keep from slipping. She forced the waistband down and slipped out of the pants. She felt the hammer thud into the ground beside her.

The blonde woman was on her feet. She heaved Orla up beside her.

Orla screamed as Spencer's hand sank into her hair. She tried to twist away, and he brought her skull hard against the other woman's, whose hair he also held tight in his fist. Their heads collided, and black spots filled Orla's vision.

Both women collapsed. Orla felt her head break free of Spencer's grasp.

She looked up to see a hand close over Spencer's mouth. Another set of arms surrounded him, and another. Orla blinked, dazed, as long, slender arms, pale and waxy, ending in torn, bloody fingernails, besieged the man.

Orla glimpsed the woman she'd encountered at the start of this nightmare: Susan, long blonde hair unaffected by the rain, but streaked in dark red. The girl had both hands over Spencer's face, pressing into his eyes. He was shrieking and tearing at their arms. He fell onto his back.

The blonde woman who'd escaped with Orla watched as well. They sat on the sodden earth as the rain subsided, watching young women with bloodied faces and long blonde hair drag Spencer backwards into the forest.

~

Hazel

Hazel regretted driving up the Peninsula the moment she turned onto M-22. The rain, a sprinkle in town, had become a practical monsoon as she crept along the curvy roads. She stopped twice when the windshield became a mass of pouring and pounding water.

When she pulled her car back onto the road, the rain had slowed. A steady drizzle kept her windshield wipers working. She passed Sapphire Lane and slowed at the curve, eyes drifting to the edge of the forest where sightings of Susie had occurred.

As if conjured by her thoughts, a young woman with long blonde hair burst from the woods. Hazel slammed on her brakes, believing for a second that she was witnessing Susie's ghost, but then another woman staggered from the trees. Her dark hair was plastered against her face, her eyes huge in her pale face.

"Orla," Hazel choked, jumping from the car.

Orla and the blonde woman clung together, their faces bruised and scratched.

When she looked at Hazel, she didn't seem to recognize her. Her mouth hung slack, but after several seconds, her eyes cleared.

"Hazel?" she whispered.

Hazel rushed to her friend.

"You're alive, you're alive," she murmured, holding Orla as if she might vanish at any moment.

Orla nodded into her neck and then pulled away, shooting a frightened glance into the woods.

"We have to call the police."

51

Abe

Abe woke in an unfamiliar room. He blinked at the dimmed lights overhead. A bandage partially covered the right side of his head and he reached a hand up, gingerly touching the wound. An IV ran from his left arm to a tall metal pole holding a saline bag.

"I fucking survived," he murmured, remembering those final moments in the forest as the hammer swung down.

"Yes, you did." The woman's voice startled him, and he sat up, wincing at the stab of pain behind his right eye.

The bandage blocked her from view. He turned his head to find Orla in a chair beside his bed.

She'd braided her long black hair and hung it over her shoulder. She sat with her legs pulled into her chest, her chin resting on her knees. On the table beside her, he saw the wrinkled photograph of Orla cradling the kittens in her lap. He had been carrying it in his back pocket when he'd run into the woods.

He offered her a smile.

"You did too," he murmured.

"Thanks to you," she told him.

He shook his head, grimaced at the pain and lay still.

"No. I saw you escape. I probably gave away your hiding place by following you to the kiln."

She untucked her legs and scooted her chair closer, putting her hand in his.

"I'm Orla," she said. "Hazel told me all about you."

He closed his eyes.

"Nice to meet you, Orla. I'm Abe."

~

Liz

Liz watched Orla's mother. Fiona's face was frozen, her eyes boring into the car. When Orla stepped out, Patrick grinned, but Fiona's face crumpled. Her small mouth drooped and her eyes gushed tears.

"Orla," she mouthed and took a step.

Orla ran to her parents, her arms out wide. Fiona fell into her daughter's arms. An animal wail left her body, and Patrick reached down and braced a hand around his wife's waist to keep her from falling.

Liz's breath had left her body. She couldn't move or speak. Her gaze was fixed, unable to shift from the scene unfolding, *knowing*, knowing why Fiona had collapsed, why she'd wailed at the sight of her beautiful - living - daughter.

"Liz," Abe murmured her name. He'd stepped from the car, and stood beside her. She hadn't even noticed him.

She turned and saw the sadness in his face. He too would be celebrating Orla's return, but there were so many who would never return.

"Are you okay?" she asked him, reaching up toward the bandage on his head, but not touching it.

"Better than okay," he said, gesturing at the scene before them as Orla folded into her parents' embrace.

Liz held her tears in check, strangled her own sobs and leaned against Abe, crying quietly into his shoulder.

~

Abe

Deputy Waller shuffled Abe into the viewing room. Several other officers and detectives huddled together, watching the interrogation of Virginia Crow. Detective Hansen of the Petoskey police department took the lead.

"I want to see my son!" Virginia Crow demanded.

"He's at the hospital being treated for a head wound and shock. Afterward, he'll be transferred to a cell right here," Detective Hansen told her. "And I understand you'd like to speak with your attorney. He'll be here shortly. Though I must warn you, we've discovered bones in the kiln on your property. A lot of bones. I've met some slick lawyers in my day, but you won't be wiggling out of this one, and neither will your son. Tell me, Mrs. Crow. Is Spencer your first or second-born child?"

She ashed her cigarette, her face pallid beneath the florescent lights.

"My second son. Dr. Crow's son."

"I see. But you also named your first son Spencer?"

Her lips curled back from her teeth and she glanced away, blinking rapidly as if for a moment she'd seen him, that original child, watching her from the corner.

"Was he in the kiln, Mrs. Crow?"

She laughed a high, shrill sound.

"I didn't burn him alive, if that's what you mean. He was dead already. He died a week after I had my second son."

"How did he die?"

She took another drag on her cigarette, and pushed a finger in her mouth, chewing the nail to a point.

"The real-life Adam's Family," another detective in the viewing room murmured.

"Natural causes, I'm sure," Victoria sighed, as if she'd grown bored with the whole affair.

Hansen opened a folder and spread the doctor's notes fan-like across the table.

"Administration of barbiturates, injections of insulin, submersion in freezing water, solitary confinement for hours. The child died before two years of age. You know what I would call that, Mrs. Crow? Murder."

She glared at the pages.

"He was weak," she hissed. "If he'd have been stronger, stronger like Spencer was..."

The detective stared at her.

"Are you telling me you did these things to your second son as well?"

"Where's Byron?" she demanded, ashing her cigarette on the table and ignoring the ash tray.

"I was about to ask you that, Mrs. Crow. He was last seen at the asylum earlier today. His vehicle is still there, but no one knows where he's gone. We have an eyewitness who saw Doctor Crow being escorted into a dark van by several men."

She frowned.

"Tell me about the brotherhood, Mrs. Crow."

Abe watched the woman lift her eyebrow.

"What brotherhood is that?"

Detective Hansen sighed and slipped off his blazer, hanging it over the back of his chair.

"Ben Stoops, the young man who has lived with Byron Crow for nearly two decades, spoke of a brotherhood at the Northern Michigan Asylum."

Virginia rolled her eyes.

"The young man comes from schizophrenics. You can't believe a word out of his mouth."

Abe's head had begun to ache, and perspiration coated his face.

He turned to Waller.

"What did you find at the property?"

Waller studied him.

"You look rough, Abe. Let me walk you to your car."

As they left the building, Waller answered Abe's question.

"The kiln was filled with bones. The forensics team has assembled six bodies, including the body of a small child."

Abe shuddered, remembering Orla hiding in the kiln that was actually a crypt.

"Susan Miner?" he asked.

Waller nodded.

"No confirmed victim identities, but we found a treasure trove of keepsakes beneath a floorboard in Spencer's cabin. Liz Miner identified Susan's clothes. There appears to be items from every missing girl you reported on."

Abe leaned against his car. His head swam and he closed his eyes. The head injury coupled with the horror of the findings overwhelmed him.

"How can I help, Abe? Do you need a lift home?"

Abe shook his head and patted the hood of his car. After he'd dropped Orla off, he'd driven directly to the police station despite hospital orders he go home and rest.

"You solved this," Waller told him. "Moore's off the case. He'll be lucky to work another homicide. On behalf of the entire department, I want to say thank you, Abe."

"I gave you the wrong guy," Abe muttered.

"No, you didn't," Waller disagreed. "That guy sang like a canary once Hansen put the pressure on him. He led us to you guys."

"Did he know about Spencer? And the murders?"

Waller shook his head.

"I don't think so. He was shocked when he learned what transpired after he left Orla at the cabin. Guilt-ridden, from the looks of him."

"And Spencer? The detective said he's in the hospital."

Waller nodded.

"Yep, we found him blubbering like a baby out in those woods. He was in the kiln, bleeding mightily from a wound to the back of his head. Looked like somebody nailed him with his own hammer, though Orla and Amber denied it."

Abe shook his head, tried to imagine it, and realized he didn't want to.

"Do you think he'll confess?" Abe asked.

"Already has - chicken-hearted to his core. Not a signed confession yet, but man, he talked and cried something fierce the entire drive back from the Peninsula. He told us he feigned a broken arm at Fountain Park to get Amber Hill to his car. He asked her to help him load some wood in his trunk. He's a clever scoundrel, I'll give him that."

"That's why we never found anything," Abe muttered. "He talked them into helping him. I should have figured as much. I was all wrong about Ben. I had it all mixed up."

Waller put a hand on his shoulder.

"That story had so many twists and turns, we likely won't ever know the full truth. How you got this close blows my mind. You did good, Abe. Go home, take a long nap, and when you get up, tell your dad to take you out to dinner. You deserve it."

~

rla

Orla wanted to hug Ben, to pull him aside and thank him, but her dad held her close as four police officers and Detective Hansen waited for Ben's directions.

Ben led the group from the asylum into the forest.

Orla shook, and her father petted her head and murmured little words of encouragement.

"You can do this," he whispered.

She didn't respond. It was not bravery she lacked in that moment. A disconcerting sense that someone, or something, watched them surrounded her.

Ben paused, pointing at a tall Willow tree, and started down the hill that led to the chamber.

Orla saw Ben's eyes darting anxiously, and she wondered if he felt it too.

Blanched trees, bare of their leaves, grew out from the earth and lay tangled in a heap across the prickly summer vegetation.

Ben walked to a wall of brush and gestured at it.

"The door's in there," he murmured.

Detective Hansen stepped forward and reached into the foliage.

He moved sideways, pushing his arms into the brush up to his shoulders. He searched for several minutes.

"There's nothing in there."

Ben frowned and stepped forward.

He reached into the brush.

After a moment, Orla broke away from her father.

Ben looked at her puzzled.

Orla, her hands protected by gloves, pulled at the twisted bushes, ripping and clawing. She created an opening in the overgrowth, but only more forest lay beyond it.

"Are we at the wrong place?" Hansen asked.

Ben shook his head.

"This is it," Orla insisted, continuing to tear at the branches. "I remember that willow. This has to be it."

"It is," Ben nodded. "There isn't another place in the forest like this."

But they backtracked and searched for another willow. After two hours, sweaty, scratched, and exhausted, they returned to the asylum grounds.

Ben hung his head, but Orla took his hand.

"I'll send out more men tomorrow," Hansen told them. "If there's a hovel in that forest, we're going to find out."

Orla looked at Ben and she saw her own doubt reflected in his face.

The police would never find the chamber. Not if the chamber didn't want to be found.

52

Orla

"Did you find these?" Ben asked Orla, looking at the photos in astonishment.

The first photo depicted a young woman posing in front of an aspen tree on the asylum grounds. A blanket-wrapped bundle rested in her arms, a tiny face peeking out.

Orla shook her head. "I wish I could take credit for it, but it was all Abe."

"I figured it was the least I could do, since I got you arrested," Abe told him. "Your records were in the garage at Misty Lane. Byron Crow was vile, but at least he kept detailed records."

Ben stared down at the photo, and then shuffled to the second and third.

"Your mom's name was Marilyn Stoops," Abe said. "She gave birth to you in the asylum on May 7th, 1951. Her siblings," Abe gestured at the second photo, which revealed Marilyn as a young woman, arms linked with her two sisters and one brother, "never knew about you. You lived in the nursery for two years, several of the nurses shared you, and your mom saw you every day. Then she contracted tuberculosis and died. When you were three, Dr. Crow started to take you home."

"There's no record that he ever did experiments on you, Ben," Orla told him. "And your aunts and uncle are dying to meet you. It devastated them when Marilyn went into the asylum."

"Why did she?" Ben asked shyly.

"Because she was pregnant out of wedlock," Abe scowled.

"It's sickening," Orla murmured, "and unbelievably sad."

"There's a bit of good news, though," Abe said, handing Ben a folder.

Ben opened the folder and looked up, confused.

"It's a deed, Ben. Byron Crow put his house in your name three years ago. He was being investigated for tax fraud. The house on Misty Lane and his part of the property are yours."

Ben wrinkled his brow and shook his head.

"Why would he do that?"

"To prevent the government from seizing his property if they decided he'd committed fraud. They never did, but he also never transferred the property back."

"It's yours, Ben," Orla said, taking his hand. "You have a home."

Ben looked ready to cry.

"I don't want it. I never want to go back there again," he whispered.

"You don't have to," Abe told him. "The police are still searching the house, but once they've released it, you're free to sell it. Buy a new house. You'll get a pretty penny out of that house and property. You'll be set for a long time."

"What if he comes back?" Ben murmured.

"Do you think he will?" Orla asked.

"No, I think he's probably dead. I think the brotherhood killed him," Ben admitted.

"Man, I want to know more about this brotherhood," Abe muttered, "I searched Crow's files, and didn't find so much as hint of this group."

"In the meantime," Orla cut in. "Our roommate, Jayne, is moving to Australia. We've got a vacancy in the house, and I thought you might like to stay with us for a while."

Ben looked away. When he spoke, his lower lip quivered.

"Are you sure?" he asked.

"I'm way more than that." Orla smiled.

~

Hazel

Calvin had set up a long table in Hazel's garden. A silver and pink tablecloth, sewed by Orla, lay over the top. From the flowering trees, Hazel had hung white string lights.

Everyone brought a dish to pass. Liz supplied garlic rolls. Fiona had made a shepherd's pie and brown bread. Abe brought freshly baked pies from Grady's Diner. Even Orla, the guest of honor, made zucchini potato pancakes.

Hazel had set the table with her mother's Aynsley Wilton bone china, piped in blue and gold. Her mother had cherished the dinnerware. Every Friday night, in the year before her mother's death, Hazel served she and her mother dinner on the set. In her final days, weak and ravaged by the cancer, Hazel's mom had dropped one of the saucers and shattered it. Her mother had sobbed for hours. Hazel had wrapped and boxed the dinnerware, and had not taken it out again until just this morning, when she realized her mother would want nothing more than to see Hazel's friends laughing and eating from her beautiful plates.

As the sun set, her guests arrived.

"Not the head of the table," Orla said, when Hazel pulled out a chair. "Please."

Hazel saw the trepidation in her friend's eyes and pulled her close.

"I didn't think, I'm sorry," Hazel whispered, kissing her on the cheek.

Orla leaned her head on Hazel's shoulder and sighed.

"That's not true at all," Orla told her. "Look at all this. You dreamed it, and here we are."

Orla sat in a chair next to Abe. He leaned over and kissed her cheek, and Hazel watched them, the way their eyes lingered on one another's.

Liz and Jerry took chairs near Pat and Fiona. Liz complimented

Fiona on her lovely green dress, which she'd sewn herself. Orla, too, wore the beautiful red and orange dress she'd made just days before her abduction. The backless dress revealed a large yellowish bruise fading from her right shoulder.

When Ben, the shy, dark-haired man who'd freed Orla from the asylum, appeared, Orla jumped from her chair and ran across the lawn. She threw her arms around him, and they toppled over backwards. He blushed red, but Hazel saw he was pleased.

When he stepped to the table, he held up a bag of cherries.

"I stopped at a fruit stand. I don't have a kitchen and I don't really know how to cook..." He trailed off, and Orla took the cherries, opening the bag and inhaling.

"I love cherries," she told him. "And when you move in, you can do all the cooking you want. Let me grab a bowl." She disappeared into the house.

Ben started to sit next to Calvin, but Patrick stood and pulled him roughly away from the table. Hazel cringed, thinking Pat might hit the young man. Instead, he gave him a hug, patting Ben's back.

"Thank you. We haven't had a chance to tell you, but thank you for saving our daughter."

Ben nodded, letting his hair fall over his face, and sat quickly down.

They ate, drank wine, and shed more than a few tears. Hazel started to clear the plates from the table as Calvin sliced the pies.

As she stepped onto the porch, she glanced toward the road and saw an ethereal woman, with long blonde hair, walking up the driveway. Hazel's mouth fell open and she froze, wondering if she stared at a ghost, but as the woman drew closer, Hazel recognized her.

"Hattie," she whispered.

The woman saw her and smiled. She wore a long, crocheted white dress, her hair flowing behind her.

"Hi," Hazel said breathlessly as she met her in the driveway.

Hattie gazed at the table of people.

"What a beautiful party," Hattie murmured.

"Thank you," Hazel told her, wondering why the woman had come.

"I've had a visitor the last few nights," Hattie said, gazing deeply into Hazel's eyes. "She would like to say goodbye to her mother."

Hazel stared at her, puzzled, and then awareness took hold.

"Susan?" she whispered.

Hattie nodded.

"May I borrow Liz Miner?"

Hazel nodded and walked back to the table.

She rested a hand on Liz's shoulder and leaned down.

"Liz, there's someone here to see you."

Liz looked up, confused, and followed Hazel's gaze to the woman in the driveway.

Without asking, she stood and followed Hazel to Hattie.

"Liz," Hattie said, taking Liz's hand and holding it for a long moment. "I've heard so much about you."

"You have?" Liz cast a surprised glance at Hazel.

"Walk with me," Hattie said, moving off down the driveway.

Hazel nodded at Liz, who turned and followed Hattie into the dark street.

~

Liz

Liz watched the woman who moved with such lightness, she appeared to float.

"How do you know me?" Liz asked.

Hattie stopped, tilted her head and nodded.

"This way," she told Liz, gesturing to a white archway that opened into a small park. Liz followed the woman, who stopped near a flowering apple tree.

"I'll give you a few minutes," Hattie said.

Liz started to argue and then froze, when another voice emerged from a shadow behind the tree.

"Mom." Susie's voice drifted from the darkness. She sounded far away, as if she called from the bottom of a well.

As Liz gazed into the purple twilight, her daughter materialized behind the white blossoms.

For a few terrible, wonderful seconds, Susan stood before her, solid and real, glowing as if she basked in the midday sun.

"Susan," Liz gasped, stepping forward, but her daughter faded.

For an instant the shadow was only darkness, and then her child, her green-eyed beauty, appeared once more.

"I'll be waiting for you, Mom. It's time to live again." Susan's voice emerged from her trembling shape. "I love you."

And then, Susan Miner disappeared for the last time.

EPILOGUE

SIX MONTHS LATER

Abe

Abe's mom stood in the baggage claim of the Spokane International Airport, waving excitedly when she spotted him. She wore an eye-popping yellow turtleneck beneath a red sweater vest and matching red pants. Her hair, long the last time Abe had seen her years earlier, was now cropped above her ears.

"Abraham," she gushed, grabbing and hugging him, pulling away to look into his face and then crushing him against her.

"My God, you're all grown up. You look just like your father," she cried, fat tears rolling from beneath her round spectacles.

"Mom, I was grown up when I left Washington."

"But you didn't have this beard, and these clothes…" She touched his shirt, and then stopped as if remembering Orla, who stood next to him, smiling. "You're Orla?" she asked, wiping at her face and smiling.

Before Orla could answer, his mother embraced her, crying into her shoulder. "Abraham, she looks just like Cher from Sonny and Cher. My goodness, you are lovely. Look at her, Abe."

Abe smiled apologetically at Orla.

"I've seen her, Mom," he assured his mother. "You are lovely, though." He lifted Orla's hand and kissed her palm.

His mother beamed at them, her gray eyes enormous and shining.

"Thank you. It's a pleasure to meet you, Mrs. Levett."

"Call me Bernice," his mother insisted, grabbing Orla's arm and steering her toward the door.

"Don't worry about me," Abe called after them. "I've got the bags."

"I'm making my legendary beef burgundy," Abe's mother announced. "Has Abraham told you all about it? I made it every year for his birthday, until he left, of course. You're not vegetarian, are you?"

Oral laughed and winked at Abe.

"No, I'm a meat-eater, and Abe *has* mentioned your legendary beef burgundy. Sounds amazing, Bernice. I can't wait to see your home. Abe tells me you raise miniature Schnauzers."

"Oh, I do, Orla. I do. They are the most precious things. I have six pups right now, three weeks from adoption, bless their little hearts."

~

Orla

"You don't have to do this," Abe said for the tenth or eleventh time since they left his mother's house to make the short drive to the Spokane police station.

"Abe." Orla put her hand on his knee. "I want to do this. It's the right thing. And not just for you. I met Liz. I saw what the families go through. I want to do it."

Abe clutched the wheel, his knuckles the same white as his face.

A detective met them in the lobby before leading them to a basement room filled with cold case files.

A single table stood in the center of the dimly lit room. A cardboard box sat on top. The name Dawn Piper was written on the side in black marker with a case number listed beneath it.

"This isn't standard procedure," the detective grumbled, looking at Orla and then Abe. "But since I have your mom to thank for my Schnauzer, Sugarplum, I'm making an exception."

"Sugarplum?" Abe asked.

Orla gently elbowed Abe in the ribs.

"That's an adorable name," Orla added.

The detective eyed them for another moment.

"This box stays here. Everything in it needs to be there when I come back from lunch. It's an open investigation. If we ever find the perp, a defense attorney could call this evidence tampering."

"Our lips are sealed," Abe said.

Orla peered into the box. She wore her gloves, sliding her hand over documents, pulling out small plastic bags. When she lifted a baggie containing a black button, she knew she'd found it.

She opened the bag and took the button out. Removing one glove, she held the button over her naked palm.

"Here goes nothing," she murmured, dropping the button into her hand.

The image rocked her. In an instant, she was transported to a long-ago summer night, to a dusty parking lot near a convenience store.

A large man, his breath stinking of whiskey, held Dawn by her hair, pulling her towards his truck. His eyes were bloodshot, and his lips big and heavy. Dawn cried out, clawing at the man, tearing at his hair, screaming for help. In the struggle, she grabbed his shirt and ripped it. The button flew to the ground.

Orla felt both their energies, the man's lust and the girl's terror.

Despite the years, the energy was strong - strong enough for Orla to follow the trail.

He dragged Dawn to his truck and forced her inside. In her mind, Orla spun the truck, memorized the license plate. The button was giving up its ghosts. The struggle continued inside the cab as they sped down the road and passed Abe. Orla saw his car spin around. She felt Dawn's exhilaration, her hope at seeing Abe. The man lifted a wrench from the console and struck her in the head. She slumped against the passenger window. The vision had begun to fade, but there was paperwork on the dashboard, letters. Orla read the name *Jasper Moran*.

The button fell from her hand.

She took in a shaky breath and opened her eyes. The dark night and Dawn's screams had dissipated, but the lingering terror made her heart thud against her ribs.

"Did you…?" Abe started and seemed to choke on the words. He looked like he might be sick.

Orla knew he could see it in her face, the truth - that yes, she knew who abducted and murdered Dawn all those years ago.

She rattled off the license plate number, and Abe wrote it in his notebook.

"His name was Jasper Moran," she told him.

~

Abe

"It's Dawn," Abe's younger sister, Trudy exclaimed, pointing at the television.

She jumped up from the Monopoly game they'd been playing, Abe getting his butt handed to him by Orla, who'd put a hotel on Boardwalk one roll before he landed there.

Trudy adjusted the volume.

A bright-eyed male reporter, wearing a tan trench coat, stood in front of a ramshackle house with peeling blue paint and a large, black tarp covering one corner of the roof. Old tires, steel barrels, and bags of garbage spotted the yard.

"I'm standing in front of the home of Jasper Moran, a local Spokane man suspected in the disappearance of eighteen-year-old Dawn Piper, who was abducted from Daryl's Convenience Store on June 11th, 1966. The police recently searched Moran's property based on an anonymous tip. Skeletal remains were located in a sealed drum in the home's basement."

Abe stared at the house in the background, but he felt nothing - no relief, no indignation. A strange numbness settled over him.

"Though dental records have not confirmed the match, police believe they've found the skeletal remains of Dawn Piper, missing for ten years in June. Despite an exhaustive search in 1966, including an eyewitness statement, Moran was never a suspect or a person of interest in the case. Fingerprints lifted from the phone booth the night Dawn went missing have been matched to Jasper Moran. Additionally, a distinctive gold necklace, containing a gold lamb pendant, was located with the remains. According to sources close to Dawn, she wore a necklace fitting that description."

Trudy glanced at Abe, her expression pained.

"They found her," she murmured.

Abe stood and turned off the television.

He returned to Orla, knelt in front of her, and laid his head in her lap. She leaned down and kissed his temple where a small scar from Spencer's hammer remained. He sighed, feeling as if a decade of sorrow had finally begun to shake loose and fall away.

READ MORE BY J.R. ERICKSON

The Northern Michigan Asylum Series

- Some Can See
- Calling Back the Dead
- Ashes Beneath Her

The Born of Shadows Series

- Ula
- Sorcière
- Kanti
- Sky Mothers
- Snake Island

ACKNOWLEDGMENTS

Many thanks to the people who made this book possible. Thank you to Rena Hoberman of Cover Quill for the beautiful cover. Thank you to Sonya, my copy editor. Many thanks to Irvene, Donamarie, Will, and Barbara for beta reading the original manuscript. Thank you to my amazing Advanced Reader Team. Lastly, and most of all, thank you to my family for always supporting and encouraging me on this journey.

ABOUT THE AUTHOR

J.R. Erickson, also known as Jacki Riegle, is an indie author who writes stories that weave together the threads of fantasy and reality. She is the author of the Northern Michigan Asylum Series as well the urban fantasy series, Born of Shadows. Some Can See, the first book in the Northern Michigan Asylum Series, is inspired by the real Northern Michigan Asylum, a sprawling mental institution in Traverse City, Michigan that closed in 1989. Though the setting for her novel is real, the characters and story are very much fiction.

Jacki was born and raised near Mason, Michigan, but she wandered to the north in her mid-twenties, and she has never looked back. These days, Jacki passes the time in the Traverse City area with her excavator husband, her wild little boy, and her three kitties: Floki, Beast and Mamoo.

To find out more about J.R. Erickson, visit her website at www.jrericksonauthor.com.

Printed in Great Britain
by Amazon